Spectacular Praise for Duane Swierczynski and the Charlie Hardie Series

"More exciting than whatever you're reading right now."
—Ed Brubaker, Harvey and Eisner Award–winning author of *Criminal* and *Incognito*

"Duane Swierczynski puts the rest of the crime-writing world on notice. So learn to spell the last name. He's going to be around for a while."
—Laura Lippman

"Oh, what style!"
—Kirkus Reviews

"Duane Swierczynski has ideas so brilliant and brutal that one day the rest of us will have to tool up and kill him."
—Warren Ellis

"So bloody satisfying."
—Booklist

"Swierczynski has an uncommon gift for the banal lunacy of criminal dialogue, and a delightfully devious eye for character."
—Dick Adler, *Chicago Tribune*

"Duane Swierczynski is one of the best thriller writers in America, and probably my favorite."
—James Frey

"A major new talent."
—Richard Aleas

"Duane Swierczynski is one of the best new things to happen to crime fiction in a long time. A ⌐ ⌐ ⌐ ⌐ ⌐ ⌐ ⌐ ⌐ ⌐ ⌐ ⌐ ⌐ills and the instincts of a seasoned ⌐ ⌐ ⌐ ⌐ ⌐ ⌐ He's going places."
—⌐ ⌐ ler

"Swierczynski seems to get suc⌐ ⌐ ⌐ ⌐ ⌐ ⌐ ⌐ ⌐ ⌐ tric crooks, it's almost criminal."—J. Kingston Pierce, January Magazine

"Duane Swierczynski is the bomb...the hottest new thing in crime fiction."
—Joe R. Lansdale

"Swierczynski steps on the gas early in this pulse-pounding contemporary thriller and doesn't let up...an unforgettable climax....The sequel's appearance won't be too soon for many readers."
—Publishers Weekly (starred review)

"Cool, suspenseful, tragic, and funny as hell, *Fun and Games* is Duane Swierczynski's best yet. I haven't had this much fun reading in a long time."
—Sara Gran, author of Dope and Come Closer

"An audacious, propulsive thrill ride that kidnapped me on page one and didn't look back."
—Brian Azzarello, Harvey and Eisner Award–winning author of 100 Bullets and Loveless

"This book could not be more perfect."
—Simon Le Bon, lead singer of Duran Duran

"This book has it all....I declare this book fastest read of the year. I want part two, *Hell and Gone,* now."
—Ruth Jordan, Central Crime Zone

"Duane Swierczynski leads an insurgency of new crime writers specializing in fast-paced crime rife with sharp dialogue, caustic humor, and over-the-top violence."—Garrett Kenyon, Spinetingler Magazine

"Brilliant...one hell of a roller-coaster read. Mr. Swierczynski writes like Elmore Leonard on adrenaline and speed."
—New York Journal of Books

"Swierczynski's style is muscular and very readable, pounding the rhythms of hard-boiled prose like he's working a heavy bag."
—Warren Moore, The American Culture

HELL AND GONE

Also by Duane Swierczynski

Secret Dead Men

The Wheelman

The Blonde

Severance Package

Expiration Date

Dark Origins (with Anthony E. Zuiker)

Dark Prophecy (with Anthony E. Zuiker)

Fun and Games

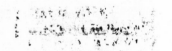

HELL
AND
GONE

DUANE SWIERCZYNSKI

MULHOLLAND BOOKS

Little, Brown and Company
New York Boston London

For David Hale Smith

Copyright © 2011 by Duane Swierczynski
Excerpt from *Point and Shoot* copyright © 2011 by Duane Swierczynski

Mulholland Books / Little, Brown and Company
Hachette Book Group
237 Park Avenue, New York, NY 10017
www.hachettebookgroup.com

First Edition: October 2011

Mulholland Books is an imprint of Little, Brown and Company, a division of Hachette Book Group, Inc. The Mulholland Books name and logo are trademarks of Hachette Book Group, Inc.

The publisher is not responsible for websites (or their content) that are not owned by the publisher.

The Hachette Speakers Bureau provides a wide range of authors for speaking events. To find out more, go to www.hachettespeakersbureau.com or call (866) 376-6591.

Library of Congress Cataloging-in-Publication Data

Swierczynski, Duane.
 Hell & gone / Duane Swierczynski. — 1st ed.
    p. cm.
 ISBN 978-0-316-13329-6 (pbk.)
 1. Ex-police officers — Crimes against — Fiction. 2. Kidnapping victims — Fiction.
3. Prisons — Fiction. 4. California — Fiction. I. Title. II. Title: Hell and gone.
 PS3619.W53H45 2011
 813'.6—dc22   2011028246

10 9 8 7 6 5 4 3 2 1

RRD-C

Printed in the United States of America

Ma prima avea ciascun la lingua stretta
coi denti, verso lor duca, per cenno;
ed elli avea del cul fatto trombetta.

—Dante
Inferno, canto 21, lines 137–39

Save me darlin'
I am down but I am far from over

—Frank Stallone
"Far from Over"

HELL AND GONE

Dear Julie,

  This is going to be hard to explain, but

1

She had crossed to the other side. She was part of the land. She was wearing her culottes, her pink sweater, and a necklace of human tongues.

— Tim O'Brien, *The Things They Carried*

JULIE LIPPMAN WOKE up early the day her boyfriend died.

As she forced her eyes open and searched her memory bank for the date, she was relieved to discover it was Sunday, the last day of Christmas break, and she had absolutely nothing to do until that evening, when a bus would (she hoped) bring Bobby back to campus. Nothing to do was good, because she was hungover to the point of active nausea and her head throbbed from all the blow and the lack of sleep. It had all seemed like a good idea at the time. A kind of exorcism, a final wiping of the slate before a return to what she prayed was normalcy. God, what a week.

She hadn't seen Bobby since the day before break. He had left in the middle of the night, the day before Christmas Eve, without a word. She had been vaguely aware of him kissing her forehead before slipping downstairs and out the town house door into the brisk December morning, leaving nothing but the start of a lame good-bye note that she later fished out of the wastepaper basket in his dorm room.

At the time, though, she thought he was being a dick.

Still, Julie was willing to give him the benefit of the doubt. Maybe the semester has stressed Bobby out, and he needed a little time to himself. So she decided to be a good girl the first week. Went home, did the Christmas thing. Got mildly buzzed on some good white wine—like her father would ever miss it—watched cable TV, even tried to read a little of next semester's lit anthology.

But by New Year's Eve, she'd grown bored with the good-girl thing. Was she supposed to live like a nun? Just because Bobby was off somewhere with his panties in a bunch? So she finally called and agreed to hang out with Chrissy Giannini, and that led them to a rooftop party somewhere, and that led her to a white tile bathroom with a group of people she didn't know, and that led to a toilet lid with a line of blow on it. She was drunk enough to get down on her knees, feeling the cold tile through her black stockings. Drunk enough to lean forward and snort. And with that first hard snort, the good girl inside her settled down for a long winter's nap.

Week two was all very *Less Than Zero*—Julie could practically hear the Bangles singing about a ha-zy shade of pure blow. Only she was coming back east from school out west, and Main Line Philadelphia was not exactly L.A. Her life became a dizzying succession of parties, from house to apartment to dorm room. She met up with a high-school boyfriend she thought she'd never see again; they spent what seemed like an eternity on a mattress in a high-rise apartment near the University of Pennsylvania campus, Julie insisting he keep his hands above her waist; the ex stubbornly, drunkenly refusing, a smile on his face the whole time. Later that night she crawled into the hallway, dragging her clothes with her, wishing her head would stop throbbing, using a dirty wall to support herself as she dressed, feeling a wave of regret wash over her. What the hell did I do? What am I *doing?*

The shame dogged her all the way back to her dad's house, which was empty and cold and quiet. The Philadelphia winter had frozen her favorite quiet spot, the garden out back. There was nowhere left to go but school. Two expensive cab rides later, she was at the airport and flying back to campus, wishing she could erase the past week. Once home, she curled up next to her apartment's heater and tried to read and sip coffee but all she could think about was Bobby, and how she would never do something this stupid again.

So now it was morning, Sunday morning, and she had the day to kill. Bus was due midafternoon.

But the bus never came.

By evening, the news was spreading around campus: a charter plane had crashed in the Nevada desert, just outside West Wendover, killing twenty-four people. All Leland University people, coming back from a holiday service project, building new housing for the impoverished.

Students were smoking on the lawn, some holding candles, some crying. Everyone looked dazed. A series of conflicting emotions washed over her. There was relief that Bobby hadn't traveled by air—in fact, she'd once laughed when he said he'd never traveled by air before. Like, *ever.* She was also in shock at the idea that she may have known someone on that plane. Worry that Bobby still wasn't back yet—and that was mixed with guilt. Maybe he'd heard somehow. Heard how she *really* spent her Christmas vacation, and now he'd never be coming back.

Come on, Bobby. Where are you?

Just before midnight someone had cobbled together a list of names; they used the copy machine in the student-union building and started to circulate the flyers. A page was pressed into her hand as she walked past the lawn. She glanced down, bracing herself for familiar names, and . . .

No.

Not possible.

Not even *remotely* possible.

Julie punched the combination—24, 3, 15—into the metal buttons on the outside of Bobby's door, turned the knob. The room hadn't been occupied for two weeks and smelled like it. Julie scanned the room for the culprit. Someone had tossed a half-eaten sandwich in the plastic wastebasket. There was the usual assortment of Pepsi cans covered in cigarette ashes. Bobby's roommate, Pags, used them as impromptu ashtrays while he sat cross-legged on the floor and listened to Cure albums nonstop. Smoke and decaying meat; one hell of a combination. Julie covered her face with a sweater sleeve, pitched at least a dozen Pepsi cans into the wastebasket, then carried the wastebasket to the end of the hall, dumped it. Though she wasn't sure why she bothered. Neither of the occupants of this dorm room was ever coming back.

What Julie couldn't understand—and what kept the grief frozen, at least temporarily—was the mystery of Bobby being on that plane. He shouldn't have been anywhere near a plane. She assumed he'd been home, working part-time with his dad to make up the tuition difference. He wasn't off building houses for the poor. Hell, Bobby *was* one of the poor, basically putting himself through an expensive Ivy.

Why was he on that plane?

Maybe there was a clue somewhere on Bobby's desk. Shoved into the corner, near the window, it was a gentle mess, covered in papers, notebooks, paperback editions of novels. He was an English lit major, and this semester he had taken a course on war literature—which, as he put it, was "all about being fundamentally depressed down to my soul twice a week." Secretly, though, he loved it. On top of the stack was a book Bobby had written a final paper on—Tim O'Brien's *The Things They Carried.* Julie wasn't much of a reader. Bobby all but forced her to read his favorite story from the collection: "Sweetheart of the Song Tra Bong," about a guy in the Vietnam War who somehow manages to import his girlfriend over to the war zone. And once she arrives, she goes native—strapping on a gun, smearing camouflage paint over her pretty skin, and stalking the humid jungle for enemy soldiers.

"You'd do that for me, wouldn't you?" Bobby had asked.

"Pass the ammunition, stud," Julie had replied.

Bobby faux-squealed—his goofy Prince imitation, which was a hit at parties. It was this absurd chickenlike squawk that started in an upper register, then briefly dipped down a few notes before ascending to the heavens again. It sounded nothing like Prince, but an accurate imitation wasn't the point. Julie had once admitted to being a Prince fan in her preteen days, and Bobby teased her mercilessly about it. Then would come the cheesy hand signals, straight from *Purple Rain:*

I

Would

Die

4

U

And with that last letter, he pointed right at her. And every time, she'd giggle, despite herself, and call him a dick. But he was just a big goofball, her boy Bobby.

But now, sitting in the empty dorm room...

There were no plane tickets or date book or anything that would give Julie a clue about where Bobby might have gone. No notes, no receipts. After a while she sat down on his bed. Pressed his pillow to her face. She could still smell him. She started to cry.

U would, wouldn't U?

She wished she could take back so much of what she said at that party...

As it turned out, nobody on campus knew that those twenty students—along with two grad students and two professors—had been off building houses for the poor. Those involved had kept it a secret from everyone, including their families. Like Bobby, they had given their relatives and friends some kind of cover story to explain their absences. An impromptu vacation. A job opportunity. A work-study program on campus. A road trip.

All of it: bullshit.

The university president explained it away as a "secret mission of kindness—these students and faculty did not want to broadcast their good deeds, merely complete them."

Yeah, Julie thought. *Right.*

"Secret mission of kindness."

Did nobody else realize that this whole thing made no sense whatsoever?

At the funeral, the casket was closed. Made sense to everybody. After all, Bobby had been inside a speeding tube of metal that had been hurled toward the earth at ridiculous speeds. Nobody wanted to see what kind of damage that would do to a human body.

Nobody except Julie.

As she sat there in a black dress—the same one she wore to a sorority social, Bobby at her side, just a few weeks ago, and until yesterday a Polaroid snapshot capturing that moment had been wedged in the corner of her mirror—Julie couldn't stop staring at the coffin.

She had no proof, no evidence of any kind. But she knew that coffin was empty. She could *feel it.*

Gathering proof became Julie's focus that semester. She stopped attending classes and photocopied newspaper articles about the crash—every piece she could find, no matter where the story may have appeared. The university library had a thriving periodicals section; Julie practically lived there for a week. After that, she traveled to the crash site, which didn't feel right, either. Had Bobby been here, ever? Had he been in the middle of that pile of burning, wrecked metal? Julie didn't think so. Again, she had no proof other than the unease in her stomach.

When she traveled to the site of the houses that Bobby had allegedly helped build, near Houston, Julie became convinced that someone was following her.

Everything at the housing site checked out; the project manager even gave her a tour of the home that the Leland University students and professors ("God rest their souls, all of them") had helped construct. Guy named Chuck Weddle was the manager, and he claimed to remember Bobby. Weddle even showed her the backyard patio that Bobby had worked on. "He mixed cement like a pro," Weddle said. Julie did everything in her power to nod politely and not break into anguished scream.

Bullshit, BULLSHIT, *BULLSHIT!*

A man in a black sedan followed her all the way back to the hotel room, and then to the airport.

The university cut her loose in early March. Her parents claimed not to understand, but then again, they didn't ask too many questions, either. They continued to pay her rent and send her living-expense money.

Julie continued investigating.

* * *

Spring break—of course Taylor would come out and visit her in beautiful California.

Taylor Williams was the high-school ex, and Julie was sure that visions of their time together on that mattress in the high-rise were dancing through his head. She insisted that he bring a friend. She didn't exactly specify *why,* but from the excited "yeah" she heard over the phone, she assumed Taylor had put things together. Either Julie had a friend who was looking to hook up, or Julie wanted to try a little ménage action.

Neither was the case. She thought it would be easier with three shovels instead of two.

Taylor arrived with his pal Drew Nardo, a case of Miller Genuine Draft, a bottle of Jack Daniel's, and a gleam in his eye. Julie didn't exactly rush them, but before Taylor and Drew knew it they were all driving out to Stockton to do her a little "favor." Predictably, the boys freaked a little when they heard what Julie had in mind. I mean, seriously—a graveyard? But Julie was convincing. She told them that she'd given Bobby her father's college ring (a lie), something she didn't have permission to do, and unknowingly, his family had buried him with it (another lie). And now her father was asking about his missing ring, and Julie couldn't bring herself to tell him the truth (the third lie). The boys seemed to buy it. Julie also implied a wild night if they'd just help her with this one little thing, even though it was a little creepy...

The dirt was cold and hard-packed. In the two months since the burial, the earth had frozen and refrozen, thanks to some freak cold blasts in this part of California. The boys worked hard, though, fortifying themselves with swallows of Jack as they went along.

"Do they really bury coffins down six feet?" Taylor asked. "I mean, did you do your homework on this one? Because we've been out here all night."

"I did," Julie said quietly. She'd been graveside during the funeral. She saw exactly how deep the hole went down. It took a tremendous amount of self-control to resist running toward the casket and prying it open and looking, just to confirm to herself that she wasn't losing her mind, that Bobby was just missing, not dead...

And that was the point this evening: to unearth the coffin and see if Bobby's remains were indeed inside.

They'd only made it three feet down when bright lights flashed in the distance. A truck engine revved.

"What—what the hell's that?" Taylor asked, wiping the edge of his wrist across his forehead.

They weren't alone. Shadowy figures swept across the graveyard, too many to count. Flashlights in their hands, beams cutting through the gloom. Thick dark forms moved around headstones and mausoleums with precision. They weren't trying to hide. They were trying to make it clear that they were in control, and that running would be futile. Of course, that didn't stop Taylor from trying, screaming drunkenly and kicking up dirt as he scrambled into the darkness. He didn't make it far.

The life Julie Lippman knew was over when the crack of the first gunshot echoed throughout the graveyard.

SIXTEEN YEARS LATER

2

Death is only an experience through which you are meant to learn a great lesson: you cannot die.

—Paramahansa Yogananda

DURING THE PAST fifteen minutes Charlie Hardie had been nearly drowned, shot in his left arm, shot in the side of his head, and almost shot in the face at point-blank range.

Now he was sprawled out on a damp suburban lawn handcuffed to a crazy secret-assassin lady who liked to sunbathe topless.

He figured things could only go up from here.

The police arrived, along with a flotilla of EMTs. Somebody used a key on the cuffs and separated Hardie from the crazy secret-assassin lady, who was named Mann. (Go figure.) Somebody else checked Hardie's neck, his vitals, shone a light in his eyes, and then he was loaded onto a gurney and carried through the Hunter home.

The rest of the people inside the house weren't doing all that great, either. The psycho brother-and-sister team was still groaning and writhing, even though they would most likely survive their gunshot wounds. Same deal with the two nameless gunmen—which meant that Hardie was losing his touch. When he shot people, he preferred them to stay down for good.

Of course, all of this was very déjà vu, in a bizarro-universe kind of way. Being shot and beaten to the brink of death, then carried through some innocent family's home. Just like when he was carried through Nate's home, after all the shooting had stopped three years ago...

Maybe this was it, finally, at long last—the closing credits that had been waiting three long years to crawl across the screen.

Please, God, let me just fade out and realize that the past three years have been an elaborate imagined fantasy sequence as my dying brain fired off its last few neurons. Please tell me I actually died at Nate's house, and all this has been some kind of fire I had to pass through before making it to the next life. Please tell me this was meant to purify my soul, and now I can rest in peace.

God—if listening—declined to respond.

Some time passed. Hardie wasn't sure how long, exactly. A minute maybe. He felt his eye go out of focus. His mind wandered, as though he were on the edge of sleep. His life didn't flash before his eyes. There were no last-minute revelations or epiphanies. Everything was just gray and soft and pleasantly numb.

An EMT appeared next to him. He ripped open some plastic. Pulled out a syringe. Pried off the plastic top. Slid the needle into a glass bottle. Flicked the syringe with a finger. Drew back the plunger.

"Oh, they're going to have fun with you," the EMT said, then slid the needle into Hardie's arm.

Blackness—

And then Hardie was choking her again.

His beefy hands around her thin, soft neck, squeezing as though he were trying to get the last dollop of toothpaste out of the tube.

Hands around *his* hands, forcing him.

Voice in his brain:

Look at her. You've wanted her from the minute you saw her. Haven't you, Charlie? Your little celebrity.

His useless rubber-meat hands on plastic bones, being forced to squeeze harder and harder and harder—

Go ahead, Charlie. You know she wants it. She's practically begging for it.

Gloved thumbs guiding his own useless digits into the middle of her soft throat, pressing down—

Feels good, doesn't it, Charlie? Choke that bitch out. Go on. Break her little scrawny neck.

Feeling her hips jolt beneath this . . .

Murdered by you, Charlie.

Hardie snapped awake sometime later in the back of an ambulance. Above him, bright lights gleamed off steel hardware. Plastic tubing that didn't quite fit into cubbyholes jiggled as the vehicle hit bumps in the road. He could feel every jolt as it traveled up the undercarriage of the vehicle and through the gurney. He tried to lift an arm and discovered that he was strapped down. He turned his head, saw the back of another man—part of his white shirt and vest, dark blond hair. The man was in the middle of a conversation with the driver.

"What are you doing? Take the surface streets. Why are you messing around with the 101?"

"Because it's big, it's anonymous, it's perfect."

"Yeah, and it's slow."

"So what? Our guy's stable, isn't he?"

"For now. He could crash at any moment. I'd rather get him to where we're going before that happens, let him be somebody else's headache."

Hardie didn't like the sound of that. The ambulance driver and the EMT didn't exactly sound like they had their hearts in their jobs. He could have interjected, but the driver spoke first.

"But he *is* stable, right? So leave the driving to me. I don't go around telling you how to stabilize people, do I?"

There was a pause as the EMT considered this, then blew the driver a raspberry.

Get a room, you assholes, Hardie thought.

"Pretty amazed he is so stable. Dude's been shot twice, once in the goddamned head, and yet his pulse is strong and he's still breathing."

"All we have to do is keep him that way until we get there."

Yeah yeah, keep talking, Hardie thought. He could still feel with the fingertips of one hand—his right. Now, his left arm and hand, they were pretty much useless. Fingertips numb, hand inert and dead. A bullet in the bicep will do that.

But his right hand...

Hardie curled his wrist up until his index and middle fingers could touch the strap. It was thick, almost rubbery. He curled even more and was able to press the pads of two fingers into the strap and push. The strap slid a tiny bit. It was something. It was a start.

"Shit, I told you. Look how jammed it is up there!"

"Don't worry. It'll move. We'll get there."

The strap gave another inch. If he could just get it to clear the loop, maybe he could pull it enough to slip the prong out of the metal-ringed hole...

"Oh, man."

"Will you relax? Do you ever drive in L.A.? I mean, except around Sherman Oaks, or wherever the hell you live?"

"Hey, now. No personal stuff, remember?"

"Well, you're getting on my *personal* nerves with your driving advice."

...and then if he could get his right arm free, well, then, Hardie was in business. Because he was jammed up against the cabinets and supply shelves on the right side, and he could stick his hand up there and maybe dig out a needle or scalpel or something else sharp. EMT turns around, Hardie could nail him in the thigh—or no, better yet, point it at a testicle, either one, didn't matter—and order his driver buddy to put the ambulance to the side of the road and hand him a cell phone. Otherwise, Hardie would be serving up some *shish-ke-ball*...

And right at that moment, as if some kind of extrasensory perception had kicked in, the EMT with the dark blond hair glanced down at Hardie and did a little involuntary jolt.

"Fuck, his eyes are open!"

"What?"

"He's moving his hand and shit, he's trying to undo a strap."

Who? Me? Undo a strap? Hardie let his hand drop and prepared to feign ignorance or incoherence...whatever would work best. He rolled his eyes around in a faux daze, swallowed, asked, "What time is it?" Everything depended on getting his wrist free...

"He's doing what?" the driver asked.

"Oh, he's definitely awake." The EMT snapped his fingers in front of Hardie's eyes. "Can you, like...see me doing this?"

"Please," Hardie said. "What time is it?"

When the EMT leaned in close, Hardie started in with his right fingers again and he was overcome with a wave of dizziness. His head pounded and his vision went all blurry. Maybe he was strapped down for a reason. Like, he shouldn't be moving his head or something. Screw it. He didn't want to hang here in the back of an ambulance with these idiots. He may be at death's door, but there was no reason to die in the company of assholes. He tried pushing the strap again, curving his hand around until it felt like his tendons were going to pop...

Above him, the EMT rummaged in a box and came out with a syringe, then rummaged around in another box until he found a vial.

"Let's try a few more cc's," he said, glancing down at Hardie. "Believe me, buddy, you're not going to want to be awake for any of this."

"Please, listen to me..."

"Shh now."

"Listen to me, you fucking fu—"

The cc's blasted down the central line; something cool and wet ran over the top of his brain.

Hardie heard one last exchange before fading into black:

"Christ, he shouldn't have woken up. Like, not at all. Not with the amount of shit I shot into him."

"You see strange things all the time in this business."

The next time Hardie woke up he saw a shotgun-blast pattern of lights. No, not lights—stars. Lots of them. Moving. Which meant *he* was moving. Being wheeled somewhere. Hot wind brushed his face. Hardie tried to turn his head to the left and only made it a millimeter before something went *squish,* which was not exactly reassuring. They'd put a stabilizer on his neck. He tried his wrists. He was still strapped to the goddamned gurney. Wrists and ankles, too. He felt pains in his chest and his heart racing until he remembered Deke.

His old pal Deacon "Deke" Clark, FBI superstar. He'd called him what...hours ago, from that hotel on the fringes of Los Feliz.

Deke would be looking for him...right?

Of course Deke would.

Deke probably arrived at the Hunter home not long after they took Hardie away. Food in his hand (the man was always eating, always with a hot dog or a bag of chips or a soft pretzel or *something*), touring the scene, trying to figure out just what had happened during the past twenty-four hours.

Hell, even Hardie had a difficult time putting it all together in his own mind. The details of the previous day floated around like pieces of a book he'd once read but couldn't fully remember. He'd been hired to watch a house up in the Hollywood Hills. That's what he did—babysat the homes of the rich. He'd been doing it for the past two years. He watched old movies and drank and made sure the places he watched didn't burn down. The last gig, however...the house more than burned down. Hardie had made enemies of a group of killers who called themselves the Accident People. They made murders look like something else. They were led by Mann.

Oh, she was a piece of work.

Mann had been hired to kill famous actress Lane Madden—and this is what made Hardie's head hurt even worse. Had he really been in that house with Lane Madden, or was this some half-remembered fantasy?

No. That had been real.

Hardie and Mann had gone back and forth, trying to outwit each other at every turn. But in the end, the Accident People had caught up with him. Forced Hardie to do the unthinkable, then left him for the gas chamber. Only then did he piece together the second part of their scheme: the carefully planned execution of Jonathan Hunter and his family.

Which had turned out...well, you know. Kind of a mixed bag.

But Hardie had managed to call his pal Deke Clark earlier in the day, convinced him to leave Philly and help him out here in L.A.

So Deke would be looking for him...right?

3

DEKE CLARK STOOD in the middle of LAX's Terminal 4, fresh off the cramped, hot plane, canvas go bag in his hand, and he was staring up with a stupefied expression at the flat-screen TV hanging from the ceiling. You couldn't hear every word the pretty blond girl was saying, not with all the noise in the terminal. But the news crawl along the bottom, along with the photo in the upper right-hand corner, filled in all the vital details. Lane Madden, actress—recovering addict—found strangled to death in a Hollywood hotel room.

Okay, so let's get this straight, Deke thought.

Buncha hours ago, I'm on my back deck in Philadelphia, grilling up some carne asada, thinking about throwing some peppers and mushrooms on there, sipping a Dogfish Head.

Call comes from a guy I haven't spoken to in years. Guy I haven't wanted to speak to, tell you the truth.

Charlie Hardie.

Don't like him much now, never really did back in the day, either.

He says:

"I'm kind of fucked, Deke."

Says:

"You don't think you can get out here sometime tonight, do you?"

Here, meaning: Los Angeles, California. All the way across the country.

Hardie explains the trouble. So of course Deke packs a bag, that's the kind of guy he is, can't say no to a man full of trouble. Goes to the airport. The whole flight out to L.A. he's thinking about the crazy story Hardie told him. That Hardie was house-sitting in the Hollywood Hills and there was a squatter in the house—only the squatter turned out to be famous actress Lane Madden, and that people were trying to kill her. Like, with exotic knockout drugs and speedball injections and shit. And now Hardie and this world-famous actress were on the run, somewhere in L.A.

Fresh off the flight, Deke stumbled up the jet bridge and into the terminal and saw Lane Madden's face on TV. Lane Madden, found dead in a hotel room near...

Only the news people weren't talking about *killers.* They said police were on the hunt for a *killer,* singular:

Charles D. Hardie.

Goddamn, Charlie, what are you getting me into?

"I know how this sounds, Deke. About ten hours ago, I wouldn't have believed me, either."

Got that right.

The local FBI-LAPD liaison was all over his ass when Deke told him over the phone that he'd heard from Hardie just a few hours ago—the liaison pumping *Deke* for information rather than the other way around. Deke said unh-unh. First you're going to walk me through what they have on the murder, what kind of evidence you have on my boy.

The liaison: Well, how about the fact that witnesses saw the victim and your boy at Musso & Frank, both looking like they were coming off a weeklong heroin binge?

A security camera catching your boy stealing a car from the back of Musso & Frank, and the vic playing Bonnie to his Clyde?

Another security camera catching the vic and your boy sneaking into their hotel?

Then there was the matter of your guy's fingerprints all over the vic's neck—and his DNA all the hell over her naked body.

Annnnd we found your boy at the scene, drunk off his ass, slumped shirtless in the corner of the room, vic's DNA all the hell over *him.*

And then finally the big one—the one that kind of clinched it for everybody involved—your boy mounted a daring and violent escape out of a moving squad car, incapacitating both officers with some kind of crazy poison gas and damn near killing them before jacking the car and heading off to who the hell knows where.

So…evidence against "your boy"? Pretty damned compelling.

Deke had to admit: Yeah. Sounded pretty damned compelling.

But Deke also knew Charlie Hardie. And even though he thought Charlie Hardie was kind of a dick, he also knew Hardie wasn't capable of something like this. Deke told the liaison so, added: "I talked to Charlie Hardie earlier today. He said was trying to keep Lane Madden safe from people who were trying to kill her."

"Did he say who these people were?" the liaison asked.

"No," Deke lied.

"So why did he run?"

"I don't know."

"Where do you think he might have run?" the liaison asked. "Did you give him a place to hide? Give him a contact out here?"

"No, I didn't, and fuck you very much for asking."

The liaison softened up a bit after that. He told Deke the address of the hotel, some dump on the fringes of Los Feliz, and gave him the name of the LAPD homicide dick working the scene. But Deke didn't want the address or the name. He wanted to figure out where Charlie would run next.

Because although he didn't lie to the liaison, he also left out a key bit of info.

Namely, the deal with the killers; Hardie had called them the Accident People.

Hardie had told him:

"They're smart, they're connected, and it's only a matter of time before they find us again."

Deke didn't know *who* they were, but Hardie said they wanted to kill Lane Madden to cover up a three-year-old hit-and-run.

That would be the hit-and-run of Kevin Hunter, the eldest child of TV executive Jonathan Hunter, who would later create a hugely popular series called *The Truth Hunters*—dedicated to catching people who got away with crimes.

The actress, Lane Madden, was apparently involved. At least, that's what Hardie had claimed. How was she involved? Deke had no idea.

Now Deke Clark was rocketing up the 405 toward Hollywood. He could have probably commandeered an agency car from Wilshire Boulevard, but that would have taken too much time—forms, mileage check, all that. Better to stay light on his feet and intercept Hardie as quickly as possible. Deke merged onto the highway, which in the gloomy night twitched and crawled like an army of slow-moving lightning bugs. He tried to put himself in Hardie's mind:

I've just been accused of killing an actress.

I called my FBI pal. (Would Hardie consider him a "pal"? Probably not.)

Help is more or less on the way.

So I hole up, right? Wait for my FBI pal to contact me?

No. That didn't sit right. Hardie wasn't the kind of guy to sit still. He'd go after the people who'd killed the actress. For revenge, if nothing else. That was the thing that Deke both admired and loathed about Hardie. He did the things you wish you could do. Thing was, you weren't supposed to actually do them. Just because it *felt* good didn't make it legal.

So that's what Charlie Hardie would do.

And then Deke remembered one of the last things he'd said to Hardie on the phone:

"Hell, if they're already going through all this trouble, why not just bump off the Hunters, too?"

Deke arrived in Studio City as twitching, bleeding, moaning bodies were being carted away from 11804 Bloomfield. The address came from the L.A. field office; he was given another name to *liaise with* at the scene. Deke didn't want to be caught in some interdepartmental clusterfuck. So instead he flashed his FBI badge and pinned down an LAPD uniform, who gave him a terse rundown of what had happened. The whole thing was turning out to be a bloodbath, the uniform said. At first the body count didn't seem too high, the uniform explained, but two of the suspect/victims went into cardiac arrest on the way to the hospital. The two others were alive, and still en route. Two plus two equals four. Was Hardie one of these four? Deke interrupted him to ask:

"Which one of them was Charles Hardie? Which hospital they send him to?"

The uniform didn't know. "We think the family's okay, but they're missing. No sign of them at the scene."

"Family"—the Hunters. Was Hardie with them? Did they make

their escape together? Were they waiting until it was safe to make contact?

Before he went back outside to find someone who could give him answers, Deke scanned the living room. Tastefully appointed, if you ignored the broken furniture, the blood on the rugs, the shattered patio doors. The thought went through his mind: *What would I do if someone broke into my house and started shooting at my family?*

Outside, Deke pulled aside an EMT, flashed the badge again, got the skinny: There were actually *five* people carried away in ambulances: three men, two women. None of them members of the Hunter family.

"Any one of them named Charlie?

"Charlie?"

"Yeah, Charlie Hardie."

The EMT had no idea, told him he should speak to the liaison on the scene.

"What hospital?"

"Everyone went to Valley Presby."

Deke nodded, looked it up on his cell phone, hopped back into his rental, and sped out there, listening to his phone tell him where to go. He didn't know L.A. Thank Christ for GPS units. Deke thought he'd better check the hospital first, see if Hardie was there or not. If not, then he was probably out with the Hunter family. Maybe they all went to the Cheesecake Factory, enjoyed some chicken française and a bottle of Pinot Noir to celebrate their most recent escape from death.

Or maybe more of these mysterious killers had caught up with them, and the family minivan was somewhere in the hinterlands outside of L.A., parked in front of a motel, and inside a room would be the cold and blood-splattered corpses of the Hunter family, and a revolver in the dead stiff hands of his "boy."

* * *

More bad news at Presby:

Only *four* victims had shown up.

"I was told they sent you five," Deke said.

The harried supervising ER doc shook his head. He looked like he hadn't slept, combed his bushy hair, or shaved his gaunt face since the previous weekend. Strangely, his teeth were freakishly straight and white and perfect, as if he were merely an actor playing a harried ER doc on TV.

"No. We got four. Three were DOA. The other one doesn't look too good."

"Where's the fifth one?"

"We weren't sent a fifth one. Just the four."

"I mean the fourth. Let me see number four?"

The ER doc swept his arm out in a help-yourself gesture. He'd probably dealt with cops and feds before. He knew the futility of arguing for patient privacy.

Deke was directed down a hallway into a receiving area. At first he thought he'd been misdirected, but then he came to a room where he saw three bodies on gurneys. There hadn't even been time to cover them with sheets. All three of them, dudes. None of them Charlie Hardie.

Back out in the ER, Deke tapped shoulders until he finally had someone take him to the fourth victim from the 11804 Bloomfield massacre. Deke wasn't sure if he was relieved or disappointed that it was a woman, and definitely not Charlie Hardie. She was a plain-looking thing, tiny face and deadly serious eyes. She was dying, the ER doc whispered.

Deke looked at the woman. A girl, really. The doc was telling the truth. She couldn't even speak, and she kept fading in and out of consciousness.

* * *

The idea of a fifth victim nagged at Deke.

What if the ER staff had been mistaken, and Hardie had been brought here? Maybe he was languishing away in one of these rooms while Deke kept spinning around out here. It was something to check out, at least. Otherwise, Deke had nothing. No choice but to return to 11804 Bloomfield and *liaise* with everybody.

But after checking a series of rooms again and finding no sign of Hardie, Deke had a brainstorm to check the security footage from the ER. Maybe Hardie had been here and gone. The man had an uncanny ability to survive an insane amount of injury. Unkillable Chuck, they called him back in Philadelphia, and Deke couldn't disagree with that. Considering what Hardie had been through.

Deke went to the security office and had the old man with the runny nose behind the desk roll back the last two hours.

And there he was.

Charlie Hardie, in a neck brace on a gurney, rolling right into the front doors. Goddamn it, he *had* been the fifth victim. He *had* been brought here.

So where was he now?

The old man rolled the footage forward; Hardie was not seen again. Deke asked if any cameras covered any other exits. The old man groaned and nodded, then cued up the footage from a side exit. After a few minutes of fast-forwarding, Deke told him to stop. There was Hardie again, same neck brace, same gurney, only rolling *out* the doors of the hospital and into the back of a waiting ambulance. The camera angle, of course, only revealed part of the vehicle. A partial license plate, not much else.

"Get what you wanted?" the old man asked.

"No," Deke muttered. "Not at all."

4

I don't know if I'm alive and dreaming or dead and remembering.
—Timothy Bottoms, *Johnny Got His Gun*

KENDRA HARDIE NEVER liked it when her husband got sick.

Which wasn't often. A cold in the summer, usually, sometimes a minor bout with the flu in winter. But when it hit, Kendra pretty much left him to die. For the longest time he couldn't figure it out. Weren't wives supposed to be all mothering and shit when their spouses were ill? Was she just keeping her distance, afraid she'd fall ill, too? No, it was more than that with Kendra. She'd seem actively *mad* at him, as if he'd done this to himself, going out and licking subway seats or running naked through the streets of the Philadelphia badlands during subzero season.

So three years ago, when Hardie been nearly shot to death and was clinging to life in an ICU, Hardie half expected the reaction he received: the cold shoulder. Didn't mean it hurt any less. Here he was, going through the most traumatic moment of his life—the senseless slaughter of his closest friend and his family—and still, Kendra kept her distance. As if he had nothing more than a bad cold.

The day he arrived home from the hospital Hardie wanted to

shout at her, Please, put me out of my misery. What's going on? Why aren't you speaking to me? Isn't this what you wanted? Me, not working with Nate? Me, home more often? Was she furious because the Albanian hit men had shot up their house—and it was a stroke of luck that she and the boy weren't home? If so, fine, let's have it out, yell at me, do something...*don't ignore me.*

But at the time, Hardie believed himself too weak for an argument. He merely asked if she'd call his doctor to find out whether he would up his pain meds a little. She did, and the doctor said no, he should try to cycle down, in fact. Kendra Hardie didn't like her men sick.

The next time Hardie woke up he was staring at a bright light, listening to the murmured conversations around him. For a moment he thought it was three years ago, that he was at Jenkintown Hospital, fighting for his miserable life, and that his recent limbo-style existence was just a fever dream. He blinked. The light was fiercely bright, ridiculously bright. Like the shining gleam off a tooth in God's own pearly smile. The voices kept murmuring, which was rude. Didn't they know he was dying over here?

"...seen anything like this, have you?"

"Hmm."

"Don't you wonder?"

"Wonder what?"

"Where he'll end up."

"Does it matter?"

"I've been hearing stories."

"Oh, boy."

"No, seriously, I hear that these near-death cases we get, we end up patching them up just good enough so they can be transported to, like, Kosovo or Thailand, only to be pulled apart again a piece at a time, packed in ice, and—"

"Hand me a suture, will you? Anyway, I recognize him. We've got a minor celebrity here."

"So who is he?"

"If you don't know, you don't want to know."

"Give me a hint."

"I did, actually, and no, I will not give you another."

"Dick."

"What time is it?" Hardie asked, his voice dry and weak and cracked.

"The hell?"

"Was that . . . ?"

Hardie tried to blink, as if that would help his eyes adjust.

"Christ on a cracker. Our guy's awake."

"You're the anesthesiologist. What did you give him?"

"Not enough, apparently."

"What time is it?" Hardie asked.

"Take care of it. He's fucking open, man!"

Hardie's eyes rolled around in his head. He couldn't feel his body, not really, but he had the sense that it was still there, that he wasn't some disembodied spirit rushing up toward the immaculate light. No. That would be too easy. He'd been given something. The guy in the ambulance was going on about cc's.

A man's face appeared in Hardie's vision. A white mask covered its lower half. Fuzzy caterpillars clung to the man's brow line.

"Shh," he said. "Everything's going to be all right."

Hardie was not put at ease. He knew "everything's going to be all right" was code for "everything's fucked up beyond all recognition, and it's not going to get any better."

"What time is it?"

"Let me give you something."

Really, he wanted to know what time it was. Was that such a hard question to answer? Not knowing where he was, or what condition he was in—Hardie could deal with that. But time meant everything, and it bugged him to the point of insanity that he couldn't connect the dots on the time line in his brain. Had an hour passed since he was in the Hunters' living room, getting blown away? Two hours? Or had it been a day? Hardie didn't know which answer he'd prefer, to be honest. A day would imply he was out of the woods, that he was stubbornly clinging to life. An hour could mean he was on his way out, and it just seemed like this whole *death* thing was taking forever.

"Just relax," the masked man said.

No.

Hardie would not relax.

In fact—fuck this shit.

He needed to move his hands. Where were his hands?

But before he could find them the man was pumping something else into his veins and he felt the horrible cool rush all over his body, not a reassuring peaceful rush, but the rush of icy death, your body's way of saying "fatal system error," warning you that this shit was real, you may not come back from this...

And as he went under he thought of his wife and his son and Deke, praying once again that Deke had doubled up the protection like he'd promised and that he'd follow the bread crumbs and figure this shit out.

Because Hardie was okay with death; he probably deserved as much. But not his wife. Not his boy...

5

You know why so many people came to my funeral?
They wanted to make sure I was dead.

—Larry Tucker, *Shock Corridor*

DEKE CLARK DROVE up and down the 101, burning gas.

Deke didn't know what he expected to see, really. The mystery ambulance? Not a chance. Some little random forensic clue that would unravel the case? Yeah. Like that ever happens. Besides, he'd done as much of the forensic-type work as he could, tapping traffic cameras everywhere from the Studio City crime scene all the way out to the hospital, and then out again to the major highways. He'd spent days trying to account for every ambulance on camera, retracing their routes, trying to find his phantom vehicle. It was a hard task, and hard to stay focused, since he kept pausing to check his cell phone and e-mail accounts—both official and private—hoping to hear from Hardie. Nothing. Exacerbating the whole situation was an awkwardness with his wife. When she'd call to check in, Deke would invariably be distracted, and it would leave his wife hurt. Later he'd feel bad and want to call back, but then would feel guilty about not using every waking minute to search for Hardie. Five days in, and nothing to show for it except half a license plate.

Deke knew who would have been great at this: his buddy Nate Parish.

Until his untimely death, the man was the secret genius of the Philadelphia police department.

Nate and Charlie Hardie had worked together—only semi-officially. Their mission: clean up the streets of their hometown, using whatever legal or extralegal means necessary.

Deke himself had almost busted the two of them during the infamous mob wars that permanently finished the Italians, crippled the Russians—but also opened the way for the Albanians.

Only reason he didn't bust them was that Nate knew what he was doing, and he was doing the right thing. And he wouldn't work without Hardie.

So what would Nate Parish do?

He had this gift for boiling things down to their simplest and purest form. Crime was not complicated, he'd say. Sure, criminals would obfuscate and try to make it seem as clever and confusing as possible, but it always boiled down to something simple. Almost always money. If you can strip away the drama and the clues and bullet casings and the blood-splattered walls, boil it down until the fat and meat fall right away from the bone...what do you have? You have some kind of financial transaction.

That's when it hit Deke—the ambulance.

Keep digging until you find out who owns it.

Whoever owns it might know who was driving it.

Whoever was driving it would know where Hardie was.

The ambulance was owned by a small private company based out in Arcadia, California, now defunct. Calls to that company were directed to a San Francisco law office called Gedney, Doyle & Abrams.

Deke called GD&A.

GD&A stonewalled.

The essence of their exchange: .

> **GD&A:** We don't own ambulances. We handle insurance litigation.
>
> **Deke:** I'm looking at the papers right here; you represent the company that owns this ambulance.
>
> **GD&A:** Must be a filing error. Because we don't own ambulances. We handle insurance litigation. Can I ask what this is regarding?
>
> **Deke:** You may not.
>
> **GD&A:** Well, go fuck yourself and have a great day.
>
> **Deke:** This company in Arcadia, do you still represent them?
>
> **GD&A:** No, really, go ahead and fuck yourself and have a super-awesome day.

Four hundred miles away, in San Francisco, in a hotel suite overlooking Union Square, Gedney was deep into another one of his conversations with his partner Doyle about the events of the past few days.

As usual, a bottle of Johnnie Walker Blue sat unopened on the marble desk between them, along with a fine array of artisanal cheeses and hand-carved meats. The management was trained to send it up no matter what. Neither Gedney nor Doyle ever touched the stuff. Not when they met in this room, anyway. This was reserved for private discussions; the Industry had equipped this room with the latest anti-eavesdropping devices and bug detectors. It was an utter dead zone. Plus, the view was nice.

"How's the asset?" Doyle asked. He was wearing a suit but still had traces of grease under his fingernails.

Gedney sat on the edge of the bed, his feet barely touching the floor. "Surgery went very well, I hear. He's going to make it. Just like I thought he would. I told you about what happened to him in Philadelphia three years ago, right? The man is a born survivor. Maybe it's good fortune he crossed our path."

"Yeah," Doyle said. "I'll be sure to pass that sentiment about *fortune* along to our friends over in Burbank. But you still think he's right for our project?"

"He will be in a few months. Soon as he's healed we'll begin training."

"Can he be trained? I worry about all that tech. Not that he can really do anything, but he's kind of the proverbial bull in a china shop. I just want some assurances that he'll behave."

"Anyone can be broken," Gedney said. "And if not, we'll flush him down the toilet. Whatever."

"We have any other loose ends? For instance, is anyone looking for the asset?"

"Asset apparently has a friend in the FBI—Philadelphia field office. But that won't be a problem. In fact, it may work to our advantage in other matters. We're looking into it."

"The Hunters are still missing."

"They'll be found and eliminated. They're staying underground, which is good. Some of the teams have worked up about a half-dozen scenarios that fit the situation. Sooner or later they'll emerge, and then..."

He allowed the statement to hang in the air for a few moments, spreading his hands as if they were blown apart by an invisible explosion.

"Good," Doyle said, nodding.

Outside, down on the square, a saxophone player started running up and down some scales, warming up. The notes bounced off the buildings.

"Well, anything else on the agenda?" Doyle seemed eager to leave. Gedney knew he was a lawyer in name and degree only; what he really loved was screwing around with machine parts.

"Go with God," Gedney said. "I'll keep you posted on the asset."

6

WHEN HARDIE WOKE up for the third time, he was in bed, tucked in tight under warm blankets.

Kendra always loved to tuck in the sheets and blankets at the bottom of the bed, forming a kind of pouch, which was great unless you were a adult human being the size of Hardie, which made going to bed like trying to slide a .357 Magnum into a holster meant for a .22. So Hardie would push his feet down and try to unwedge some of the sheets from between the mattress and box spring so he could actually straighten his legs while he slept. This only pissed off Kendra, because he was ruining the whole pouch effect. Every night they fought this battle, for their entire marriage, sometimes one side surrendering to the other (Hardie would spend a few weeks at a time simply curling up like a fetus; Kendra would occasionally skip the pouch thing, if it was warm enough). The happiest nights of their marriage were the months after Hardie had been shot and almost killed. For a few weeks he was in a hospital bed at the hospital; then later he was in a hospital bed in their spare bedroom. Kendra was free to slide into that pouch without fear of someone ripping it open in the middle of the night.

Now, though, it felt like more than a pouch. He was really wedged in tight—strapped down, maybe? Hard to tell. Sometimes when you sleep, a body part will go numb; Hardie's entire body felt numb.

But what came back online almost instantly were his memories, the whole thing, in a violent blood-splattered flood: the explosion in the house, the race up the Hollywood Hills, the hotel room, the crashing police car, the gunfight at the Hunter home, the cold chill at the bottom of the pool...all of it. The fact that he was being held against his will by people he did not know and in a place that he didn't recognize.

And even if his body were completely numb, 100 percent paralyzed from the Adam's apple down, he was going to escape from this place. Even if he had to decapitate himself and drag himself along the floor using only the suction of his tongue, one inch at a time.

They were *not* going to win.

He had been thinking about Kendra and he was overcome with worry about her now. On the phone, Deke had promised to double her protection. She and the boy, Charlie, Jr., lived in a quiet, non-flashy Philadelphia suburb, a small but pretty house, built in the late 1940s, the dawn of the postwar boom. Hardie had never set foot inside it—he had only driven by it. And Kendra didn't know about the protection provided by Deke and his fellow Father Judge High School boys at the FBI. That had been part of a complicated deal in which Hardie had given up essentially everything—his career, his past, his life—in exchange for his family's safety.

But that old deal had been struck when Hardie was worried that the men who'd shot him (and killed Nate and his family) would come after Kendra and Charlie, Jr., just to be dicks. An FBI presence, even a light one, Hardie reasoned, would be enough to convince the Albanian mob that such a move would not be cost-effective.

Now Hardie had new enemies, and his stomach felt like a bottomless pit because he didn't know a damn thing about them.

Clearly, he was not just duking it out with Mann and her killer boy toys. She had a boss, and that boss had enough juice to have a team of EMTs, surgeons, and this secret hospital facility. All put into play tonight to keep him alive...

For what?

If they were worried about him snitching, they could have given him a shot in the ambulance and been, like, *Whoopsie, cardiac arrest, bummer, man.*

They were keeping him around for something. Which probably meant they wanted to ask him questions. And if they were going to ask him questions, they were going to need something to threaten him with.

Kendra and Charlie, Jr.

Their address was secret. Although it wasn't anything near witness protection, it was fairly secure. But such a secret wouldn't last forever. You try hard enough, you can find anything.

They would find it.

They would find his wife and son.

They would let Hardie know that they'd found his wife and son.

And they would say:

So what do you want to do now, tough guy?

Hardie stared at the ceiling above him, which was nothing more than a fuzzy white arrangement of tiles. The lights were off; there was no clock in the room. Not one that he could see, anyway. Kendra used to keep a fancy Bed, Bath & Beyond alarm clock on her bedside table that projected the time on the ceiling in ugly red digits. When Hardie would wake up in the middle of the night—without fail, go ahead and set your atomic clock by it, federal government—the bloodred digital display would read 3:13 a.m. His personal witching hour.

When the night terrors would come.

Was that something in his lizard brain, the lizard brains of all men, dating back to the dawn of time? Did prehistoric men wake up and realize how alone they were, how tenuously they clung to life, how everything they knew and loved could be snatched away from them by a smiling predator, teeth gleaming? Hardie kept a firm lock on his emotions during waking hours—especially when he was working. As if there were a fat steel pipe in his brain with EMOTIONS embossed along the side, Hardie would pull the heavy switch and, *shhhhhhUNK,* turn it off every morning. After a while, he didn't even have to pull.

And every night, at exactly 3:13 a.m., he'd pop awake and find that someone had turned the damn thing on again.

And he'd push his legs and try to undo Kendra's pouch, because, goddamn it, you could not suffer proper night terror if you were tucked in like a joey in a mama kangaroo's front pocket.

There was no clock in the room now, but Hardie would bet anything it was 3:13 a.m.

7

I genuinely feel these people are trying to kill us.

—Evi Quaid

IN HIS AIRPORT hotel room, Deke's cell phone buzzed. It was his liaison at Wilshire, telling him to find a TV or laptop and check the news immediately.

The Jonathan Hunter story had exploded everywhere—Web/cable/TV/Facebook/Twitter—quickly eclipsing the Lane Madden murder. There was only so much attention you could give to a dead celebrity, except maybe run some clips of old movies or snatch a sound bite from industry people the dearly departed worked with. People expected celebrities to die, usually in threes, and unless you were administrator of the Official Lane Madden Fan Club website (of which there were three), the news probably shot through your eyeballs, tumbled through your brain, and quickly turned into synaptic compost. The "killer on the loose" angle was interesting, because that meant there would be a sequel to the story, but in this case it wasn't all that shocking. Not Manson-worthy. There would not be books written about the Lane Madden murder; she'd be a chapter in a celebrity death roundup book.

The Hunters, though...

Oh, man, people would be puzzling this shit out for ages.

They turned up in Vancouver, at a small video studio. Hunter agreed to talk, but only to the news networks—which pissed off his own network, to be sure. If he was going to break some major news, why not throw his own people the bone?

The press conference was teased a full hour in advance—and speculation had run wild for hours before that. There had been Hunter family sightings up and down the California coast, out in the Southwest, as far south as Mexico, and as far east as Times Square in Manhattan.

Last America heard, there had been a hit attempt at the Hunter home in Studio City, California. On family movie night, no less! Many shots were fired, many pints of blood spilled. None of it matched that of the Hunter family, which was good. But the Hunters? Totally missing. Along with their beloved family minivan. Where had they gone? Why hadn't they called anybody—not even their attorneys? Nobody knew! It was a proper mystery, and America loved its mysteries.

When Jonathan Hunter finally appeared on camera, the on-screen titles claimed he was broadcasting live from Vancouver, but he quickly shot that down. He announced that the press conference had been previously taped, and that he was no longer anywhere near the Vancouver area...and all America was, like, *Ah, I see what you did there!* and they loved it.

But they really went crazy for the next part.

"My family and I are being hunted by a group of elite assassins who specialize in murdering celebrities and their families. These individuals broke into my home and attempted to slaughter my wife and children. I will not be speaking about particulars at this time, because I believe that doing so will further endanger my family."

No. No way—he did *not* just say that...

"But I will say that a man named Charles Hardie, who I understand is a security guard, helped us out. Again, I cannot go into details, but the same people who tried to murder my family also killed Lane Madden. It was these celebrity whackers, not Mr. Hardie. He is innocent and he is a hero."

An hour later, Deke was in Barney's Beanery in West Hollywood, eating a loaded western omelet and sipping a Shiner Bock—his body clock was hopelessly off, so what the hell. Clever son of a bitch, that Jonathan Hunter.

Hunter had more or less confirmed what Hardie had told Deke over the phone...more or less. Sure, the man had added a little smidge of crazy to his speech, which was appropriate. Because Jonathan Hunter, creator of *Truth Hunters,* did not want to be believed. He *wanted* to be ridiculed.

Which was brilliant, because he had just created his own life-insurance policy.

If there were real "celebrity whackers" out there, then they wouldn't dare kill Hunter and his family now. *Because that would publicly prove their existence.*

Brilliant, daring, insane fucking move.

And a boon to Hardie. Deke hoped, prayed, *please, God, please,* let him see this broadcast. Because if Hardie had any brains in his head, he'd realize that now he could come in from the cold, show his face, and everything would work itself out.

Come on, Hardie.

Walk in through that door.

Sit down and have a Shiner Bock with me.

We'll have a beer, then we'll all go home to Philadelphia and clear up the mess that is your life.

8

I hope you ain't going to be a hard case.
—Clifton James, *Cool Hand Luke*

WHEN HARDIE WOKE up the fourth—and, as it turned out, the next-to-last time—he was on a gurney and being wheeled down to a cold, bright garage.

Still no idea where he was.

There were lots of people around him. Sodium-vapor lights. Hurting his eyes. The smell of gasoline, stale air. Somebody said, "Right this way." "Pull it up." "The black one." Hardie rolled his eyes around and saw angry red taillights. He blinked and the image became a bit clearer. They were wheeling him toward a Lincoln Town Car. Big, black, and gleaming. Hands opened up a trunk. Other hands under his arms, lifting him up to his feet. "Come on." Hardie looked down at himself and was mildly surprised to discover he wasn't wearing any clothes. His body was naked, pale, weak, withered. They made him walk anyway. Hardie jolted involuntarily. "He's a fighter, this one. Be careful." The same hands carried him closer to the car. Close enough so that he could see what was in the trunk: tubes and pads and plastic bags, none of it making sense. Not at first, anyway. Then when Hardie's brain finally made sense of it, the things in the trunk ceased to worry him. What worried him was the thing that was *not* in the trunk.

Namely, his own body.

The entire trunk of the Lincoln Town Car was a kind of mobile life-support system, with tubes and wires and pumps and IV bags, as well as enough space for a man to curl up into a fetal position.

A man about the size of Charlie Hardie.

Hardie's weakened body bucked, jolted, kicked, punched. The men around him yelled, "Whoa whoa whoa." But Hardie refused to go into that trunk. They pulled him closer. He was *not* going into that trunk. A hand pushed the top of Hardie's head down; shoes kicked the backs of Hardie's knees so that his legs buckled. *I am not going into that trunk.* More hands pushed him over the hard steel edge and into the space—many, many hands holding him down. *I am* not *going into that trunk.* A hand came near his mouth. Hardie tried to bite off a finger. A fist struck the side of his head. Something was forced into his mouth, chipping teeth. A gloved finger dug out the shards. Then the thing was forced down his throat, gagging him. A needle jabbed his bare arm. "Give him more—we don't want him waking up halfway through." Cool yet white-hot water cascaded over his brain. *I AM NOT GOING INTO THAT TRUNK...*

Hardie had no choice; he was too weak to fight and too fuzzy-headed to do anything at all...

...except go into that trunk.

They weren't taking any chances. They checked on the acceptable amount of sedatives for a human being the size and weight of Charlie Hardie... and then they *tripled* it.

The driver saw this and started to freak out a little.

"Whoa whoa whoa—how much you giving him?"

"Trust me. This guy needs a heavier dose than usual. He woke up on the table. And the EMT told us he also popped awake on the gurney like they'd given him nothing stronger than an Ambien. Dude here has a high tolerance for knockout drugs."

"That still looks like a lot. I don't get paid if I deliver a slightly chilled corpse."

"He'll be fine. And if he's DOA, that's on me. But you're going to thank me. You don't want to be cruising out on the highway with this guy waking up in the back, banging on the trunk, trying to figure a way out."

The three of them stared down at Hardie's naked body curled up into the fetal position. The breathing tubes were humming along fine, and his pulse was being carefully monitored and regulated. IV tubes fed him nutrients; another set of tubes took away waste products. He could exist for days, in near-suspended animation, and not require any additional care. Even when the car was parked—so long as the backup battery was still working.

"Poor fucker."

The trunk lid slammed over his head and locked shut. Hardie thought that if he could somehow will himself to stay conscious, everything would be okay. If he could stay awake, then he could figure a way out of this. Hardie once read a Batman comic when he was a kid in which Batman is all tied up in some freezing basement, and Robin is freaking, but Batman is totally calm, and he tells Robin: "Every prison provides its own escape."

Of course, you had to be awake to be Batman.

This was Hardie's last conscious thought for a long, long time.

9

The bastard you hate, but don't dare kill. The bitch you detest, who deserves a fate worse than death. We are at your service.

—Oldboy

DEKE CLARK SAT in the Chinese restaurant waiting for his date.

Her name was Alisa Z. Quinnell—a reporter for a New York news aggregator that specialized in what passes for investigative reporting these days. He nursed an Amstel Light, picked at a bowl of cold sesame noodles, and stared out the window. Across Second Street was the old City Tavern, the legendary Philadelphia watering hole where George Washington and John Adams first met. A revolution that would change the world had been launched in that building over pewter mugs of porter and plates of roast pheasant.

Here, Deke was having some revolutionary thoughts of his own.

He'd gotten nowhere interdepartmentally; he thought it was time to bring some outside heat to the situation. Charlie Hardie had been missing for two months now, and Deke had nothing to show for it except half a phantom license-plate number and a lot of phone calls. So Deke decided on a course of action he thought he'd never pursue in a billion years: bringing the media into this. Maybe with some pressure, the department would be forced to get off their asses and look for Hardie.

Quinnell was right on time. She sat down, ordered a salad (which seemed suspect to Deke—who orders a salad in a Chinese noodle joint?), asked if he minded a tape recorder. Deke shook his head. No, he didn't mind.

"So you're talking to me now?"

Quinnell had been dogging Deke for years, wanting to write a book about the slaughter of Nate Parish and his family. Deke had ignored her. She'd tried doing end runs around him, but Deke had spread the word: nobody talks to Quinnell. Then she dug up a lot of interviews with felons who'd been busted by Nate and Hardie. She kept digging and poking; Deke kept shutting her down. So her surprise made sense.

Sometimes, though, you have to enlist the enemy's aid to win the war.

"I need your help," Deke said.

"Finding your friend Charlie Hardie."

"Yeah."

"What do you know?"

Deke ran down what he saw in L.A., and that since then he'd run into brick walls everywhere—including within his own department. A cold feeling washed over Deke. Cold raw shame. He'd never talked to reporters before, and it felt as bad as cheating on his wife. Quinnell tried not to gloat too much, but Deke could see she was struggling to fight back the smiles. Every now and again she'd pause to clarify a fact, but otherwise she kept Deke talking. His cashew chicken cooled as the Amstel in his bottle grew warm. When they were finished, Deke realized he wasn't hungry. Quinnell offered to take care of the tab; Deke let her, just like a good date.

After they said their polite good-byes, Deke stood up, straightened his jacket, and turned . . . to see Jack Sarkissian, the special agent in charge of the FBI's Philadelphia field office, sitting two tables away, stabbing at noodles with wooden chopsticks.

Sitting there, staring at right at Deke.

Deke walked by his boss without a word. He almost lost his footing on the cobblestone path outside the restaurant. The world swam around him. Instead of turning left, which would take him to Market Street and eventually to his office on Sixth Street, Deke hung a right, toward the Society Hill Towers. Around South Street he turned right and kept walking until he found a quiet bar. Then he went inside and ordered a beer and wondered how long it would be until he was fired.

Two Yuenglings later Deke walked back to the office, ashamed at being such a coward. What the hell was that about? Deke had never hidden from anything in his life. He took the elevator up and walked right into Sarkissian's office, sat down without being invited. His boss was staring at his laptop screen, mouth openly slightly, mind on vacation somewhere.

"Hey, Jack."

Sarkissian looked up at him. The disappointment just oozed from the man's face.

Deke reached into his jacket pocket, pulled out his badge, then unclipped his gun and put both on the desk. "I'm guessing you're going to want these."

"You don't have to do that."

"Yeah, I kind of think I do. I don't want to embarrass myself and pretend you weren't there. So, there we go."

"What's Ellie going to think?"

"I'll explain it to her, like I always do. There are no secrets between us."

Sarkissian considered this. "Okay. Fine. So what are you going to do next?"

"You and I both know what I'm going to do. What this department doesn't seem to want me to do."

"And what's that?"

"Come on, Jack. You were there in that noodle bar, you heard me. I can't believe we're not going to do a thing about the Charlie Hardie situation. Especially after the long and tortured history we all share."

Sarkissian turned his laptop so that it faced Deke. The screen showed a breaking-news website.

"What's this?" Deke asked, but he was already leaning in and reading. First thing he saw was the photo, the mangled car. Oh, God, no. Had to be a mistake...but then he saw the headline, and the one-paragraph story. It had all happened so quickly—about twenty minutes ago, based on the dateline—there hadn't been time for the website to put together a proper piece.

A. Z. Quinnell, auto accident on the New Jersey Turnpike, found dead at the scene. Just two hours ago she'd left the noodle bar with her tape recorder and hopped in her car and headed back up to New York City and then...they'd gotten to her. That fast.

Charlie Hardie had a name for them:

The Accident People.

"What you need to do," Sarkissian said, "is pick up your stuff and get out of my office and go back to work and forget Charlie Hardie. It's not our fight. I'll let you keep the detail on his family, but beyond that, leave it behind. This is not your mess to clean up. Nor is it the department's mess."

"I can't believe it. You're actually *afraid* of these guys."

"Fuck you, Deke. You have no idea what you're talking about, who you're dealing with. Can't you see that?"

"Coward."

"Let this go."

"No."

Which was when Deke did something he never imagined he'd do: Quit the FBI.

That night he sat on his bedroom floor, hugging his knees. Ellie was already asleep, a book fanned out on her chest. Deke had never been more afraid in his life. Afraid for his family. Afraid for the world in which he was raising his kids.

Afraid for what he had to do next, because he really had no choice.

Because, damn it, as much as his rational self pleaded with him, Deacon Clark would *not* let this go.

Deke returned to his soon-to-be-former office and started packing his personal belongings in a kind of daze. Was he really doing this? Yes, he was. An e-mail *ding* snapped him out of it. Deke looked at the sender, but didn't recognize it at first: assistant at dgausa.com. He clicked it open, which immediately opened up a Web browser window. *Damn it*. At first he thought he'd unleashed a virus that somehow had made it past the FBI firewall. But when the horrific image appeared, and his cell phone rang, Deke knew he was dealing with something altogether different.

"Agent Clark?"

"Yeah," Deke said quietly, eyes transfixed on the image before him. He had never seen anything more horrific.

"Is your Web browser open?"

"Yeah."

"So you're seeing the image."

Yeah, he was seeing the image, which only partially resolved the question of what had happened to Charlie Hardie. There was a time stamp on the image, meant to suggest that the photo had been taken just a few hours ago. There were tubes and tape and other gear implying medical care, but Hardie looked pretty fuckin' far from *cared for*.

"Is he alive?" Deke asked. "What did you do to his—"

"Let me show you something else."

The image changed. Now Deke was staring at his own backyard. Not just his backyard, like an image stored in Google's street view. This was Deke's backyard as it appeared today, best he could tell. Deke could still see the tan grilling mitt he'd forgotten to bring into the kitchen last night. Last night he'd cooked chicken for Ellie and the kids, preoccupied with thoughts of what he'd tell the reporter the next day. None of that mattered now. Not when they were showing Deke his own house.

"Don't do this," Deke said.

"We're not through yet."

The image switched again. Now they were inside Deke's empty living room. He could see the clock on the wall—an oversize, classy thing that Ellie had picked up at Restoration Hardware. Deke tried to figure when they were in his house. Then he noticed the time on the clock; then he looked at the digital clock on his computer. Same exact time. The feed was *live*.

"Get the hell out of my house, you son of a bitch."

The screen jumped back to the original image of Charlie Hardie, which was horrifying on its own.

"You are currently investigating a certain group linked to white slavery. This group has ties to Eastern Europe. You know the investigation, Agent Clark?"

"No. There's no way I can—"

"You will curtail that investigation immediately."

"I don't have that authority."

"Your boss, Agent Sarkissian, will go along with it. As for your colleagues, you will simply have to convince them that the matter is not worth pursuing at a federal level. Do you understand me?"

"You know what? I'm going to pursue you at a federal level, you son of a bitch."

The scene image jumped again, cutting away from Hardie. Now Deke was staring at his own bedroom. Ellie's robe was draped over the bed. She usually showered late in the day, working from home until it was time to pick up the kids from school. She was in the shower right now and had no idea there was someone in their living room...

"And we can continue on to the next scene, Agent Clark. Would you like us to do that? Or perhaps you'd like to skip ahead a little?"

Scene jump: the view outside his daughters' school. About forty-five minutes until the dismissal bell rang. Deke knew that they would be waiting inside until Ellie pulled up in the car line. But if these thugs were inside the house, then they could easily take the car. His baby girls would have no idea until...

"Would you like us to continue, Agent Clark?"

An invisible, crushing weight pushed down on his chest. Deke was not an emotional man, but he recognized the symptoms of utter heartbreak. He thought of Sarkissian, the strange look on his face, and understood. He thought of Charlie Hardie lying there on that gurney, technically still alive but pulled apart in the most ghastly way Deke could imagine. But he thought more about his wife, Ellie, in the shower, and his girls waiting for their school day to end.

"No," Deke said softly.

10

Your place or mine?

—Popular saying

THE NEXT TIME Hardie woke up he was surprised to find himself sitting in a metal chair and wearing a fairly nice suit.

He couldn't remember how he ended up in this room, or why he was wearing this suit. Nothing more than fragments. Flashes in a black-and-gray fog. It wasn't quite amnesia, because he remembered his name and who he was and what he had been doing just a short time ago—namely, being shot to hell in Los Angeles, California, and being patched together by these two jackass doctors. But after that...?

Was there a car?

He swore there was a car involved.

Pieces of it floated around in his mind, like half-remembered parts of a nightmare. A black car. Needles. Blood spraying out the side of someone's head. The more he thought about it, the more his heart raced. His brain struggled to put the fragments together into linear order. His brain struggled like a computer trying to reboot itself.

He tried to focus on the memory of the car. There was a car, wasn't there? It was coming back now. Yeah. Definitely a car. A big, black, scary Lincoln Town Car.

Or was that just a memory of a nightmare?

Relax. It'll come. Don't force it, don't freak yourself out.

You're only in a suit you don't remember buying, in a room you've never seen before.

No reason to panic at all.

The room was wide with a low plaster ceiling. Paint flaked off the walls. The molding looked like real wood, reminding Hardie of his grandparents' house in North Philadelphia. There was something very 1920s about it. The only nod to modernity was a fluorescent light above him, which flickered every couple of seconds, as if warning: *I could go out at any moment. Appreciate me while I last.*

There wasn't much here, except the chair Hardie was sitting in, a metal table, another chair, and a filing cabinet tucked in the corner. The fading paint on the walls made it seem like other pieces of furniture had been in this room at some point, long enough to cause discoloration.

Hardie tried to listen for any sounds that would give him a clue as to his location—and somewhere was the faint swelling of violins. Maybe. Those could also be in his head.

His head.

Another piece of memory.

Right. He'd been shot in the head.

Hardie tried to reach up with his right hand and it stopped short. Metal dug into his wrist. He looked down with throbbing eyes and saw that he had been handcuffed to the metal chair.

Well, at least that settled a few things. This wasn't some dumpy hospital room. He was being kept here, and someone had thought Hardie was enough of a security risk to slap some handcuffs on him. Which was funny, because Hardie felt ridiculously weak, down to the middle of his bones. He couldn't remember ever feeling so drained. Yet he was still conscious. So at least there was that.

His left hand was free. Hardie tried to lift it, but the muscles in his arm screamed in protest. He forced it anyway, to the point where his fingers actually trembled as they touched the side of his head. The side where he remembered being shot. His hair had been cropped very short, and he could feel the rough edges of a ragged scar on his scalp. No stitches; just the bumpy mountain of skin. Hardie's fingertips traced the wound about five or six inches around toward the back of his head until it faded.

So he'd been out of it long enough to heal. Which was weird.

Because it felt like he'd been shot only a few hours ago.

Right?

Hardie felt the rest of his head while he was at it, and yeah—someone had given him a crew cut. He'd hadn't had such a short-cropped haircut in twenty years, since back in his military days. He felt the rest of his face, and it was hard. The skin rough. When had they cut his friggin' hair? Why didn't he remember that? How long had he been out, anyway?

Hardie sat in the room, trying to put all these memories together, wondering where he was and what they had in mind for him. Because it was clear he had pissed off somebody important—somebody who wanted to go through all this trouble to save his life and bring him to this room, dress him up in a suit, handcuff him to a chair.

But . . . for what?

There was murmuring elsewhere in the building. Hardie tried to focus on it, but the sounds were too faint. Were they even voices? It almost sounded like the string section of an orchestra, hitting notes that were too far away to place. Maybe bells, too?

After what seemed like an eternity, the door opened. A woman stepped into the room, closed the door behind her with a metallic *snick.*

It was, of course, Mann. Holding a long cardboard box about the size of a golf club.

"Hiya, Charlie," she said.

And in that moment, Hardie knew he was really, really fucked.

So this was a revenge thing. Plain and simple. His life had been spared so that Mann could toy with it.

Whatever positive thinking he'd managed to muster up was gone. Mann was here, and she was probably going to torture him before killing him. Probably using whatever was in that box. Or she'd kill him and desecrate his dead body. Or maybe come up with some slow agonizing torture that would eventually, and only eventually, kill him.

"Uh, hi," Hardie responded.

Mann slinked into the room, strolled right up to the table between them, and rested the box on top. She looked healthy, a little more filled out. And she seemed to have both of her eyes, which was kind of a shock. One of them was a brighter, otherworldly blue.

"Mind if I sit down?"

Hardie wanted to gesture with his hand—*Be my guest.* But the handcuff prevented him. And he didn't feel like trying to lift his left arm again.

She took the chair opposite Charlie. The metal legs scraped against the concrete floor as she moved a little closer. "Good to see you."

"Yeah."

"No, really. You're a sight for sore eyes."

Memory flash: Mann with an eye patch. She wasn't wearing one now, though.

"You're looking better," Hardie said.

"Why, thank you."

"Not to interrupt the pleasantries," Hardie said. "But if you're here to kill me, I'd rather you just go ahead and do it. I'm not into small talk."

Mann smirked. "Me? Kill the unkillable Charles Hardie? I wouldn't dream of such a thing. Besides, whatever happened between us is... well, *ancient history.*"

"Doesn't exactly feel that way to me."

"Of course it wouldn't."

"I'm sure it doesn't feel that way to the Hunters, either."

Her eyes narrowed, and now Charlie could see it—the glass one. Her right eye. The unnaturally blue one. So she hadn't emerged from their little battle unscathed. She'd lost an eye. What was that old saying? It's all fun and games until someone loses an eye? Hardie supposed the fun and games were over. Now it was something else.

"That's ancient history, too," Mann said. "Look, as much as I'd love to sit back and reminisce, I'm here for a reason. They wanted you to talk to a familiar face, so that you'd know they were serious."

"Again with the *they.*"

"It's always *they,* Charlie. Don't you know that? They run everything."

"Kind of surprised *they* didn't have you killed for screwing everything up so badly."

This time Mann giggled before catching herself. Her cheeks turned red, and she fought for her composure. "Oh, Charlie, I've missed you. No, they didn't have me killed. They don't waste assets. And I'm an asset to the Industry. Just like you."

Hardie tried to put his face in his hands, wanting to press his own eyeballs in to see if they'd stop throbbing. But then he remembered he was half handcuffed. Still, he used the palm of his left hand to rub his forehead. The movement was awkward; his left arm seemed to want to do its own thing, not be pressed into service.

"Do you have a headache?" Mann asked with something resembling genuine concern in her voice.

Hardie said nothing and continued rubbing his head. "Yeah. You wouldn't happen to have any aspirin, would you?"

"That's an unfortunate side effect of the memory shot they gave you."

Hardie looked at her from between his fingers. "Memory *what?*"

"A shot to erase your short-term memory. Which is why you're so confused right now, and why you have a really bad headache. They didn't want you remembering anything about your trip here. Not the sounds of tires on the road, or the way the air felt or smelled. Nothing. So they blanked out your recent past. It's a security precaution."

"Exactly how much of my recent past?"

Mann smiled and hummed playfully. *Hmm hmm hmmmmm.*

"Great," Hardie said. "You sure you don't have any aspirin?"

Hardie had to admit it: he didn't understand a thing about what was going on. Why was Mann smiling and chipper? That made him uneasy, far more than the ache in his skull and the handcuff around his wrist.

Now Mann leaned forward, sizing him up with her eyes. "You're going to behave, right, Charlie?"

He took a moment before responding. "Sure."

"Goody."

Mann fished in her pocket and produced a small key. She stood up, scraping the chair back across the concrete floor, then moved around the table to Hardie's side. He flinched. She told him to relax, then leaned forward. Her breasts brushed against his shoulder.

Hardie blurted: "You know, you still have a nice rack."

It was a dumb inside joke between them—at least Hardie thought so. The first time they'd met, she'd been topless, sunning herself on a patio high up in the Hollywood Hills. He hadn't known she was a professional assassin back then. He just thought she was rich and eccentric and an exhibitionist.

But Mann stepped away and frowned. Dark clouds formed in her eyes. Even, impossibly enough, the glass one. Okay, Hardie thought. Here it comes. Here's the Mann I know. He braced himself for a punch in the head or a chop to the throat.

Instead, her hands came up and started to unbutton her blouse.

Now, this wasn't what he expected.

"What are you doing?" Hardie asked.

"For old times' sake," she said, then removed her blouse to reveal her bra—disappointingly white and rather matronly. Mann reached around to the back and unhooked it.

"Look," Hardie said, "I know this is a cliché, but when I said I had a headache, I really meant that I had a—"

When Mann's bra came away from her chest, one of her breasts came with it. It took Hardie a few seconds to realize that the bra had padding on one side to perfectly match her remaining breast. The left part of her chest was glistening with fresh scar tissue, pink and raw-looking.

"God," Hardie muttered. "What—"

"The big *C*. Runs in the family, sad to say. You can run away from many things in life, but you can't run away from your genes. Happened a short while ago. I'm still getting used to one of the girls being gone."

Hardie didn't know what to say. What could you say? *Sorry you lost one, but the other looks great?* Mann wasn't a high-school girlfriend.

She was a cold-blooded killer. She had racked up many notches on her gun. She'd tried to kill *him.*

Then it occurred to him. When did she find the time to, like, *survive* breast cancer? How long had he been out?

"It's not all bad," she continued. "Amazon warrior women used to remove a breast willingly, so their tits wouldn't get in the way when drawing back an arrow. Mind you, I prefer a gun, but I'm tempted to give archery a shot. Certainly would make for a great cocktail-party story, don't you think?"

Hardie couldn't look anymore. Mann rehooked her bra, slid her arms into the blouse, rebuttoned it. "Anyway, I just wanted to make sure you know that you're not the only one who's lost something, Charlie."

"What do you want?" Hardie said. "Why are you here?"

"They wanted you to see a familiar face. They wanted you to know this is for real."

"What's for real?"

Mann smiled. "Your new life."

"We're in the vestibule of site seven seven three four," Mann said. "This is a secret maximum-security facility, known only to an extremely limited number of people in the world. We're somewhere deep in the earth, in the middle of absolutely nowhere. Even I don't know where it is."

"Right."

"No, I'm serious. They stuck me with the same memory shot they gave you. When I leave, they're going to give me another shot, and I'll wake up in a hotel room somewhere else in the world. Hopefully someplace with a spa and excellent room service."

"*They,* again, huh?"

Mann leaned forward, raised her eyebrows. "Creepy, isn't it?"

Unconsciously, Hardie's trembling left hand went to the crook of his right arm and then he realized what he was searching for. The needle jab. Sure enough, there was a fabric bandage there, and wine-dark bruising around it. Somebody had given him a shot. Somebody had been giving him *lots* of shots. Sticking him up as though he were a college student trying to make some extra bread over a weekend.

Mann leaned back. "And when I wake up, my bank account will be fatter. I'll probably go have a cocktail in the hotel bar. I'm not supposed to say anything to anybody, ever, so I'll raise a silent toast to you, Charlie. Because you're going to be away a long, long time."

"So this is my punishment, huh?"

"Punishment?"

"For messing up your big Hollywood murder plans."

"Oh, *that,*" Mann said. "Geez, I'd almost forgotten all about that."

Uh-huh, Hardie thought. *You forget all about about losing an eye. Forgive and forget. Turn the other socket.*

"This isn't about punishment, Charlie. It's simple economics. You cost our employers a great deal of money. So they're going to put you to work to recoup some of the losses."

"*Our* employers?" Hardie said, but already his mind was reeling. Was Mann actually here to recruit him? Have Hardie join their little team of assassins? Good God—no. *Hell,* no. Put a bullet in his brain right now, be done with it. Or maybe he'd play ball just long enough to get his hands on a gun so that he could finish off Mann here, once and for all.

"You'll be briefed down below—and let me tell you, the staff is looking forward to meeting with you."

Now his patience had run out. "I'm not going to work for you. You can forget it."

"Work for me? Oh, that's funny, Charlie. Seriously. No, I don't think you'd be a good fit for my team."

"Then what's this about a staff?"

"I think you're going to find working with them extremely rewarding. I mean, they're all truly good people. Heroes, really."

Again, Mann was fucking with him.

"Oh, almost forgot. I have a present for you."

At long last she opened the long cardboard box on the table. Hardie thought there could be anything in there. A shotgun. Dozen roses. A slender chain saw.

Instead, Mann removed a black cane and gently slid it across the table toward Hardie.

"A little parting gift."

"You can shove that up your ass," Hardie replied.

"That's extraordinarily tempting," Mann said. "But before I do that, why don't you try standing up? It's why I removed the handcuffs, you know."

Hardie put his palms on the table and stood up. Immediately his right leg gave out and he slammed his ribs into the edge of the table before slipping down even farther. Mann flew forward and caught his head in record time, her hands grabbing his ears. She yanked forward. Hardie struggled to find his footing, but it was as if his right leg weren't even there. Left arm—useless.

"You've suffered some pretty serious neurological damage," Mann said, her breath hot in his face. "Your leg probably won't work all that well for the rest of your life."

"Bite me."

Mann bared her teeth. "You saying you don't want the job? Because it doesn't matter to me. In fact, it would thrill me if you spit in my face and tell me you don't want this job."

Hardie obliged her, launching a wad of saliva that struck her cheek and began a lazy roll down her face.

"I don't want the job," he said.

Mann reached out her tongue and slowly licked the spittle from her face, as if savoring it.

"Wonder if Kendra will spit in my face, too, when I show up in her bedroom tonight. Maybe I'll force her to lick my face, ask her if she tastes her dead husband. Think she'd like that?"

Before Hardie could reply, Mann let go, and Hardie's own body weight pulled him down fast, the edge of the table slamming into his jaw. Vision went white for a second. The pain like a firecracker in his skull. He spun, landed facedown. Mann was over the table and straddling him as he struggled to roll over. Again, she leaned in close.

"Nothing would make me happier than to kill you, then go kill your family. Because you're right, Charlie. No such thing as *ancient history.*"

"You so much as even look at my wife or son I'll—"

Mann grabbed Hardie's ears and slammed his head into the floor hard enough to make him bite his tongue.

"Don't write a check your ass can't cash, old friend. In about sixty seconds, I'm going to leave this room, take an elevator to the surface, where I'll receive my shot, and be on my way to have that drink I mentioned. Right after that, they're going to seal up the entrance-way nice and tight and permanent. With cement and steel, just like they do whenever there's a new arrival to site number seven seven three four. There's no way out, Charlie. None. That's the point of this facility—no escape. *Ever.* All you can do is grab your cane and take the elevator down to your new life. Don't worry. I'll be toasting you back in the real world. And if you fail to perform your duties, just know that I'll be the first one they'll call. And then I will *delight* in destroying your family."

Mann climbed off Hardie's body, staring at him carefully, waiting for a reaction. Hardie didn't give her one. After a few moments she made a *pfft* sound with her lips and left the room.

* * *

Sure enough, after a few minutes Hardie could hear the sound of construction: the banging of steel, the muffled scrape of mortar hoes against some hard surface, the shrill buzzing of power saws.

Which was more than a little troubling.

Hardie pulled himself up off the ground, using his only good arm and only good leg to steady himself on elbow and knee. Balancing himself on that single knee, he reached out and grabbed the edge of the table, slowly working himself up again. He took the black cane from the tabletop. His right leg was still numb and fluttery, like a phantom limb. He needed the table.

He took a series of wobbly steps and, by way of sheer luck, eventually crashed into the door that Mann had used to exit. Hardie balanced himself, grabbed the handle. Locked tight. Somewhere above him, some unseen construction crew labored. Clanging. Pouring. Welding. Sealing.

"HEYYYYYYYYY!" Hardie screamed, so hard that he lost his balance, a misstep exacerbated by a sudden coughing fit.

"HEYYYYYYYYY UP THERE, CAN YOU HEAR ME?"

No response came. Either they were unable to hear him above the din of the power tools or the construction crew was dedicated to doing their job and their job alone.

Hardie made his way back to the table and sat down and considered his options.

He didn't have to think long—because his options sucked.

So little of this made sense. It was like snapping awake from a horrible, sweat-soaked dream, only to discover that the world was about to end, the H-bombs were dropping everywhere, and boy, you're about to wish you'd stayed in that bad dream.

The elevator door was the only way out.

Out was not up; out was down. Deeper into the bad dream.

To his *staff*—is that what she'd said? What the hell did she mean by that?

The stubborn knot in Hardie's gut told him to stay put. Just sit here and do nothing. Eventually he'd dehydrate, maybe even be lucky enough to pass out. Just to spite Mann. Write a little message on the wall for her before he finally expired. *Hope you choke on the olive in your fancy-ass cocktail.*

Yeah.

Sometimes after a tough case Hardie would find himself hanging out on Nate Parish's broken couch in his Philly PD office. One of the fabric-covered arms had long ago snapped, leaving a perfect V in which Hardie could rest his aching head. Hardie would crash on that couch, sipping a can of lukewarm beer, too keyed up to go home, too tired to move. Once, he'd said to Nate:

"We've been really busy lately."

"We're always busy. Remember what Pascal said."

Hardie had no idea who Pascal was—some South Philly mobster he'd never heard of, maybe?

"What's that?"

"All human evil comes from a single cause—man's inability to sit still in a room."

Nate turned out to be right, of course.

Hardie stepped into the elevator cage, slid the old-fashioned accordion-style gate shut. His grandmother's old apartment building used to have an elevator like this. As a kid he'd constantly worry about getting his fingers chopped off when the gate slid open. That never prevented him from running his fingers over the greasy gate anyway. He pressed one of only two buttons in the elevator—ancient semen-colored circles of plastic adorned with the chipped words UP and DOWN. He seemed to already be UP. That left DOWN. Hardie pressed the button, which lit up. Somewhere, ancient machinery kick-started; pulleys and cables started turning. Hardie's body jolted as the car slid downward. Here we go.

Going down.

Down.

Down.

Down.

What was down here? Hardie tried to decode Mann's cryptic statements about this place—site 7734, she'd called it. A maximum-security facility. Buried deep in the earth. (If the length of this elevator ride was any indication, she was telling the truth about that, at least.) But for what? Was he being sent down for human experimentation? Imprisonment? Torture?

Suddenly Hardie got the idea that he may have been better off sitting up in that waiting room and withering away slowly.

After what seemed like an absurdly long time, the cage touched down at the bottom of the shaft. The air was noticeably cooler down here. Hardie braced himself with the cane, realizing that, yeah, he really should have stayed up top. He stabbed the UP button, but now it refused to work. Something clanked, but the mechanism failed to restart. Well, he was stuck with his choice now. Time to see it through.

Hardie reached out with this right hand to slide open the gate. He took a step forward, supporting his weight with the cane. The moment he stepped out of the elevator, he heard the strangest noise.

Applause.

11

{When he} heard the cell door banging shut, he'd been scared.
Like a little kid he had wanted to shout: I take it back!
———Malcolm Braly, *Felony Tank*

FOUR PEOPLE IN dark brown uniforms stood in a half circle, clapping their hands, all eyes focused on *him*. Hardie froze in place. They kept applauding anyway, seemingly oblivious to his shock. A bearded guy gave him a thumbs-up and mouthed something like, *Right on.*

Oh fuck, Hardie thought. What *was* this?

Their uniforms had deep red piping and cargo pockets, and were paired with black leather belts, black leather wristbands, and even black leather boots. The four of them took a collective step back, as if to encourage Hardie to take another step forward, come on, now, that's it, that's a good boy. Welcoming him into their communal bosom, all smiles and cheers and even a few *woo-hoos.* Hearty cries of congratulations in languages he didn't recognize—but the overall meaning was clear.

The bearded one broke ranks and nervously shuffled forward, still pounding his hands together. Smiling through his dark, neatly trimmed beard.

"Welcome, Warden," he said in a broad Australian accent. "Boy, are we glad to finally have you here."

Warden?

"Well, aren't you going to say something?"

Hardie looked over the Aussie's shoulder and saw cages, and two figures sitting inside those cages.

All at once Hardie realized what this was.

This was a secret prison; these were the guards.

And all this *applause* bullshit was the mockery before the crucifixion, and here were his tormenters. Fucking with Your Victim, New-Testament Style. Sure, yeah, now they were shouting and proclaiming him the King of the Jews and shit. Next they'd be dividing up his new suit in dice games and shoving a crown of sharp thorns down on his tender scalp.

Not if he could help it.

Hardie took a step forward, scanning the four guards quickly. Three men, one woman. All wearing the same uniform. Tools and gadgets hanging from their belts. Plastic restraints. Tasers. A few syringes topped with sturdy plastic caps. Still applauding and opening the circle up wider for Hardie.

No doubt getting ready to pounce his ass.

Hardie switched the cane into his other hand, using his weak arm to balance himself, hoping it would be enough to support his own body weight. Because the moment the bearded Aussie took another step, Hardie lunged out and grabbed up a fistful of the guy's uniform and then pulled him in for a violent head butt.

Skull bone made contact with nose bone; bright lights flashed. Hardie's head suddenly felt like it had been blown apart by a cherry bomb. But so what? His head already hurt like hell. What was pain on top of pain?

The Aussie guard's eyes rolled back in their sockets. He was not expecting the forehead-to-nose action. Hardie tightened his grip and used the Aussie's body to support himself as he spun around and whipped the wooden cane across the head of the next advancing guard—a blond, pale guy. The guy cried out as his head snapped to the side. Turning his attention back to the bearded guard, Hardie gave him a push in the direction of the other guards. The Aussie became a human bowling ball; his friends the pins. Then, as fast as he could, Hardie started to make a beeline for the door he'd just stepped through.

Hardie knew it was practically useless. It was four against one, and he was down two limbs. But Hardie also wasn't about to stand around for mockery and whatever else they had in mind. He vowed to fight until he stopped breathing. At least then there was the illusion of control.

Who knows? Maybe he'd luck out, and they'd skip the torture and kill him quick.

Hardie found the handle, pulled open the door enough so that he could throw himself inside the metal cage. He half turned and yanked the door shut behind him—but two hands shoved through the space between the metal door and the frame.

Fine. Hardie let it open a few inches to give himself enough room...and then he *really* pulled the door shut.

The screams were otherworldly—strange profanity in a foreign tongue. Fingers wriggled like white worms in the crack between the door and the frame. Hardie pulled even tighter and relished the agonized screams. Oh, please. Here's hoping it made these bastards so furious that they killed him immediately rather than drag it out.

"NO!" a female voice shouted.

"YOU DON'T UNDERSTAND, MATE!"

"DO NOT GO UP!"

"NO! NO NO NO!"

Hardie let the door open a fraction of an inch, giving the wriggling worms enough room to remove themselves from the situation. As soon as the last fingernail cleared the space, Hardie yanked the door shut a final time, then staggered backward until his back collided with the other end of the cage. No one was more surprised than Hardie. He'd made it this far. Could he actually make it out of here? Somehow?

Adrenaline had carried him this far, but he felt like he'd used up his last reserves.

No matter.

All he had to do now was push the up button, figure out his next move once he was back in that waiting room. Maybe he could find a way out. Maybe he could even catch up with Mann. Snap her neck and ask her if she'd still like to meet his wife and son.

A face appeared in the grille. Bearded Aussie guy.

"WARDEN!" he shouted. "DON'T DO THIS! PLEASE DON'T DO THIS. WE DON'T WANT TO HAVE TO—"

"Fuck you," Hardie muttered, then stabbed the up button with an index finger. A second later the bearded guy sighed, unclipped something from his belt, jammed it against the outside of the metal cage, then squeezed it.

ZZZZZZZZZZZZZZZZZZZZZZZ-POP

And then:

white

hot

crazy

Nothing

A disjointed moment later, Hardie was being dragged out of the cage, drooling and twitching. Slowly he pieced together what had happened. A Taser. They must have jammed a Taser against the metal cage, pulled the trigger, and the electricity that sailed through the cage must have shocked him unconscious.

Now rough hands were dragging him along the cold concrete floor. Any minute now the beatings were likely to commence. Hardie knew it. He'd tried. Lost. Welcome to your new life sentence, dumb ass. You should have stayed upstairs. Starved yourself to death. Would have been the classy, stoic move. Better than being thrown into a secret prison cell for the rest of your life.

But instead of a punch—

The bearded Aussie cautiously touched his face. "Can you see me, mate? Are you okay?"

Hardie nodded. At least, he thought he nodded. All he knew, his head may have bobbled around as though it were attached to his body with a coiled spring.

"The hell were you trying to do?" Bearded Guy said. "Didn't they tell you about the elevator? How it's a one-way trip?"

Hardie shook his head again, incoherently.

"Jesus...look, if you were to have gone back up and made your way outside, you would have triggered the death mechanism. They didn't tell you about the death mechanism? Anyway, listen to me now. If you had gone up, you would have...well, you would killed everybody in here. *Everybody.* Including me."

The other three guards glared down at him, a mixture of disappointment and checked fury on their faces. All like, *How dare he almost trip the death mechanism?*

Finally Hardie's lips stopped trembling enough for him to attempt a few words in the English language. "Would have...tripped the...death *what?*"

"The death mechanism, mate. They didn't tell you about it?"

Death mechanism. The words apparently carried some kind of meaning, but Hardie didn't understand.

Utter exhaustion washed over him. Hardie could tell his body was trembling, but he didn't actually feel it until a few moments later, as the guards stooped over to pick him up from the cement floor. His vision went woozy, and the muscles in his neck stiffened, as if to choke him into unconsciousness in a desperate attempt at self-preservation. No. He had to stay awake, soak up every detail.

What was this place?

Where was it?

Why was he here?

He had no idea.

The guards guided his stumbling ass through a confusing series of rooms. One looked like a cafeteria. The next was a laundry room furnished with—strangely—refrigerators. Then somebody's spartan bedroom, followed by a room that looked like a primitive security-department control booth, then another bedroom, then a third bed-room, which was apparently his, because they eased him onto a creaky bed there and told him to rest a while. There was a lot of work ahead of them.

Hardie had no intention of sleeping. Just wanted to ease back for a few seconds, take a few deep, cleansing breaths, close his eyes, maybe, for a microsecond or two...

12

This is hell, and I'm going to give you the guided tour.
—Donald Sutherland, *Lock Up*

A NOISE—

(clanging chains?)

—jolted Hardie awake.

He bolted upright, immediately forgot that one of his arms didn't work right, and collapsed back down to the mattress. Beneath his head, ancient mattress springs groaned. *Fuck me.* Using the hand attached to the arm that *did* work, Hardie rubbed his eyes and tried to clear his mind. He was going to need a clear mind if he was going to get out of here.

Where was *here,* though?

Hardie imagined a map of California—specifically, Los Angeles, where this all began. He wondered how far away he might be from the City of Angels. There had been a ride in an ambulance, with the driver talking about taking the 101. There had also been some time in a hospital—which had to be within driving distance, right? Because he didn't remember any planes.

Hardie allowed his mental map to zoom out to encompass

the entire American Southwest. Lots of desert. Lots of places to hide.

If you were going to set up a secret prison on American soil, the middle of the desert wouldn't be a bad place. Is that where he was? Somewhere in Death Valley?

Of course, there were gaps in his memory—there *had* to be a whole bunch of missing time he couldn't account for. (Otherwise, his head wound sure did heal up freakishly quick.) There had also been that hellish ride in the coma car followed by...more missing time. So yeah. He could have *easily* missed a plane ride. Extradition, the good old-fashioned American way. A one-way trip on a torture taxi. Last stop: your sorry ass in a secret prison.

The mental map zoomed out further to include the entire United States, then North America, then further still, the globe spinning, the Atlantic whizzing by, and Europe and Africa and the Middle East swinging into view...

He could be anywhere.

And at the same time...*nowhere.*

Okay.

Forget the location for now.

Didn't matter where he was.

What mattered was finding a way out of this place, and *then* worrying about finding his way back home to Kendra and the boy.

Hardie blinked crust out of his eyes and twisted his body up into a half-sitting position, supporting his upper body weight with his right arm this time. His left arm was still numb, his right leg throbbed, and oh, how his head still pounded.

Now that Hardie could see it properly, the room turned out to be no bigger than a college dorm. Bed, sink, desk, small beat-up wooden dresser that looked like it had been painted back in the 1950s. There were no bars in the doorway, so it wasn't a prison cell—but there wasn't a door, either, which meant no privacy.

Hardie swung his legs over the side of the bed and rested his feet on the concrete floor for a few moments until he felt like trying to stand up. Uh...no. That wasn't going to happen right now. Apparently Old Man Hardie needed his cane first. Someone had helpfully left it hanging from the metal bedpost. As he reached for it Hardie could feel the blood rush to his extremities. Out of nowhere, his heart began to race. He took a deep breath, which is when a voice startled him:

"A bit more calm now, mate?"

It was the Aussie guard, the one with the neatly trimmed beard and bright blue eyes, perched in the doorway, a nervous smile on his face. He was either Australian or he enjoyed faking the accent.

"You gave us kind of a scare. Never had the new warden, uh, *attack* us before."

"Why are you calling me that?" Hardie said.

"What?"

"Warden."

"Uh...because you *are* the warden? I mean, why else would you be here?"

"Vacation."

The Aussie was dumbstruck for a moment before cracking a broad smile and nodding. "Ah, you've got a sense of humor. That's good. It'll serve you well down here."

Hardie thought about this. He had to play it carefully. Either the Aussie knew the truth—that Hardie had been sent here against his will—or he didn't. For now, Hardie thought it best to reveal as little as possible. The moment you open yourself up is the moment your problems multiply. He rubbed his eyes again. Why couldn't he wipe the gunk away? Maybe he'd slept longer than he thought, because his eyes were seriously crusted over. The Aussie just stood there, grinning and waiting patiently.

Hardie had to break the silence. "So what do you want?"

"Just wanted to introduce myself," the bearded guy said. "I'm Victor."

"Right," Hardie said. "I'm Ch—"

"Uh uh uh." Victor interrupted. "Can't know your real-world name. We don't know your name, you don't know ours. It's better that way."

"You just told me your name."

"Victor's not my real-world name. It's just a handle. All the guards have them. There's me, Whiskey, X-Ray, and Yankee. This protects our identities as well as our loved ones out there in the big bad world, you know?

"Whiskey? X-Ray?"

"You know—the NATO alphabet? Hey, it's better than colors, for fuck's sake. Anyway, when a new guard arrives, they're given the next letter down. Next guard will be Zulu. Then Alpha, Bravo, Charlie, and so on. What's funny is, I've been Victor so long it's starting to feel like my real name."

"So that makes me...what, Zulu?"

"No, that makes you the *warden*. So from here on out, we call you Warden. They didn't explain this to you?"

No, they—or in this case, Mann—had neglected to add this little detail. *Warden.* Hardie shook his head in disbelief. He'd spent two years as a house sitter. Now, if this bearded dude with a fake name was telling the truth, Hardie was in charge of running the Big House. It was almost a joke. Was God up there laughing? Did God even exist?

"Right," Hardie said. "Okay. Well, if I'm the warden, pardon me while I take a look around the place."

And look for the fucking exit.

"Hang on," Victor said. "Got some prezzies for you."

The guard reached into his pocket and pulled out a pair of goggles and a small plastic teardrop.

"What's this?" Hardie asked as Victor dropped the items into his hand.

"The goggles help block out some of the fluorescent lights, since they never turn them off—even in our quarters. You'll also want to wear them when dealing with the prisoners. Some of them have been known to, uh, spit."

They reminded Hardie of a child's plastic swimming goggles. He turned them over and saw that the insides of the lenses were indeed dark—pitch-black as the screen on a busted TV.

"And the earpiece"—Victor tapped his right ear—"is how we communicate with each other. You want to call the other guards, just make a single whistle and click twice. That engages the system. Watch."

Hardie sat there, watching.

"Well, you have to put the earbud in first," Victor said.

After turning it around with his fingers, Hardie gave in. *Sure. I'll put the stupid plastic thing in my ear.* And sure enough, the daffy bastard whistled, a kind of a *Star Trek* communicator–style trill, then made two fast clicking noises. Now Hardie could hear Victor's voice coming from two distinct locations: right in front of him, and directly inside his ear canal.

"Pretty neat, huh?"

Another male voice quickly chimed in: "Everything all right, Victor?"

"Yes—sorry, mate. Just giving the warden an earpiece demonstration."

"Is he awake?"

"Yes, Yankee, he's awake," Victor said. "And he's listening."

Victor made two clicks, and the earbud went dead.

"I think Yankee was taking a little nap there. Sucks to have to wake the others, but communication is everything in this place. If something happens, you want to know the other guards will come running immediately."

"Right."

So there was some kind of wireless system down here. Hardie wondered if he could figure out a way to broadcast a signal beyond these walls. This would do no good if the secret prison were buried in the middle of nowhere, of course. And Hardie had no idea how cell phones worked, let alone how to hijack a wireless communications system and make it broadcast out. But it was something. A possibility.

Hardie finally wrapped a hand around his cane and steadied himself. He wished Victor weren't here. If Hardie was going to fall on his ass, he'd rather do it in peace and quiet. He tried waiting a few seconds, not making eye contact.

But Victor wasn't the kind of guy to take a hint. So Hardie steadied his right hand on the cane, then used his left leg to push himself upright. The world went a little fuzzy for a few seconds... and then it only got worse. Hardie thought he was in real danger of passing out.

Victor smiled and clapped him on the back, massaging him for a second, which was a second longer than Hardie liked.

"You're a real old-school badass, aren't you?" Victor asked.

"How about you don't touch me?"

Hardie moved the cane, then his good leg. Cane, good leg. A few more steps and he had a system going. By the time he reached the doorway, however, a guard was blocking his path.

* * *

It was the female guard. Arms crossed, cold, hard stones in her eyes. Hardie couldn't help but think: this is it. They would admit they had been kidding about the whole *warden* thing. And then they would savagely beat his ass, and he'd be forced to defend himself with his old-man cane before being thrown into a cell.

Instead, Victor made a hasty introduction.

"Warden, this is Whiskey."

She just stared at him, eyes slicing straight through his skull.

"Not my brand, obviously," Hardie said.

Standing behind her was one of the other male guards—one with black Brillo-pad hair and a white mitten of gauze around his right hand. He must have been the one who had gotten his paw caught in the elevator door.

"Hello, Warden. I'd shake your hand, but..."

"Yeah," Hardie said. "Understood."

"That's Yankee," Victor said.

Victor.

Whiskey.

Yankee.

Was all this for real?

But the biggest absurdity was the idea that *he* was in charge of these people. If this was all legit, and *they* (that word again) actually put Hardie to work as the warden of a secret prison to work off some perceived debt, then *they* could have done a lot better with somebody else. Like, *anybody* else. Hardie was a born loner. Not only did he not play nice with others, he couldn't fucking stand others. Everyone except Kendra, the boy, and Nate Parish. And Nate was dead.

Besides that...all Hardie wanted to do was get the fuck out of there. Like he'd spend a single second doing something *other* than trying to escape?

Victor smiled and said, "All we're missing is X-Ray. But you can meet him later."

"Yeah," Hardie said. "X-Ray. Sure."

The female guard stepped forward, said, in shaky English: "Warden."

Already, the *Warden* shit was getting real old fast. "Look, guys," Hardie said. "Why don't you just call me Ch—"

"Hey, now," Yankee said, shaking his head. "No names. You know that. Victor, he knows that, right?"

"He knows," Victor said, wagging his finger at Hardie. "You know...right?"

Whiskey reached out to touch Hardie's arm. "We need...heat."

"What?"

"On gelé," she said. "It is...too cold."

"So find the thermostat and turn it up."

Yankee gave him a confused look. "Only the Prisonmaster can do that."

"Who?"

"The Prisonmaster," Victor said. "The man in charge of sending down food, medical supplies, and new clothing as needed. And only the Warden can talk to the Prisonmaster to make these requests."

Victor and Yankee exchanged a brief look. Hardie probably wasn't meant to catch it—but he did.

Turning his attention back to Hardie, Victor said, "Look, I was getting to that. This is how it works down here. You call it in, the Prisonmaster has it sent it down. He also controls the environmentals—heat, cooling, water temperature. Without a warden, the Prisonmaster's been just sending down the bare minimums, enough to keep the facility running. Even environmental requests were ignored."

"So you want me to talk to this Prisonmaster guy and ask him to turn up the heat?"

"If you would," Yankee said with a smile that was meant to be charming but came off as slightly overeager, bordering on homicidal. "And there's also the food situation."

"You're out of food?" Hardie asked.

"No," Yankee said. "We have plenty of food. But it's the same food—breakfast all the freakin' time. Muffins, white bread, orange juice, grits, oatmeal, and the most awful slab of gray meat you've ever tasted. We've had it. We need something else."

Already Hardie's mind was racing. Food. Prisons needed food, and the food had be delivered from somewhere. Garbage hauled away, too, right? There was no such thing as an escape-proof prison, because to sustain life inside a prison you need support from the outside. This was good.

"Okay," Hardie said, trying to give the impression that he was actually giving a shit. "No breakfast. Got it."

Victor smirked. "That was your predecessor's big idea, too. He thought breakfast was comfort food."

"Okay, heat and different food. Can I do anything else for you?"

An extremely awkward moment followed. All three guards stared at Hardie, as if trying to figure him out. And Hardie did the same. Were they putting him on with this bullshit about heat and breakfast?

Hardie decided, fuck it, and pushed past them. Cane, leg. Cane, leg.

Of course, he didn't make it far.

Once Hardie crossed the next room—which also had a bed and sink—the door was locked.

"Wait," Victor said, just catching up behind him. "Where are you going?"

"If I'm the warden, I should tour this place, shouldn't I?"

"Of course. But you gotta put these on, mate."

Victor pressed something into Hardie's hand—the stupid goggles.

"No, thanks," Hardie said.

"You don't understand. It's a rule. Besides, you don't want them gazing into your eyes. Windows to the soul, and all that."

Hardie could only imagine what he must look like in his suit, with his walking stick and the dorky spaceman goggles in his hand. Something out of a 1980s new-wave music video, most likely. Maybe Mann's bosses didn't want to work him to death. Maybe they just wanted to embarrass the living shit out of him.

Victor fitted his own goggles on his face, double-checked his belt and plastic restraint cuffs, then pulled a set of keys out of his pocket, which were attached by a short length of chain to a metal stud on his black leather belt.

"Besides, you're not going to get very far without keys."

"Don't I get a set?"

"I'm sure they'll send your set down soon. Anyway, they're electronically coded. You slip a key in the door, the mechanism unlocks, and you're good to go. There are door keys, cell keys, all kinds of keys."

Victor hesitated.

"You sure you're ready for this?"

"Just open the door."

"All due respect, Warden, we've got the smartest monsters you'll ever encounter. Our survival in this facility depends on following the rules. You show any of them weakness, they'll exploit it. They will try to befriend you, crawl inside your mind with just a glance. But you cannot listen to them, any more than you'd listen to a rabid animal. Do you understand?"

"Sure."

Victor laughed, shook his head. "I can tell you don't believe me. That's okay. When I first arrived, I didn't believe the warden, either. But here's something I've come to realize. As bad as the outside world might be, with nutty bastards blowing up day-care centers and terrorist technicians constantly trying to find the best way to hide liquid explosives up someone's ass so they can fart and take out a jetliner...as bad as that is, it could be worse. Far worse. There could be more serial killers, more bin Ladens, more monsters roaming the planet...if not for facilities like these. We're the first and last line of defense."

Hardie said:

"Just open the door."

13

Knowledge of the outside world is what we tell you.
    —Patrick McGoohan, *Escape from Alcatraz*

As HARDIE HOBBLED forward into the small, cramped room housing the control panel and looked through a dingy partition of thick, shatterproof plastic onto the rest of the facility, he finally got a sense of the place.

He'd seen prisons before. But none like this.

The entire site was one low-ceilinged room, about the size of a cafeteria in a shitty inner-city high school. This control room, like his own quarters, was one of a series of small rooms on the outer perimeter—like luxury boxes in a sporting arena, only minus the luxury. Cement floors with chipping paint, cement walls with chipping paint, steel supports with chipping paint.

And the prisoners? They were crammed into poorly lit rusty cages. They sat on metal floors and had metal masks strapped to their heads.

Two of them, in three cages.

"The hell...?" Hardie muttered, thinking: *This is it?*

"Told you," Victor said.

None of it made sense. *This* was supposed to be the most secure prison facility in the world?

There had to be more to it than this. Something Hardie wasn't seeing. Maybe force fields, or invisible electronic barriers, or some other high-tech sci-fi bullshit. Mann's employers, whoever they were, seemed to have an unlimited budget. So what was with this cheap-ass prison?

"We mostly watch them from inside this control room," Victor said. "There's one on the opposite side, too, facing the other row of cells. Six cells, four prisoners on the floor. Of course, we do go in there to feed them and do roll call and drag them to the shower room when the smell gets too strong. But yeah, the idea is to minimize contact. These are clever fuckers. They'd crawl inside your skull and hot-wire your brain if they could."

"Huh."

"Like everyplace else, we're tragically understaffed. We work in four shifts, six hours each, but you often end up watching someone else's back."

Hardie said, "Where exactly are we?"

"What do you mean? We're in site number seven seven three four."

"No, I mean geographically. The place we're standing. Where is it?"

Victor squinted as if he'd bitten into something sour. "Where is it? Are you kidding? We don't know. None of us knows. That's the whole point of an escape-proof facility. Didn't they explain any of this to you?"

"How did *you* get here?"

"Like everybody else. Like *you* did."

Nobody, Hardie thought, *got here like I did.*

Yankee and Whiskey wordlessly slipped past both of them and unlocked a door that led out to the cages.

"Anyway, this is good timing," Victor said. "You'll get to see how we do roll call."

"All right, lights..."

Victor reached for an ancient control panel and stabbed a dirty plastic button. An insanely bright light filled the three cells facing them.

"Cameras..."

Yankee and Whiskey unclipped little plastic devices the size of TV remotes from their belts.

"And action."

Inside the first cage was a pale-skinned, lanky, yet muscular man whose head was hanging low. He was stark naked except for the metal mask that was strapped to his head like a welder's helmet. There were breathing holes, but otherwise the mask was featureless. The prisoner sat with his back against the wall, feet flat on the floor, knees a good three feet apart so that you could see his limp cock and slightly larger-than-average balls just hanging there, gently resting on the cold concrete floor.

"Meet Prisoner Four," Victor said.

After an awkward silence, Hardie asked, "Can't you get him something to wear?"

"Wanker refuses to wear anything," Victor explained. "He's renounced all material possessions, or some such shit. We give him clothes, he rips them up into strips."

"Yeah. He's just oozing honor there, isn't he?"

At which point the lanky man—Prisoner Four—lifted his head. He could sense the other two guards approaching. Yankee barked his orders at the prisoner, his voice sounding tinny through the small speaker in the control room.

"Number Four, back against the bars."

"No names for these guys, either?"

"Nope. Just numbers. But we do have nicknames, which relieves the tedium of the numbers. We sometimes call this one Bollock. As in 'bollocks'?"

"Yeah, I get it."

"Sometimes Americans don't."

Once the prisoner's back was against the bars, Whiskey reached out and yanked Bollock's head backward, pinning it to the bars and keeping it still. Yankee took a key from his ring and inserted it into a small lock that joined the straps on the back of the prisoner's mask.

"What's the deal with the masks?"

"They're only allowed to remove the masks when they eat and when there's roll call, which we do with digital photographs."

Yankee said, "Now turn around. Back against the wall."

Prisoner Four, aka Bollock, complied. With the mask off, he turned out to be a long-faced, grim man, with unruly, wispy blond hair. Yankee lifted his digital camera and snapped a photo just as Bollock hoisted a long, bony middle finger at them.

"See what I mean?" Victor said inside the control room.

Whiskey's response was quick and brutal. The bird was flying for only two seconds before a baton jabbed Bollock in the stomach. As the prisoner doubled over, Whiskey removed the baton then jammed it into the hollow of his throat, choking him. Yankee snapped a new photo.

"Say 'cheese,' scumbag," Victor muttered.

"Over on the left is Prisoner One. Also known as Horsehead."

The heavily muscled man inside the cell lazily rubbed the back of his head. Unlike Bollock, this prisoner wore a plain smock. But it didn't cover the scars and puncture wounds that snaked up and down his arms and legs, and presumably his torso, upper thighs, and many of his major internal organs, too. He was a large, thick slab of scarred muscle.

"Horsehead?" Hardie asked.

As if on cue, Horsehead's masked head whipped up to attention. Moved a fraction of an inch to the right, then the left, then the right again, as if his brain were a satellite trying to tune in to a signal. Then he began to jibber excitedly in Italian, the words almost sounding operatic as his voice rose and fell in pitch with every sentence.

Victor rolled his eyes. "Talkative bastard. It's so ironic."

"What's that?"

"Well, you know how the mob's always sending enforcers to scare potential witnesses?" Victor leaned in. "Rumor has it old Horsehead here was the worst mob enforcer of all. When they wanted to frighten somebody into stone-cold silence, they'd send him. Forget severed animal heads in your bed. This guy would do the sickest, most twisted shit you can even imagine. Vile acts that you can never scrub out of your brain, not matter how hard you try. He wouldn't say a word. He would just show you, and instantly, you'd get it."

"Uh-huh."

"Now listen to him. Singing like a canary, ever since they put him down here. Or so I've been told."

Yankee and Whiskey stepped into the frame to repeat the routine. "Prisoner One, back against the bars," Yankee said. Horsehead stopped jabbering and meekly complied with their demands. This time, Whiskey inserted the key.

And nothing happened.

Yankee shook his head sadly. "Shit. Let me try," he said. He took the keys from Whiskey, jammed one into the slot in the back of the mask. Nothing. Jammed it in repeatedly, like he was trying to churn the world's smallest batch of butter. Still nothing.

In the control room, Victor shrugged. "Another wonderful bonus of this facility. Stuff breaks down all the time. And it's not as if we can get a repair crew down here to fix anything—security being what it is. So usually, we have to make do with what we've got."

Hardie watched the guards struggle to open the mask for another few moments. How was this son of a bitch supposed to eat?

"Come on. We've got to walk around to the other control room. Your leg doing okay? You want to go back?"

"I'm fine," Hardie lied. His leg was killing him. But the sooner he saw the rest of the place, the sooner he could figure out how to escape.

The next door Victor opened revealed another guard's living quarters—Yankee's. Same spare furniture as Hardie's and Victor's rooms, only this space smelled like body odor and mold. Hardie couldn't help but think that the guards' rooms were not much better than the prisoners' cells. Granted, you didn't have to sit in your room with your balls touching a cold metal floor, but this wasn't exactly easy living, either. For the past three years—right up until his run-in with Mann and her crew—Hardie had guarded fairly posh residences, stuffed with wall-to-wall audio and video entertainment. It distracted him from the shambles of his own life. If Hardie had to sit in an empty room and just contemplate shit, he might lose his mind.

Yankee's cell led into a much bigger corner room lined with small metal doors, each of them a bit smaller than a cafeteria tray.

"This is where we receive food and fresh clothes," Victor explained. "And any trash goes down here."

"Who sends the stuff down?"

"The Prisonmaster, like I said. Our only link to the outside world. Only he knows where we are."

"How do we talk to this Prisonmaster?"

Victor tapped his ear. "You don't call him. He calls you."

Hardie checked out the doors, which reminded him of both old-fashioned Automats and mausoleum crypts. Neither a very pleasant association.

"Aren't you worried about, uh, prisoners escaping and crawling up the supply path?"

Translation: Maybe I could find a way to escape by crawling up the supply path?

Victor shook his head. "Impossible. The pathways are lined with razor-sharp metal—kind of like those traffic spikes you see in parking lots. The packages are fine coming down. But try to go up one of those things and you'll be cut to pieces."

Awesome.

The next door led to the saddest break room Hardie had ever seen. And Hardie had spent countless hours in the sad, soul-draining break rooms of many Philadelphia police departments. The centerpiece was a long wooden table with metal legs that looked like it wobbled all the time. Hardie made his way over and pressed two fingertips down on its tacky surface. Yep. It wobbled.

"We spend our leisure time in here," Victor explained.

"Leisure, huh?"

"It's actually nice to get out of your room every so often."

"I'm sure."

The door at the other end of the room led to the corner room that Hardie was already familiar with: the elevator vestibule, where he'd been shocked into unconsciousness. Good times, good times. Hardie looked at the elevator mechanism and once again wished he'd stayed in that stupid room upstairs. At least he could wither away in peace.

Now Hardie and Victor were on the other side of the room, and once they made their way through Whiskey's accommodations—just as spartan as the others—they stood inside a second control room, facing a row of three cells.

Through the hard plastic window, Hardie could see a woman in the cage on the right.

Victor said, "That's Prisoner Two."

She wore a mask and a drab cotton smock, just as Prisoner One did, but she didn't look particularly uncomfortable. She sat with her legs arranged in the lotus position, backs of her wrists resting on her knees, head perfectly straight, raven-dark hair touching her shoulders. She didn't move. At all. From all outward appearances, she could have been a fiberglass mannequin, modeling the latest in prison attire.

"Watch this," Victor said, a mischievous little smile on his bearded face.

He stabbed a button. There was a static pop and then—

SQWEEEEEEEEEEEEE

—a hideous siren filled the room, the sound from coming from a speaker directly above the cells. Even inside this control room it was loud enough to burst eardrums. Out there, Hardie thought, it must be unbearable.

"Did you see that?"

"What?"

"I SAID, DID YOU SEE THAT?"

Hardie shook his head; Victor killed the siren.

"She didn't even twitch," Victor said. "It's like she zones out of this place entirely. Sometimes we think she's playing dead—and of course, one of us has to go in there to check on her. Creepy, isn't it?"

Hardie watched the woman, who was utterly still. Not even a strand of her raven-black hair moved; everything was perfectly arranged, and she was somehow at peace with her surroundings.

"Don't let her fool you," Victor said. "She's been trying to screw her way out of this place for months now. When her mask is off she gives you these eyes—and for a minute, you'll be thinking, wow, maybe I should just forget this job and go for it, right? Give her a go, who's to know? Well, let me tell ya, brother—I hear that's how we lost one of your predecessors. It wasn't pretty."

"What's she in for?"

"What?"

Hardie asked, "What did she do?"

"What does it matter?"

He wondered what her face looked like under the mask. Strangely, he found himself picturing his ex, Kendra, under the mask. His curiosity was soon satisfied as Whiskey and Yankee ordered her through the same drill as the others. Back against the bars, head kept still while they unlocked the mask. She slipped it off and turned around to face the guards.

Prisoner Two was absolutely gorgeous.

Prisoner Two was not in her cell.

Instead, she was sitting in a beautiful, lush suburban garden on the warmest day of spring.

Back in college, her philosophy professor had invited the entire class—seventeen freshmen—to his own backyard for a Friday afternoon barbecue. The professor and his wife lived in a beautiful little California oasis, complete with a koi pond and perfectly manicured hedges and stone gardens. At one point the entire class had gathered in the professor's living room for dessert, but the woman now known as Prisoner Two had lingered in the yard for a short time. Not more than a few moments, nowhere as long as a minute. But enough time to permanently record the scene in her memory; she traveled back there now and relished every detail. The smell of the grass. The harsh, smoky scent of charcoal as it hung in the air. The late-spring sun on her forearms. The memory of a shy smile from a boy in her class, and the warm feeling in her stomach. The knowledge that the weekend was ahead of her, and she could do whatever she wanted. She was eighteen years old and healthy and people told her she was beautiful and had yet to experience all the good things that could happen to her.

Barking commands jarred her back to cold reality.

They were here to photograph her again.

She took a deep breath and held it, trying to clear her mind. It was time for her little game. She both looked forward to it and dreaded it. The mechanics were simple—a matter of conjuring the right memory. But the aftereffect was painful.

When they removed her mask, Prisoner Two broke out into the world's silliest grin, like she didn't have a care in the world.

Boys had always told her she had a beautiful smile.

And the trick to smiling like she meant it was traveling back in time two decades, back to when she was a teenager and truly *didn't* have a care in the world, and she'd sit out in the backyard sipping screwdrivers while listening to her drunk friends crack crude jokes. She transported herself back there and smiled, almost feeling the slight chlorine burn in her nose and the warmth on her face and the sweet orange juice and bracing Absolut in her mouth...

"The hell is she doing?" Hardie asked.

"Absolutely *mental,* isn't she?" Victor said. "I'm telling you. Keep your distance from that one. We call her Fatale, for obvious reasons."

The smile didn't last long. Whiskey unclipped something from her belt and sprayed something into Prisoner Two's face that made her recoil.

The mace.

Yeah, that was the painful part of her little game. It sealed her eyes instantly and went to work on the pores of her skin, burning little trails that felt like they bored all the way to her skull. She choked down a scream; she wouldn't give them that satisfaction. They snapped her photo like that, her face a rictus of pain. That didn't matter, though.

Her mask was off. And it would stay off for a while. A half victory. The other half would come later.

Just as there was on the other side, there was an empty cell between the two prisoners. While Two curled up into a ball, hands on her face, Whiskey and Yankee moved down to the last prisoner.

"And there's Prisoner Three. An absolute nightmare."

The figure in the cell was a fearsome-looking bruiser type, even with the mask on. Tattoos of black bones ran up his arms and legs, as if he were the Visible Man from biology class. He had biceps enough to easily snap a neck. Thighs, too, for that matter. The inked-up monster was sitting on the floor of his cell, arms crossed, feet flat on the floor, and his knees locked together.

"Christ," Hardie muttered. "What's *he* in for?"

"Haven't you been listening? They don't tell us. Doesn't matter. This one's been trouble from the beginning. We usually have to shock him into submission just to get him to do something simple, like take a dump."

"Shock him?"

"The metal floors of the cells are electrified, and we carry these bad boys," Victor said, tapping the baton strapped to his belt.

"Doesn't this guy have a cute nickname or anything?"

Victor made a sour face. "The word *cute* doesn't even apply."

Outside, Yankee and Whiskey prepared their routine. "Prisoner Three. Back against the bars." Prisoner Three didn't stir.

"Come on," Yankee said. "Let's not do this again. It always ends the same way. You know this."

No response.

"Oh, so wanker's being stubborn again, is he?" Victor muttered. "Showing off for the new warden. Well, he wants to play it this way, fine."

Victor stabbed a blue button. Static popped. "Guards, stand clear." His voice boomed throughout the facility. Yankee and Whiskey nodded and took three giant steps backward, as if playing a schoolyard game. Victor stabbed the next button in the row—a big red one.

ZZZZZZZZZZAT.

First you heard the shrieks, followed by the jerky movements of their bodies. Hardie could almost could smell the ozone and singed flesh. Prisoner Two had lost her Zen and was screaming in pain. Same with Prisoner Three. They seemed to want to do anything, anything at all, to avoid contact with the floor—which clearly was the source of the electrical shocks. Prisoner Three was shouting something—"All right! All right!"—but it was hard to tell over the screaming of the other prisoners.

"Goddamn it, that's enough," Hardie said.

"No, it's not."

Hardie balanced his weight on the cane and lunged out for Victor's hand. He whipped it up and away before contact could be made.

"Don't ever do that," Victor said. "*Ever.* All due respect, you don't know how to handle these monsters. Show of mercy like that will get your shit twisted up down here."

"You like torturing people? Is that it?"

"Hey, they know the rules, and they know they are expected to follow the rules. All our punishments are nonlethal. If one refuses, all will be punished. Leverage is the only thing that seems to work. They can take almost anything individually. But start in on the others, and their resolve crumbles. Honor among thieves."

"Right," Hardie muttered.

"Hey, we're not the bad guys here," Victor said.

Out on the floor Prisoner Two crawled over to the corner of her cell and curled up into it. Her body was trembling violently. Prisoner Three, meanwhile, slid over on his ass so that he could place his back against the bars, as requested. Whiskey unclipped the baton from her belt, pressed the end into the back of Three's neck, and unleashed a harsh jolt while screaming something in French. Three's body twitched, and he grabbed the bars of his cell to steady himself, but he did not move. Yankee held up a hand to Whiskey, then unlocked the back of Three's mask.

"Come on," Victor said. "You've got one more prisoner to meet."

14

ONE MORE? HAD Hardie missed something? He'd counted six cells on the floor—three on each side, four occupied, two empty. Where did they hide the fifth prisoner? The break room?

Victor led Hardie through the next room—which belonged to the guard named X-Ray. He was on the bed, oblivious to their presence, plastic goggles covering his eyes and a thin smile on his face. "Hey," Hardie said, not expecting a response. Victor explained that X-Ray only spoke German, so Hardie shouldn't expect much in the way of conversation.

The next door led directly into a shower room, which reeked of mildew. The lighting was poor, which was probably a good thing. The ancient crud caked onto the tile looked disgusting even in shadow. They kept to the wall and walked the length of it. Hardie's cane slipped on the tile floor a few times. He moved slowly, trying to redistribute his body weight.

Victor gestured grandly. "This happy place is where we shower, too. Nothing but the best for us."

They reached another locked door. Victor used a key to open it, revealing another long space, much like the break room. Only this room was utterly barren, except for a small table and a series of wall-mounted electronic fixtures.

"When we're done taking the photos of the prisoners, we plug the cameras in here to upload."

Another possible connection to the outside world. Food and clothes come down one way, photographic images go out another. This could be useful. Hardie wasn't sure exactly how yet, but he kept it in mind.

Nate, if you want to give me any hints, feel free.

On the other side of the room was a door that looked like it belonged on a submarine, complete with a metal wheel in the center. Victor put his hands on the metal wheel, then paused. "I have to confess, this is the reason I'm glad you're finally here. Because in the absence of a warden, I've had to step in here once a day, and I'm not going to miss it in the least."

"What is that?"

"Where we keep Prisoner Zero."

"Zero is the oldest prisoner in this facility," Victor continued. "In fact, a lot of us think the facility was created specifically for him. We don't know what he did in the outside world, or where he comes from, his age, what language he speaks...nothing. We don't even know if he's fully human, because none of us understands how a human being could survive these conditions for as long as he has. There's a rumor that he can't be killed. Which is why he's down here, away from everything except us."

Hardie thought about it. *Can't be killed.* This was going to be like one of those old Universal monster-movie matchups: *Unkillable Chuck versus the Prisoner Who Couldn't Be Killed.*

Victor must have caught the expression on his face because he said, "Look, I know it sounds like complete and utter shit, but believe me. The guards are vastly relieved they almost never have to deal with him. Which is why I'm vastly relieved you arrived. And I don't want you dead, so please take care with him."

"What am I supposed to do?"

"Just check his IV and piss-tube lines."

"And look for what?"

"Something that looks wrong."

"Hey, I'm the furthest thing from a doctor. I don't think I'd know what to look for. And even if I did—"

"If you see anything weird, call for X-Ray. He's an actual doctor—or at least has some medical training. But the rules are the rules. Only the warden deals with Zero. Better you meet him now while I can stand guard outside. Most of the time you'll be headed in there alone."

Victor cranked open the door and stepped out of the way.

"You're not coming?" Hardie asked.

"Going to stay out here, if it's just the same to you. And seriously, put on your goggles."

Hardie ignored him and cane-leg-stepped into the dark room.

"Fine, don't listen to good advice," Victor said as the door closed behind Hardie and clanged shut. "Just knock when you're ready to come out."

Hardie steadied himself with the cane. The room was shrouded in darkness. Right away he could hear something breathing, lungs chuffing and chortling.

After his vision adjusted Hardie could see that the dark room was a steel octagon. Prisoner Zero was in the center, on a rusty hospital-style bed. He neither reclined nor sat up fully; his body was halfway between the two. *Body:* funny word to use. As Hardie's eyes adjusted, he could see that Zero had a head, covered with a mask. A torso. An arm—the left. And maybe stumps where legs used to be. That was it. The prisoner was hooked up to a confusing series of tubes and wires. The only signs that he was still alive: the gentle motion of his chest, almost too slight to be considered breathing, and, of course, the sound of the breathing itself—sickly, congested, disgusting.

"Hi," Hardie said into the darkness.

Zero said nothing, just as Victor warned.

Hardie couldn't help but think of that old Metallica video, the one that used clips from *Johnny Got His Gun.* Perhaps Zero here would communicate by Morse code, banging his head against the table, tapping out *K-I-L-L-M-E-N-O-W* one dot and dash at a time.

"Can you hear me?" Hardie asked.

Hardie inched closer. Zero's mask, like the others, had no eye holes. But through the breathing cutout Hardie saw the most perfectly hideous teeth ever.

Smiling.

Without warning, the figure lurched forward and let out a fevered grunt like a sonic blast. As much as he hated to admit it, Hardie flinched. Took a clumsy step back, felt his legs weaken, tried to reposition the cane to support his weight, but the bottom slipped on the metal floor, and all was lost. Hardie stumbled backward, screaming at his own legs to listen to him, don't do this to me now, for Christ's sake...and then the cane slipped out of his hand and the base of his spine slammed into something hard and metallic and unforgiving, and then he was landing on his ass on the floor.

A few feet away, Zero started to pulsate and make a strange repeating sound:

"Huh-huh-guh-huh-huh-guh-huh-huh-huh."

Guy was either laughing or having a seizure.

Hardie used his cane to pull himself back up to a standing position, then hobbled over behind Zero's head. Victor told him: he had to check the guy's IV lines, his pee tubes, whatever. Maybe he was a gross bastard, but he could also be hopelessly insane. And ignoring him was just adding to his misery...

"Huh-huh. Huh-huh. HUHHHHHHH."

"Shh now, okay? Daddy's thinking back here."

Hardie crouched down, but he didn't know what he was looking at. He settled on looking for an obvious blockage, a sudden change in color in one of the tubes. That would mean a blockage, right? The smell here, up close and personal, was even more hideous. He'd once read that a person's sense of smell wasn't ethereal, wasn't some magical wave like stink lines in a cartoon. Atoms from whatever you were smelling traveled up your nose and adhered themselves to your mucous membranes. Hardie was literally snorting this gross bastard the longer he stayed back here. He worked his way around to the side of Zero's bed, eager to get out of this room as quickly as possible.

"Huh-HUH. Huh-HUH. Huh-HUHHHHHHHH."

And then something cold and greasy splattered on Hardie's face.

Zero had spit on him.

"Son of a—" he began, and then realized that he had opened his mouth, which wasn't the smartest thing he could have done. Something like phlegm dripped down his forehead, along his cheek, and ran toward his mouth. Hardie fought a gag reflex and turned away from Zero, wiping at his face with his left sleeve. His arm trembled; his aim was imperfect. Hardie didn't so much clean his face as spread more of the slimy, viscous fluid across it.

"Huh-huh-huh-huh-huh-huh-huh-huh-huh."

It took Hardie a few seconds to realize that Prisoner Zero was laughing.

* * *

Okay, fuck this.

Hardie recovered his cane and climbed to his feet, his right leg still wobbly and generally useless as support device. His palms were clammy and greasy from whatever grime had collected on the floor of this crazy steel room. God knows what cocktail of filth and human secretions had gathered here. At that moment Hardie's needs were reduced to two simple items: getting out and taking a hot shower. Were the showers hot in this hellhole? He was eager to find out. Gross bastard could check his own IV bags, flush out his own waste.

Good hand on the cane, Hardie rapped his knuckles on the steel vault door. The resulting sound was impossibly faint, as if he were tapping on the hull of the *Titanic* in hopes that the captain would hear it up in his quarters.

"Come on, Victor."

"Huh-huh-guh-huh-huh-guh-huh-huh-huh."

Steadying himself, Hardie banged harder.

"VICTOR!"

"Huh-huh-guh-huh-huh-guh-huh-huh-huh."

Hardie spun to look at the half-human form in the dim light. The masked head had turned to watch him.

"Don't you start with me," Hardie said.

Under the mask came some kind of mumbling.

"Yeah, that's what I thought."

The thing in the mask didn't move. He simply waited. Like a puppy expecting his master's next command.

Hardie banged again. "COME ON, LET ME THE FUCK OUT."

Across the room, an electric bolt snapped; a door popped open a few inches. Problem was, that wasn't the way he'd entered...was it? Hardie was disoriented; had he gotten turned around?

Then again, what did it really matter? It was an exit.

Hardie cane-staggered out of Zero's chamber and used his right sleeve to wipe the shit off the rest of his face. Okay, yeah, fine, Victor was right. He should have kept the damned goggles on. He blinked compulsively, convinced some vile disease was worming its way past his eyes and into his brain.

God, a shower. He'd give anything for a shower right now.

After he was convinced that his face was somewhat phlegm-free, Hardie realized he was trapped.

In a steel room the size of a walk-in closet.

Behind him, the electric bolt snapped, locking the door shut.

Come on. Seriously?

He spun around and picked up his cane to bang on the door that had just closed behind him. But that only threw off his balance. His bad leg buckled and he staggered backward until he slammed into the opposite wall, just behind him. Something sharp stabbed the base of his spine. Goddamn it.

Hardie paused to catch his breath; it was embarrassing to feel so out of control. Heart in a tight knot, guts wound up so tight it felt like they were either going to bind themselves shut forever or explode in a wet hot gush. Neither prospect appealed to him.

Calm down, Charlie.

You're just stuck in a steel coffin in a secret prison.

Could be worse, right?

Once he was steady again, Hardie smashed his cane against the door.

BANG

And followed it with a shouted

"HEY."

Nothing.

BANG

BANG

BANG

"HEY, I'M STUCK IN HERE!"

Nothing, except...

...maybe Hardie was imagining this, but he could swear he heard the faint sound of...

Huh-HUH. Huh-HUH. Huh-HUHHHHHHHHH.

"Fuck me," Hardie muttered.

The cosmic joke was still unfolding, it seemed. Instead of dying up in that waiting room, maybe Hardie was fated to die in this steel closet. Unkillable Chuck, indeed. *And that's the last anyone ever heard of him...*

Breathe, Charlie, breathe.

Remember what Batman said.

Every prison provides its own escape.

Batman, you are so full of shit.

Breathe, Charlie.

Breathe.

BANG

BANG

BANG

"FUUUUUCK!"

Hardie wasn't sure how long it was before he regained his focus and felt the muscles in his neck finally loosen—for all he knew he'd spent an eternity in that steel coffin/closet, and for some reason, none of the other guards had bothered to come looking for him. Especially that bastard Victor, his tour guide. Hardie told himself to forget

Victor and channel his inner Dark Knight. Batman would have been able to see a way out of this, like, *instantly.* Look around you.

Which, of course, is the moment he noticed the metal grate at his feet.

Hardie worked his way down to the floor, steadying himself with his cane, getting his fancy new suit even dirtier, and tugged at the grate, lifting it a fraction of an inch before it settled back down into its groove. But at least it moved. That was something.

Hardie had to sit down on the floor for the leverage he needed. His left arm was almost useless, but with enough grunting and pulling he was able to mostly use his right hand to lift the grate out of its cement groove and slide it out of the way, revealing a small tunnel that ran parallel to the floor. The space would be wide enough to fit his shoulders. Just barely. Was he really considering this? Going down into a hole in the darkness?

Yes. Yes, he was.

Although Batman would have probably sent that skinny-ass Boy Wonder in first.

He tried to stay positive. Tell himself that maybe this was a good thing. See, in every prison flick he'd ever watched—which was a lot—the escape plan depended on secret tunnels and hidden passageways. If he somehow had ended up in the ductwork of this facility, then maybe he could find a way out. Or at least create a better mental map of the place, from the ground up.

So Hardie took a deep clean breath and went down.

There was only just enough room to move his right arm and left leg, pulling himself along the tunnel, a few inches at a time. The farther he crawled, the tighter the crawl space seemed to get. Hardie was beginning to panic now. Rationally, he knew that in the worst case, he could just crawl backward the way he came. But the irrational part of his brain suggested that his feet would bump into some barrier if he did that. And no matter how hard he kicked, the barrier wouldn't budge. And he'd be stuck, beyond rescue, beyond reach...

The only sound was the steady hum of water tapping against some kind of surface; too steady to be a leak, but also too light to be a faucet. Still, it was something to go on. Hardie paused every few feet to make sure he was headed toward the sound, not away from it. The air stank like mold and wet stone. Whoever had built this place hadn't ever come back to clean it. Ever.

Come on, Hardie told himself, and pressed forward until he emerged into a small, cold, empty room, with a rusty metal ladder leading...up.

After the confinement of the tunnel, the room felt as vast and limitless as a sports arena.

You did it.

Breathe.

Breathe.

Hardie craned his neck around. There wasn't much in the way of light up there, and the smell of mold and mildew made him want to puke. It wasn't just a smell, actually. It seemed to float in the air like a living organism, a free-floating apparition made of grime.

But at least he could go up.

Hardie climbed the ladder with his good arm and one good leg, which required a series of half pull-ups that completely drained him. Halfway up the ladder Hardie began to realize the folly of his decision. There was another grate above his head and not much light; fat, greasy drops of water were dive-bombing him from the grate. In addition to the slime and phlegm and filth already covering his hands and clothes.

Either continue up, or admit defeat and go crawling back to that steel room with the grunting, spitting nutcase.

Wasn't much of a choice, really. Hardie had been force-fed defeat for the past God knows how long, and he refused to take another teaspoon of it. Using his good arm (the right) and good leg (the left), Hardie continued up the ladder until he reached the grate. He wrapped his gimp arm around the ladder, then reached up with his right hand, slipping his fingers through the openings, grabbing hold, and pushing up.

The grate, to his delight and surprise, moved.

See, things were looking up already.

The grate was heavy as hell, though. He pushed it aside until his fingers reached the concrete edge of the opening, then he slipped them out and slid the grate fully out of the way before continuing his ascent. Once he climbed out of the passageway, Hardie had no choice but to roll on the damp floor until he could work himself up into a sitting position, and when he did he was more than a little stunned to see a naked woman not six feet away, showering in the gloom.

Prisoner Two rubbed the bar of soap across the top of her head. The mace had long since worked its way into her skin, and the soap and water didn't help the burn one bit. The soap itself was a thick chunky white block that reeked of bad perfume. Better than nothing, though.

The shower was the other half of her victory.

She knew they wouldn't let her stay in her cell with the chemicals soaking into her face. Too dangerous. You could actually die from something like that, and the prisoners were not permitted to die. So a shower almost always followed.

The ability to choose when you clean yourself was a big deal, especially when almost nothing else was under your control.

She only used the cloying soap on her hair during every other shower, which worked out to twice a month, if she was counting the days correctly. Holding back on the soap was a vain attempt to keep her hair from drying out too much after washing. Vanity; she still clung to a tiny shred of it. Though that was difficult when your shower room was a subterranean pit, the tile in which was caked with funk going back to the Middle Ages, and your three-minute shower was lorded over by a cunt in a Nazi uniform who loved to end your shower session with a small but perfectly horrible electric jolt from her magic Dong Juan Stun Wand.

Speaking of, she only had about a minute left, she guessed. Better finish up. Whiskey the guard loved to drag her out when she was still tacky.

But as she bent down to rinse the soap from her legs, she was stunned to see thick fingers reaching up out of the drain in the corner of the room.

Was this a hallucination? Was she still asleep in her cage and dreaming this?

If so, the vision persisted. The fingers pushed aside the grate and a rumpled, trembling man in a dirty suit came scrambling up out of the hole.

Prisoner Two's first inclination was to scream. But then she remembered where she was and realized the absurdity of such an act. Whiskey would see him soon enough, and she'd come running over to probably shove her electrified dildo wand in his face. And probably hers, for good measure.

"Sorry," he said, sitting on the edge of the hole. "Really...I didn't know..."

What was the deal with the suit? Nobody wore a suit down here. Nobody except the warden.

God...this was the new warden, wasn't it?

And when he looked up at her, and Prisoner Two had a chance to blink some of the chemical residue out of her eyes and focus on the details of his face, she realized something else. The hair was different, and the face definitely more wan and weary than the photo she'd been given.

But she knew this man.

The naked woman said,

"Charlie Hardie?"

Which blew Hardie's mind so hard he thought his skull would shatter into tiny little bits and pieces. Never mind that nobody used real names down here; never mind that he'd never seen this woman before today—and, yes, Hardie would have remembered; never mind that the last thing he expected was to pop out into the shower room of this freaky secret prison.

But somehow, she knew his name.

How did she know his name?

"Who are you?" Hardie asked.

All at once a yell sounded from the other side of the shower. Though Hardie was no linguist, he would have guessed that the burst of words that followed was profanity, and that it was in French. He tore his eyes away from the mysterious naked lady who knew his name. Squinting in the gloom, he could see Whiskey running toward them.

The naked prisoner whispered: "You don't know me, but I was sent to look for you."

Before Hardie had a chance to respond, Whiskey had closed the distance and slammed Prisoner Two into the nearest available wall. The tremor of the blow seemed to spread throughout the tiles of the entire room. Water splattered; Two grunted; Whiskey cursed again, in French. A bar of soap ricocheted off the wall and spun to a stop in the middle of the floor. Whiskey spun her head around and started screaming:

"GO! GO NOW!"

"Let go of her," Hardie said.

"GO NOW!"

"That's enough!"

Prisoner Two stared at him, face pressed against the disgusting tile, and said, "Deke sent me."

"SHUT UP!" the guard cried, then to Hardie: "GO NOW!"

The impasse was broken by a broad yell from the other end of the room. "Whoa ho ho!" Hardie turned to see Victor stepping in the doorway, back from wherever he had gone.

"What's going on here? You're not allowed in here. Especially during ladies' shower time, mate. The fuck's wrong with you?"

"Just help me up," Hardie said.

The situation quickly defused. Whiskey dragged Prisoner Two back to her cell; Victor picked up Hardie by the arm and escorted him to the entrance of the shower cell. Hardie stole one last glance, though, and Prisoner Two caught it. She gave him a grim smile in return.

You don't know me, but I was sent to look for you.

Deke sent me.

Deke Clark?

Hardie wanted to scream for joy. Goddamn it, he'd followed the bread crumbs after all. God bless that ugly stubborn bastard. God bless the FBI. God bless goddamn America.

15

*You're my dog, see? You bark when I say bark. You fetch when
I say fetch. You roll over and play dead when I tell you to.*
— The Punisher, *Circle of Blood*

AS HE SHOWERED the scum off his body, Hardie couldn't help but
wonder why life kept putting naked ladies in his path.

The last time Hardie met a naked woman—well, topless, anyway—he'd ended up shot, abducted, then dumped here. Her sun-
tanned breasts had been an omen of many horrible things to come.

So what did *this* naked-lady omen mean?

Hardie dried the top of his head with the edge of a white terry-
cloth towel that had been bleached so many times it felt like cardboard. Inside the small closet was another suit, a duplicate of his
stained and ripped suit; below that, a drawer containing three sets of
boxers and plain white T-shirts.

As he dressed, Hardie wondered where his other suitcase was right
now. Probably in a dank police evidence locker. Tagged, bagged, and
put into indefinite storage. Unless Deke had managed to check it out
and send it to Kendra. Last personal effects and all that. All the time
that had passed—weeks, maybe even months—they had to think
he was either missing for good or dead.

No, that wasn't right; Deke still believed. Because she'd said it herself:

Deke sent me.

Hardie lay down on the stiff mattress and tried to put both hands behind his head. His left arm set off little fireworks displays of agony, as if to say *NO, YOU MAY NOT DO THAT*. Hardie settled for his right hand, balled up into a fist, behind his head, and his left arm resting loose and semistraight. He put his feet up. He closed his eyes. He tried not to think. Just for a little while...

A knock jarred him out of his reverie.

"Warden," a soft voice said. "May I see you?"

Hardie sat up, using his right arm for support. It was Whiskey. She was short, dark-haired, compact, and wore a deadly serious expression meant to offset the fact that she looked like a teenager. Hardie said nothing. She took his silence as an invitation, and walked across the room before sitting down at the edge of the bed near his feet. Okay, then, make yourself right at home. Whiskey remained seated at the edge of his bed, staring at him with big brown eyes. Hardie was confused.

"What is it?"

She inched closer, then unceremoniously placed her hand on his crotch.

Hardie acknowledged that he'd left himself wide open, so to speak. But she couldn't seriously be hitting on him, could she?

Whiskey's hand, though, pushed against his balls like she meant it. This was no accidental brush. She gave them an experimental squeeze, looking him dead in the eyes, the ghost of a smile on her face. It was the kind of strange smile that some people could make by turning the corners of their mouths downward; the smile was all in the eyes.

And then she squeezed his balls hard as a vise and pushed Hardie's entire half-crippled body up against the wall. Her other hand flew to his throat and squeezed that, too.

"You will *never* do that again."

Hardie's body didn't know to do with the pain on two fronts. His air had been cut off expertly—strongly. Whiskey's grip was unreal. But the pain in his balls was the stuff of legend. Entire organ systems seemed to want to shut down immediately. Hardie gasped. Whiskey leaned in closer.

"You will never embarrass me in front of prisoners, Warden."

Yes you crazy bitch yes I'll call just take your hands off my testicles, please…

The twin grip on his balls and throat suddenly released. Her head cocked. Someone was speaking to her through the bud in her ear. Hardie could hear the faint buzzing. Then she turned her gaze back to Hardie, said "never" one last time, and ran out the door.

As soon as his internal organs unclenched enough to allow him to do so, Hardie sat up, reached for his cane, then started after her as best he could—cane-leg, cane-leg, cane-leg, cane-leg—through Victor's empty room. Nobody was in the control booth, either, or Yankee's quarters, or the food delivery room. Instead he found all four guards in the break room, batons in hand, yelling at someone.

"The hell's going on?"

Hardie inched forward and saw that it was the prisoner called Horsehead.

Out of his cage.

The mask had slid up so that his mouth was uncovered. And he was snarling. Spitting. Cursing in Italian at them all. Holding his hands palms out, fingers curled like claws.

Victor turned his head quickly and noticed Hardie. "Stand back, Warden. We've got this."

How the hell did the prisoner escape from his cell? Granted, the bars were old and rusted, but it still didn't seem possible.

"Everybody ready?" Yankee said.

X-Ray nodded, as did Whiskey.

"Let's do it," Victor said.

Four against one—it wasn't really a proper fight. Even for a foe as formidable as Horsehead, who lashed out with a flurry of fists and elbows and even a few desperate head butts, trying his best to gouge an opening in the wall of human bodies that were standing all around him. But the guards had electrified batons and saps that quickly pounded the resistance out of the prisoner.

After the beating, two of the guards dragged Horsehead back out to the main floor, a guard on each limb. Hardie trailed behind. By the time Hardie reached the main floor, the stage was already set. The sirens were blaring, the lights flashing. The other three prisoners were stirring, climbing to their feet and moving toward the bars like toy robots with comically large heads.

"What's this, now?" Hardie asked.

"Escapes aren't treated lightly here," Victor said. "The other prisoners have to learn that any attempt will be met with an extreme—"

"You're not understanding me. What are you going to do?"

"Standard procedure."

"Do they bust out of their cages that often?"

Horsehead was on his knees, X-Ray and Yankee standing guard on either side. Whiskey carried over a rubber hose, which was attached to a wall fixture. When Horsehead saw the hose, he didn't react. Not at first. He lowered his head, resigned to what was coming, as if it had happened before.

Christ, were they going to pull the old police trick of beating him with a rubber hose?

When the hose reached him, Horsehead launched a punch into

Yankee's stomach, then spun a few degrees on his knees and tried to do the same to X-Ray. No fancy moves, just blunt-force trauma. But X-Ray dodged the blow. Horsehead climbed off one knee, foot planted on the ground. X-Ray slammed a baton into Horsehead's left shoulder blade and squeezed the trigger. *ZZZZAP.* Horsehead screamed in Italian and then Whiskey jammed her baton into his chest—almost as if the guards were trying to complete a circuit through the man's heart.

Hardie took a step toward them.

Victor, circling on the periphery, said: "He's fine. He's going to be fine. The batons are tuned to nonlethal charges."

Horsehead's body got the message. His knees slammed back down onto the concrete, and his large muscled body wobbled there for a moment before collapsing to the ground. X-Ray and Whiskey zapped him a few more times on his head, neck, and the bottoms of his feet, and Horsehead's body wobbled like a creature who'd been deboned.

"Goddamn it!"

"It's almost over," Victor said.

But it wasn't. The guards were intent on finishing what they started. Horsehead was hauled back up to his knees, held in place. By this time, Yankee had recovered. He slapped Horsehead, slapped him again, a third time, then a fourth until his mouth finally flopped open and the hose nozzle was jammed in. Another guard held it in place by squeezing the top and bottom of Horsehead's face, forcing his jaw shut. The water was turned on. The gush was violent and uncontrolled. It seemed to spray everywhere, out of the sides of Horsehead's mouth and nose as his whole body began to writhe and guards struggled to hold him in place.

"Oh, fuck this," Hardie said, and started forward with his cane.

Victor held up a hand, curled into a fist, and pointed it at Hardie. "Warden, stop."

"Let him go," Hardie said, a few steps closer now. He'd smack the guards with his goddamn cane if he had to. There was a difference between discipline and torture.

Then something squirted out of Victor's wrist, nailing Hardie in the face. By the time he was trying to wipe it away with his sleeve, his eyes and nose were already on fire. Hardie, now blinded, screamed and lashed out toward Victor with his cane. Someone tackled him from the right. He yelled and tried to spin in midair, crashing onto the concrete floor with Victor on top of him.

"I told you not do that! You don't understand! You stop this and we lose! Be sensible!"

"Get off me."

"Will you please trust me?"

"Fuck you!"

Victor punched Hardie in the face, then used those few seconds of shock and confusion to put him in a crazy super-tight headlock. The lock was so tight and expertly rendered that it both threatened to cut off his air supply and essentially paralyzed Hardie from the midtorso up. He couldn't even think a word, let alone speak it aloud.

"Listen to me, mate—I like you and all, but you've just arrived here, and you've got to learn to trust somebody, otherwise you're not going to make it. We need you, just like you need us. That's the only way this can work."

Hardie wanted to tell him to go fuck himself, but couldn't move his jaw.

He could only watch as Horsehead fell back to the ground, choking almost silently, hideous gurgling in his throat, stomach bloated. X-Ray slammed a baton into his belly. Water gushed out of his mouth and he coughed for real now, a wet furious bark. He voided his bowels. They allowed him a few moments to recover, waiting at least two seconds between each bark, which let them know it was time to begin again.

Prisoner Two listened to the water-hose torture from the other side of the floor. She tried to return to the philosopher's peaceful backyard garden, but was snapped back by the sound of the man's frenzied barking. Her nervous system wouldn't allow her to ignore that. Something about the man's voice broke her heart.

They were no doubt putting on this show to impress the new warden. This is what needed to be done, *this* was how they handled business down here. All very familiar. But the new warden didn't seem all that impressed.

Of course he wasn't. He was Charlie Hardie, fugitive hero.

What she couldn't figure out was *why* he was here.

Was it a taunt? Her abductors knew her assignment was to find Hardie. They had lured her to that hotel with the promise of new intel—a source who had claimed to know where Hardie had been hiding. Had they had him all this time, and now just shipped him here to taunt her? Or to see what he could get her to reveal? He'd been gone a long time. They could have done things to his mind. They could have completely broken it and rebuilt it from nothing. He could be here to pry apart her mind, see how much *she* knew.

Listening to Hardie's reaction to the torture, however, led her to believe this wasn't the case. The man still cared; the man was still a fighter.

She'd have to wait until they could be alone to know for sure. She just hoped he was smart enough to make that happen.

Hours later, Hardie woke up in his bed. His face and neck still ached from where Victor had punched and choked him. Whenever he swallowed, his neck muscles throbbed, to the point where he started to worry that his airway might seal itself up. His buddy, good ol' Victor, was all apologies, of course. Had to do it, Warden. You'll see. For the good of the facility. Blah blah freakin' *blah.*

Why had he bothered?

His mind should be concentrating on escape, not on saving people. Saving people was what got him into this hellhole. Freakin' Horseboy was probably a multiple murderer who skullfucked his victims and ate unborn children. And he just endured a face full of chemicals and a good old-fashioned choke-out to intervene on his behalf?

Enough of this.

Focus on getting out of this place.

Hardie had struggled up to a semisitting position when a calm voice spoke into his ear.

"Hello, Mr. Hardie."

Oh, boy.

The Prisonmaster, at long last.

Finally, someone who could tell him what was going on here. Hardie knew it was pointless to threaten him. He had zero leverage here. Instead, he had to draw him out. Learn whatever he could about what this place was—maybe even where it was. What he was supposed to do, except get the crap beat out of him by his own colleagues?

"Uh, hi," Hardie said.

"Welcome to site seven seven three four," the Prisonmaster said. "I know the staff is excited to meet you."

"Yeah. Real excited."

The voice in his ear was real, but it still felt strange, like he was talking to himself.

"I detect a note of sarcasm in your voice, Mr. Hardie. It's too soon in your tenure to be jaded, don't you think?"

"I didn't ask to be here. Do you have a name besides Prisonmaster? Who do you work for?"

"We all have the same employer. As for my identity...well, you know by now that's not how we work."

"Yet you know my name."

"Yes, of course I do."

There was a moment of awkward silence.

Be the bigger guy, Hardie told himself. Draw him out. Learn something about this place.

Instead, Hardie blurted:

"I don't understand what the fuck you want me to do down here."

There was a pause on the line. Hardie thought he heard the sharp intake of breath, as if he'd offended the sensibilities of the man on the other line. He closed his eyes, tried to channel his former partner, Nate Parish. Nate was great at this stuff. He could draw a man's deepest, darkest secrets out of him during a street-corner conversation. Hardie was never good at that. Hardie usually just hung in the background and watched, in case things got out of hand. With Nate, though, they never did.

"Mr. Hardie, we want you to do what you do best. Guard things. Wasn't that your previous job? Guarding the homes of the rich?"

"This isn't exactly a house."

"No, it is not. Your task is much more important than protecting the material goods of the overprivileged. You are, in effect, protecting *many* homes, all across the country. Because the individuals incarcerated in this facility are those worst kind of predators. They destroy without guilt. They need to be contained. And your job is to contain them."

"Don't know if you've been down here lately, but things are a little out of hand."

"Which is why you're there," the Prisonmaster said. "We want you to bring some moral rectitude to the facility. In the time without a warden, it's lapsed a bit. This facility can be great again. It's why you were chosen for the job."

"Like I have a choice? I mean, I didn't ask for this."

The Prisonmaster sighed, almost inaudibly. "Your personal circumstances really don't matter. You were selected for this job. As I understand it, you owe a considerable debt to our employers. But that's no affair of mine. I'm just here to help you run the best facility possible."

"Right. While you're enjoying the sun up top somewhere."

The Prisonmaster said nothing.

By now, Hardie thought, his dead partner Nate Parish would have deduced a hundred things from the conversation so far—if this guy went to college or not. If so, the specific college. And beyond that, which dorm complex he stayed in freshman year, and even beyond *that* he would probably be able to narrow that shit down to a handful of rooms. Hardie? All he knew about the Prisonmaster was that he was up there, and Hardie was stuck down here.

"Well, do you have any requests?" the Prisonmaster asked.

Hardie fought back the urge to request that the Prisonmaster insert his head into his own ass. But then remembered that he did have a few things to ask.

"Yeah. The food. Everyone's tired of the breakfast foods."

"Ah. This may take a while. The food service department is slow to change, but I'll see what I can do. Anything else?"

Hardie racked his brain. There *was* something else . . .

"The heat. We need more heat down here. It's freezing."

"I will see"—there was a pause, as if to imply that the Prisonmaster was eagerly taking notes—"what I can do. Is there anything else, Mr. Hardie?"

"Yeah. Tell me what this is all about. Why I'm down here. Why you're keeping people in cages in this secret prison. And most importantly, *who the hell* you people are."

The Prisonmaster exhaled so forcefully it seemed like he was blowing right into Hardie's ear.

"You may feel slightly discouraged, but remember this—the facility is what you make it. Everything in your file indicates that you bring unorthodox solutions to difficult situations. I believe you can bring great change to the institution."

"Uh-huh."

"And those *people*—by the way, they're not people, Mr. Hardie, let's make that clear from the beginning, they're *monsters,* and they are being kept in cages to make the world a safer place. You were chosen because you possess a certain skill set. You're down there to help make the world a safe place."

Right, Hardie thought. *But who's keeping the world safe from* you *bastards?*

INTERLUDE WITH A PARANOID FEDERAL AGENT (RETIRED)

DEKE CLARK HAD a knife in hand and raw chicken on the counter when he saw *something* moving in the bushes out back.

He did a double take, wondering if it was just an optical illusion in the early summer twilight. A shadow falling in an unexpected way. A crosswind. Or maybe that third beer goofing around with his mind, making him see things that weren't really out there, in the backyard, where his teenaged girls were tossing a baseball around, waiting for their father to get dinner going already.

It was nothing, Deke told himself. *Had* to be nothing. But a little voice inside Deke's head—the same voice that had been nagging at him for a long time now—told him maybe it could be something. After all, Deke had done something very naughty today.

He'd made a phone call.

Deke put the knife down and walked to the window, holding his hands in the air. He should wash them. But he needed to look first just to make sure. Deke squinted, trying to block out the sun and zero in on those bushes.

"DAAAAAAD," his youngest cried. "I'm STARRRVING."

"It's coming, baby," Deke said, still peering into the spaces between the branches and leaves, looking for movement, the gleam of metal, anything.

"Come on, DAAAAD," his elder daughter yelled, joining her sister in the faux anguish.

Nothing...

Of course, if you were an assassin hiding in the bushes out behind a suburban home, you'd go perfectly still, too, knowing that your target was now sticking his stupid head in the perfect frame of a kitchen window. Deke imagined a blast of cold black—his brains splattered on the raw chicken behind him—and the look on his kids' faces as their father's already dead body dropped to the floor, out of view. Then the assassin expertly turning his gun on them, no matter how fast or where they ran...

Because he made a phone call.

Why did he make that damned call?

Deke stepped away from the window, nudged the kitchen tap with his wrists, stuck his hands under the hot water.

For the longest time he'd played everything cool. Served his time and had done what they wanted. He didn't mention Hardie or the Hunters ever again. Not even to Ellie. He'd put the brakes on several investigations connected to activities in Eastern Europe. He'd received no resistance from Sarkissian, so it wasn't difficult. If Deke or his boss wasn't leading the charge into something, nothing got done. Their office was too scattered, the case load too great. Eventually Deke couldn't take it anymore and he pulled the plug. Said he wanted to teach, spend more time with his family. Sarkissian didn't say a word. He was probably thinking the same thing.

Still, the image of Hardie ate away at him. Deke had only seen it once—they felt no need to show it to him again—but once was enough. The pain on that man's face. Goddamn it. You couldn't see what kind of torture they were putting him through and that somehow made it worse. Deke tried to console himself with the thought that Hardie was dead; they wouldn't keep him alive. They'd kept him alive just long enough to show his image to Deke so Deke would eagerly slip that dog collar around his own neck. He cursed his own cowardice.

What else could he do, though?

Play the tough guy and wait until they grabbed one of his kids and ...

Deke couldn't even think about it.

As time passed, though, he had this troubling gut feeling that Hardie was alive. Kept in some hellhole like a POW, brought out for beatings every so often. Meanwhile Deke drank his Yards Pale Ale and cut up chicken breast for the grill, watching his kids play in his backyard ...

Finally Deke decided to do something about it.

He was careful. God, was he careful. Deke, a longtime FBI agent, knew how the bad guys could communicate in secret. He duplicated those techniques—laundering his own money, using disposable cell phones and dead drops, none of it (he prayed to God) traceable in any way back to himself.

What Deke did with that money was hire a professional investigator. Not just anyone—the best of the best. Someone he'd never met but had heard great things about. Whose track record spoke for itself. The contact was brief; the investigator seemed to understand Deke's situation perfectly, which was a little unnerving. "The next time you hear from me, I'll have found your man." Which Deke would have considered bluster, if not for the investigator's 98 percent success rate. (Confirmable, too, after a peek at FBI case files.)

But all this time later ... and no word from the investigator.

Which was why Deke made that phone call this morning, just to check on progress, and had spent the rest of the day with a growing sense of unease, half convincing himself that trained killers were hiding in his backyard, ready to punish him for the transgression. Deke hadn't even made contact with the investigator; just the answering service. Which made him worry even more that...

Oh, God.

He *definitely* saw something now, in the bushes. An arm. Had to be. What else could it be? Deke almost screamed the names of his girls before forcing his mouth shut. Don't be an idiot and tip him off. Instead Deke took the knife and ran out the back door, putting himself between his children and the bushes and screaming at them to go inside the house, NOW, don't ask questions, just GO GO GO and stabbing at the bushes with the knife and...

Whatever had been there—if anything *had* been there—was gone.

Back inside, Deke told the girls that he thought he saw a rabid dog out in the bushes and there wasn't time to explain. His elder girl rolled her eyes, thinking her dad was kidding, but then she saw his ashen face and decided not to press it. Deke also announced that the chicken had spoiled, they won't be grilling tonight, they should put some shoes on and pile into the car pronto and go out for something to eat.

Deke drove Ellie and the kids to their favorite pizza parlor, a few minutes away, his mind a jumble of contradictory emotions. Relief that nothing had happened. Regret at making that phone call. Cowardice for feeling that regret.

The entire drive, Deke couldn't keep his eyes off the rearview and side-view mirrors.

16

These walls are funny. First you hate 'em, then you get used to
'em. Enough time passes, you get so you depend on them.
—Morgan Freeman, *The Shawshank Redemption*

OVER THE NEXT dozen shifts Hardie waited, learning the patterns. There were four shifts to cover the twenty-four-hour day. Not that they truly measured days—they had timers strapped to their wrists, not watches. Six hours a shift, one guard per shift, with another serving as backup. Each "day," the prisoners removed their masks and were photographed with a handheld plastic digital camera. The guards took those cameras to the uploading room, and the images were sent to somebody in the outside world. A proof of life. Meant for whom? Who knows.

Hardie himself was on Prisoner Zero detail, checking pee tubes and IV lines twice a day and listening to the creepy son of a bitch grunt and wheeze and laugh to himself. Or to no one in particular.

Guh-huh. Huh-huh. Huh-huh-huhhhhhhhhhhhh.

No one asked for Zero's proof of life. Which was a relief. Hardie wasn't in any great rush to see what was under that mask.

Otherwise, prisoners were confined to their cells for twenty-three and a half hours a day. Some form of disgusting breakfast food, barely heated in a battered, rusty toaster oven, was served during two of the three shifts that were considered "day."

Hardie again thought about those food deliveries. If there was a way in for food and medical supplies, there had to be a way out, no matter what Victor said. And what about trash? Trash had to go somewhere.

"Whatever isn't used, we burn," Victor said. "But we tend to reuse whatever we can."

"Doing your part for the environment."

"All these questions," Victor said, a curious smile on his face. "You do realize this is a prison, Warden? Maximum security and all that? Do you think the designers of this place would leave anything to chance, and let some prisoner shimmy up a vent or something? Do you think the designers of this place haven't seen *Star Wars*?"

And Victor was the friendliest guard, in his own passive-aggressive way. The other three eyed him with suspicion. Worry. Hostility. Uncertainty. Maybe they knew what he was up to. Maybe they could sense he wasn't taking this seriously. They'd be right, of course.

Hardie needed to gain their trust somehow, put them at ease. He couldn't escape if his own staff was keeping a closer eye on him than the actual prisoners.

God help him...

He needed to hold a staff meeting.

After the fourteenth (fifteenth?) shift, Hardie asked Victor to gather everyone in the break room.

"Why? What's going on?" Victor asked.

"Just get everyone together."

"No sneak preview, Warden?"

Hardie shook his head no. Victor actually seemed hurt, then shuffled off to gather the other three guards.

"For those of you who don't speak English," Hardie said, "my apologies. Maybe someone can translate for you."

Everyone just...*stared,* as if they had all lost the ability to speak or understand English.

Christ, Hardie hated this shit. Because you know what? He was used to being the one in the back of the room, giving the ice-cold stare. He was never the leader of anything. Not for more than a decade, anyway, and back then it was different. Nate Parish had often goaded him, asking him why he didn't go legit, join the force, wear the badge and all that. One good word from me, Nate said, and you'd be in. But Hardie demurred. He wasn't a team kind of guy. He preferred to be freelance. A consultant. Whatever you want to call it. He'd often tell Nate: "Problem is, there's no 'fuck off' in 'team.'" And Nate would just shake his head and smile in that sly, knowing way of his.

Somewhere up in heaven, Nate's sides were probably killing him from laughing so hard. Look at Charlie Hardie, trying to lead a meeting.

So, Nate, what would you do?

Give 'em something. Something little. A peace offering. Let 'em know you're working for them behind the scenes.

"I finally spoke with the Prisonmaster."

Some eyes perked up a little.

"And he's working on the heat."

Yankee sighed. "Yeah, he always says that. And then it takes weeks, or more, to change it. You can push him a little harder, you know. You're the new guy. You've got a grace period. He's just testing you, see how far you'll go."

Hardie ignored him. "Food's changing, too."

"Oh, yeah?" Victor asked. "When will that little miracle happen, exactly?"

Hardie felt a little sucker-punched there. Victor was turning on him now?

"He's working on it," Hardie said.

"Same old shit," Yankee muttered.

So much for giving 'em something, Nate. Maybe he should just get to the point.

"I want to talk about the breakout from a few days ago. What you people did to Horsehead. I don't know what's gone on in the past. And I really don't give a shit. But that's not going to happen anymore. Not without my authority. You understand me?"

No one spoke at first. The four of them seemed to be waiting him out, the same way you wait for some crazy crackhead with a gun to run out of bullets before you calmly step out from the shadows and put him down with two to the chest.

Yankee coughed and raised his hand briefly. "Warden."

"Yeah."

"Respectfully, how do you suggest we control the prisoners? When they escape, do we pat their hand, tell them that's okay, everything will be all right?"

"No," Hardie said. "But you don't beat the living shit out of them, then nearly electrocute them to death."

"The batons are designed to be nonlethal," Yankee said quietly. "It's impossible to kill someone with them."

"Bullshit. I saw what you guys did. And like I said, I don't care how it was around here before, I don't care what the previous wardens did, I want it to stop."

"So," Yankee said, drawing the word out until it almost purred. "The next escape attempt we're supposed to just hang back until you tell us what to do? That will be interesting. What if you're asleep? Or taking a shit? You expect us to just wait until you're done?"

"Yeah, I do."

The moment the words left Hardie's mouth he realized it was a tactical error. Because what he said was stupid. *See, Nate, this is why you can't put me in front of a room. I'm not a leader. I'm not a policy maker. I'm a doer. You know that better than anybody.*

"Bool-sheet," X-Ray said. The German guard may not have been able to speak English, but he could understand enough of it.

"No, that's actually brilliant," Victor said. "While we wait, maybe the loose prisoner can help free his friends. And then they can come after us and kill us all, and the Prisonmaster can send down another group of guards with yet another lame-ass warden for them to torment."

"Enough!" said Yankee. "We're ignoring the real problem here, and that's the obvious plant among the staff. Horsehead didn't just walk through solid bars. He had *help.*"

"Uh-huh," Whiskey said.

"Listen to me: those cells cannot be opened from the inside. It's impossible. I've checked them. They can only be opened by a guard. So you're telling me these cell doors just pop open all by themselves? Presto, bingo? Like magic?"

"What are you saying?" Hardie asked.

"It's obvious. Someone in this room is collaborating with the prisoners, trying to engineer a revolt."

"Who?"

Yankee looked away. "I'm not that insane."

That's when Hardie realized that the staff distrust didn't apply just to him. The whole guard staff didn't trust each other. When something went wrong, like a prisoner busting out of his cell, they all started looking at each other.

"Nobody's going to say it out loud," said Yankee. "But we all know who's responsible."

"Who?" Hardie asked. He felt stupid again—repeating *who* like a goddamned owl. Wasn't this his meeting? What had happened?

Yankee now stood, smiled, and pointed at Victor. "Anybody ask Victor there where he was right before Horsehead broke free?"

"What?" Victor said, now sliding up to a full sitting position. "Fuck you, mate! Have you lost your mind?"

The room jolted, as though someone had sent a current up through the very floor.

"You haven't told him, have you?" Yankee asked.

"Told me what?"

Hardie gave himself credit. At least he hadn't asked: *Who?*

"Nothing," Victor said.

"Nothing my ass." Yankee turned to address Hardie. "Your boy there, your lead guard? He's real close with one of the prisoners."

"Shut up."

"No, it's true. Prisoner Three. You haven't heard him speak yet, but when he does, it'll be with an Australian accent. That's because the prisoner and Victor over there used to be partners in the outside world. Oh, yeah."

"Shut the fuck up, I'm warning you! Am I the only person who remembers the rules in this place?"

"Ol' Victor there's sworn his allegiance up and down, renounced his old buddy and everything, but none of us ever believed him. And we think he's taking advantage of your arrival to make his play."

"We need to question him," Whiskey said.

Yankee looked around the room. "Any objections? Shall we finally get to the bottom of this bullshit and stop these escape attempts?"

Victor slid out of his chair and started to move toward the door. Yankee moved to block the door while Whiskey and X-Ray removed their batons from their belts. Victor, back now against the wall, darted his eyes around nervously. The man knew he was outnumbered; his play for the door was more a reflex than a real plan. He muttered, "I don't believe this shit" to himself. And stole a glance at Hardie.

"Do it," Yankee said. "Warden, consider this a favor. A little welcome present. Taking care of a problem so you won't have to." Sparks popped from the end of Whiskey's baton. They moved in...

"No."

Hardie, cane and all, put himself between Victor and the other guards. He didn't know how to lead, or motivate, or any of that shit. But he wasn't going to let these people devolve into savagery.

He was no fool; he knew this would end badly. It was three on two, and he was lame and weaponless. Still, Hardie could feel the lizard part of his brain twitching. Scanning the room, building a futile plan of attack. If he could count on Victor to take out X-Ray, maybe he could use his cane and whip Whiskey across the shins, take her down. If it breaks, so be it. He'd take the jagged edge and use it as a knife...

Then something strange happened.

All three of them—X-Ray, Whiskey, and Yankee—smiled. They even started to applaud.

From behind, Victor slapped him lightly on the shoulder. "It's all right, mate. We just had to know."

Later, Victor showed up in Hardie's room, hands hidden behind his back. "Got a little surprise for you." Victor revealed his treasure: two bottles of nonalcoholic beer. Left over from a case that was sent down a long, long time ago, Victor explained. He'd hoarded them away. Hardie stared at the bottle before accepting it. "Near beer sucks," he said.

"It does suck," Victor explained, "but it's better than no beer at all."

Hardie took one, twisted off the top—of course it would be a twist-off—and took a swig. The beer tasted like it had skunked sometime around the turn of the century. If you'd been given one in a blind taste test, you'd be hard-pressed to identify the liquid as anything close to beer. Hardie drank it anyway, knowing that he'd need to down at least a case of these to feel even the slightest buzz. The near beer made Hardie miss the real thing all the more. But he didn't say anything to Victor. He didn't want to offend his new bestest friend.

After the meeting broke up, Victor had stayed behind and explained:

"Really sorry about that, but we had to be sure. A new warden comes down here, and right away he's aligning himself with the prisoners . . . well, you can see how that can be troublesome. They don't tell us anything, other than that a new warden is coming down. You understand, right?"

Hardie had nodded, his nerves still jumpy from the confrontation. Sometimes the anticipation of an ass-beating could be worse than the actual ass-beating.

"But you stuck up for me—and you just won major points in everyone's eyes. Just like I told them. I knew you'd be all right. They only send the best down here, and I suspect you're better than anyone realizes."

"Thanks," Hardie had said, then made a beeline for his room. He wanted to sleep. Think everything through with a fresh brain. So far, that hadn't happened. Every time he woke up, he felt more confused, more fuzzy. There was no sleep that left him feeling refreshed. Even when he slept through two shifts in a row.

What *was* this place? Was he really down here to reform it?

Now Victor was here with his near beer peace offering, and in the mood to talk.

"How was that?" he asked, a big grin on his face, tipping his own bottle of near beer toward Hardie's.

"Good," Hardie lied.

"I wanted to level with you up front, but we have to be cautious," Victor continued. "Prisoner Three was indeed my partner. We worked in Syd...well, you know I'm not allowed to tell you anything. Rules are still rules. But we were close. Completely different in skills and styles, mind you, but I considered him a blood brother. I didn't learn his true side, the side he kept hidden behind a human mask, until it was too late. Sometimes I think I'm here to keep an eye on him. My own personal burden, you know? As if he's still my responsibility, even though he's locked up here forever."

Hardie nodded. He'd had a partner once. A blood brother. And things had not turned out the way he expected.

"Anyway," Victor continued, "that's why I don't have a cute nickname for him. His real name is bad enough. It burns a hole in my mind as it is. Better to think of him as a number. Nothing more."

"What did he do?"

"Eh?"

Hardie looked at Victor. "What did he do, to deserve being here?"

Victor took another swig of beer, stared off at the far wall of Hardie's room. He swished the beer around in his mouth before he worked it down his throat.

"You know I can't say anything. But think of the worst kind of betrayal, at the worst possible moment...and then multiply that by a thousand. The man's a monster. He had been the whole time. And I'm ashamed it took me so long to recognize that."

Victor seemed convinced that his former pal was a monster. But *monster* was a word that was thrown around a lot. What was he—a cold-blooded hit man? A secret serial killer who dressed up in a black leather gimp suit and sliced up entire families in suburban houses?

See, the thing that bothered Hardie the most was that he had no files on these "prisoners." There was no rap sheet, no news accounts.

They were just human beings, boxed up for someone's convenience. But whose? And why? The Industry, as Mann called it, certainly had enemies.

Or was he simply allowing Prisoner Two to color his thinking? Maybe she was every bit as diabolical as Victor claimed she was. Wouldn't be tough to dig up old newspaper articles about Hardie's exploits in Philadelphia involving his good friend Nate Parish—and, by extension, FBI agent Deke Clark. She could be one of those savants who easily matches names to faces. She could be a brilliant actress, expressing surprise when Hardie popped out of that shower drain—and instantly knowing what to say to make him doubt everything.

There was, of course, a way to find out.

Before Victor left, Hardie gestured for him to come closer. "Now that I've cleared my name, I really need a favor."

"That's the last of the beer, I swear."

"Two favors, actually."

"Okay, let's hear them."

"I need a weapon."

Victor stared at him for a moment, a smile almost breaking out on his face before he turned serious again. "A weapon? For what?"

"For the second favor, which you'll hear about in a second."

Victor gave it a moment to roll around in his mind. "I don't know what to tell you, mate. Weapons are rationed out here. You're given what you're given, and that's it. You'll notice I don't carry one of those electrified baton things. That's because I broke mine during an altercation, and the Prisonmaster didn't see fit to send me a replacement. You're not going to find any other guards willing to give up their weapons, either. Even to you."

"So I've got no options."

"You've got your cane. Maybe that was intended to double as a weapon."

"Sure. I can poke a prisoner to death."

"And...oh, hell. What do you need a weapon for?"

"I've got to have *something*," Hardie pleaded. "Come on. I feel defenseless down here. What if I get into a jam?"

Again Victor let Hardie's words sink in, but this time he was looking at Hardie with a guilty expression. Finally Victor reached around, fished something out of his back pocket, handed it to Hardie. It looked like a black pen, complete with a pocket clip. Only the tip didn't feature a rollerball or anything else that carried ink.

"What the hell's this?" Hardie asked. "A pen?"

"No, sir. That's a Smith & Wesson tactical pen. Police and military version, which is longer, and skips the screw-on cap."

"This is your idea of a weapon?"

"Like I said, I lost my baton. Here. Let me show you."

Victor took the pen back, holding it up as though he were a spokesmodel. "Made from aircraft aluminum. This end's the fun end. Jam it into a nerve bundle, your opponent goes down. Jam it into an eye, no more 3-D movies." He pulled off the cap on the other end, which took a bit of effort. "Other side, ballpoint pen. You can fill out your tax forms. Genius, isn't it?"

"A pen?"

"Best I can do."

Hardie took it anyway, slid it into his right trouser pocket. Great. Now he was fully prepared to cross a street and fill out a parking ticket. "Thanks."

"What's the second favor, for which you require a weapon?"

"I need you to sneak me into a cell."

17

Get it up or I'll cut it off.

—Roberta Collins, *The Big Doll House*

HARDIE CAME UP with the plan: use Zero as a distraction. Victor could claim that some of Zero's piss tubes were loose. Victor would summon X-Ray, leaving only Whiskey, who would be asleep—in turn leaving Hardie alone with Prisoner Two. For a few minutes, anyway.

He stood there now, waiting.

A soft voice spoke from behind the mask. "Come closer. I won't bite."

She was awake. She could see him. Outwardly, she gave no sign of being conscious or even alive, her body in some kind of ultrarelaxed yoga-style suspended animation, chest barely moving. Hardie stepped closer to her cell—cane, leg, cane, leg—until he was right up against the bars. He cleared his throat and told her he didn't have much time.

"I want to hear everything, right now," Hardie said. "Who you are, why Deke hired you, how you got here—"

"Help me take this off."

With that, she stood up gracefully, made her way to the bars, and bowed her head.

Hardie paused momentarily, then put his right arm through the opening between two bars and reached around to the back of her head. She took his hand and guided it to the clasp in back, where it locked. Shit, the lock. All the masks were locked. Hardie started to tell her, "I don't have a—" when she slipped her other hand into his pants pocket and removed a thin electronic key. She pressed it into Hardie's left palm. Her fingertips were cold. Hardie had to lean against the bars for balance, but he managed to snap open the lock, then ease the mask—heavier than he thought—off the top of her head.

Prisoner Two touched her fingers to her lips, then puckered them. Pressed the fingers of both hands into her cheekbones. "Are you alone?" she murmured, her voice so quiet Hardie could barely hear it.

"Yeah, I'm alone."

"No one else on the floor?"

Hardie shook his head and was about to say no when she turned, narrowed her eyes, then spit something hard and phlegmy into his face. Some of the wet blast was blocked by the bars, but not enough.

"Been saving that for you," she said, louder.

"What? Seriously?"

Her expression changed slightly; some of the fury softened. "Hurt me," she whispered. "Pull me in close to the bars. *Now, do it.*"

"What do you want?"

Under her breath: "Someone is probably watching or listening. You don't hurt me, we're all dead. Do it *now*, fucking *hurt me.*"

In his previous life Charlie Hardie would never have hit a woman, ever. Recent events, however, had caused him to abandon that code. He'd punched Mann in the eye and didn't feel an ounce of guilt about it. So he reached inside the bars and pulled the prisoner forward, banging her head on the bars. She cried out, and seemed to lose her balance.

What the hell am I doing? Hardie thought, his stomach suddenly sick.

The prisoner rolled her eyes up to glare at him, a sardonic smile on her face. "Is that all you've got?"

"Enough of this *hurt me* shit. Who are you, and how do you know me?"

She whispered,

"The name's Eve Bell and I was hired to find you, you stupid asshole."

This disappointed Hardie on at least three levels.

For starters, the name Eve Bell sounded about as made-up as you can get. What—were Modesty Blaise and Pussy Galore already taken?

Also, it was disappointing that she didn't identify herself as a member of the Federal Bureau of Investigation. That would have meant a battalion of Kansas farm boys with heavy artillery was waiting outside for a signal, a raid would ensue, and he'd be plucked out of this nightmare.

And finally—*stupid asshole?* Really? Was this Catholic grade school all over again?

"Well, you found me," Hardie said. "Congratulations."

"Yeah."

"How did you get here?"

Eve smiled, then slammed a fist into Hardie's right ear. A tiny explosion went off in his skull. The moment he lowered his head to recoil, Eve's other hand was grabbing his shirt collar, yanking him closer, throwing him off balance. Hardie pulled Eve's head forward, pressing it against the bars, pinning it there. Both of them slid down the bars until they were on the floor.

"One night I went to bed in a chain motel in Grand Island, Nebraska, and I woke up in this place."

It took Hardie a minute to realize that Eve was answering his question.

"Why were you in Nebraska?"

"Looking for you."

"Why did you think I was in Nebraska?"

Hardie had never been to Nebraska—at least, not that he knew of. And he'd never heard of Grand Island before. How could there be an island in the middle of a landlocked state? Briefly he considered the possibility that the prisoner here, this "Eve," was making shit up off the top of her head.

But if so...how did she know Deke's name?

"I was following a lead," she whispered. "There was a rumor you were there. Turned out to be a trap, and it was a pretty good one, too. Usually I can detect a grab site from a hundred miles away."

"And you say Deke Clark hired you."

"Yeah. Which is why I was pretty shocked to find you popping up out of the drain in the shower room. Kind of thought I'd botched the case, being kidnapped and thrown into a secret prison and all. But with you standing here—gee whiz, I can finally call Deke and collect my final check."

Hardie blinked. "You're in contact with him?"

Eve gave him a squinty-eyed *duh* look, then said,

"Hit me again."

"What is wrong with you?"

"Somebody's *watching*. If you don't brutalize the prisoners, it looks suspicious. Especially with you being so new. So hit me. Later you can explain it away as punishing me for the shower-room incident."

"No."

"I can take it, believe me."

"*No.*"

"Charlie, it's vital you stay the warden if we're going to get out of this, and if you want to stay warden, you need to fucking hit me now."

Hardie removed his hands from her head, slid backward, then searched for his cane.

Eve sighed. "Then we're done talking. Come back when you find your balls and your brains. But whatever you do—stay the warden. It's our only chance."

"What do you mean, stay the warden?"

"Keep your fucking job," she hissed. "The guards are the bad guys. *We're the real guards, trapped in these cells.*"

Victor turned the corner and appeared at Hardie's side, as if he'd materialized out of thin air. "What did she just say?"

18

If you're standing out in the yard in San Quentin and some-thing's going to come down, you're scared to death and you can't show it. Inside you're dying, but outside you're saying, Bring it!
—Danny Trejo

VICTOR'S EYES DARTED back and forth—prisoner, warden, prisoner, warden—waiting for someone to answer.

"Nothing," Hardie said. "She's crazy."

"Okay, come on. Fun's over. X-Ray's coming back soon." Then turning his attention to Eve: "And you—put that mask back on."

As they walked back toward the control room in silence, Hardie glanced over at Victor. Seemed like a perfectly nice man. But didn't all the nice young psychopaths? Hardie tried to summon his inner Nate for some guidance. Nate told him: *No idea, buddy. You're on your own here.*

The situation boiled down to two possible realities, didn't it? Either Eve was lying, in an attempt to worm her way into Hardie's brain so that she could turn him against his own team. Or *Victor* was lying, along with the rest of them—and they were cunning psychopaths just toying with him before destroying them.

Neither made sense—not really. That's what bothered Hardie the most. There was a Sherlock Holmes line that Nate Parish was fond of quoting: When you have eliminated the impossible, whatever remains, however improbable, must be the truth. But that was the problem. Which possibility was more improbable? Both were absurd. This whole facility—his whole life—was maddeningly absurd.

Why couldn't Mann have just put a bullet in his face and been done with it?

"You get what you needed?" asked Victor.

Hardie just nodded.

"Hope it was worth it, because I had no other choice but to pull Zero's real urine tubes. Got piss all over myself. So not only do I have that evil bastard's waste products sinking into my skin, I've forever incurred his wrath."

They ascended the metal staircase up to the break room.

"Well, I owe you one," Hardie said.

"I should say you do," Victor said. "So what did she say?"

"Nothing useful."

"No?"

"No."

"Great. All that effort for *nothing useful?*"

They went back toward the control room. Hardie had been awake for what—three or four shifts straight? There was so much to process, to get straight in his own mind. If this prisoner, Eve Bell, was telling the truth, and the real bad guys were the guards, then what was he supposed to do? Incapacitate them one by one, then free the prisoners and restore order? He was a broken man who needed a cane to walk. And that's if he trusted her. Big if.

"Seriously?" Victor asked as he opened the door to the break room. "She didn't tell you anything?"

"No."

"She didn't say, 'Hurt me, stupid asshole'?"

The blood in Hardie's veins went frosty.

"She didn't say, 'The guards are the bad guys. We're the real guards, trapped in these cells'?"

Inside Hardie's room, X-Ray, Yankee, and Whiskey were waiting for him.

"We heard the whole thing," Yankee said.

Whiskey added, rather unnecessarily:

"You are fucked."

Hardie quickly pulled the tactical pen from his pocket—X-Ray slapped it away. The weapon flew out of Hardie's hand, bounced off a wall, landed on the cement floor, and started spinning. Whiskey, who was closest, punched Hardie in the head, drawing blood. At almost the same time Yankee attacked from behind, kicking the cane out from beneath his hand. Hardie's arms pinwheeled. He collapsed to the ground. Victor pinned Hardie to the floor with a meaty forearm.

"Thought you'd be different," he said, a childlike bitterness in every word. "I really did, mate."

"Listen to me, Victor..."

"No, listen to *this*—"

Upon that last syllable Whiskey smashed a boot into Hardie's stomach, which immediately forced his body into a fetal position. Come on, breathe through it. Breathe. *Breathe*...Hardie stretched his fingers out, grasping at the floor as though he were trying to claw through the cement. Victor loosened his grip to let him respond to the pain; Hardie took the opportunity. He'd been hit in the stomach many times before; he knew how to contract the muscles to minimize the damage. And while Victor thought he was fighting for air and trying not to puke, Hardie marshaled all the strength he could into his right arm. And then he launched it up like a guided missile directly into the space between Victor's testicles.

Victor's entire body seemed to float up in the air a moment, just a few millimeters in orbit above the surface of the floor. His mouth curled into an O shape.

Hardie blinked the blood out of his eyes and saw that X-Ray and Yankee had their electrified batons out. The ends of them sparked and snapped, like portable Tesla coils.

From the floor, Victor spoke in a quavering voice that—although not a full octave above normal, had definitely changed in pitch.

"It was a test, you stupid bastard," he spat. "After all that I told you, why couldn't you believe me? You've chosen the wrong side. This is what she does. She gets inside your mind, twists everything around."

Behind them, one of the guards spoke in a harsh language that Hardie didn't recognize. The meaning, however, was clear:

We're going to kick your ass unless you submit to us.

The other three guards moved in closer with their snapping, electrified sticks. One touch, Hardie realized, would probably cause him to wet his pants and forget who he was for a half hour. The object, then, would be to avoid being touched with the business ends of those sticks. And what then? If by some miracle he were able to overpower the guards here, and maybe knock out the Aussie cocksucker on the floor, what then? Where do you go? What do you do? Take the elevator up, so everyone else down here dies? Good guys and bad?

"Shit," was all he could say.

Because this was his last stand.

The battle was brief yet violent. The electrified ends of the batons did touch Hardie, and more than once. He did not soil his pants, but he did scream, and punch and kick and try to repeat his trick with Victor—namely, aiming for private parts. This was not effective.

Before long Hardie was pinned to the floor, and Victor picked up his walking stick. What, were they going to beat him with it? Didn't that break all kinds of disability rights laws?

Victor twisted the cane just so and removed a cover that Hardie never knew was there. At the end of the stick were two metal prongs. Victor pushed a button on the side of the cane. Electricity jumped from prong to prong and made a fat thick snapping sound. They had given him a weapon after all. Only they had forgotten to tell him.

Hardie was about to curse at them but Victor was too fast—the prongs already slamming into his chest, his entire body seizing up for what felt like forever, to the point where he thought he smelled his own flesh burning.

After they dragged him to an empty cell and began to beat him again and strip him out of his suit, Hardie realized that he probably had lost his job as warden.

As Victor ran his knuckles under cold water in the slop sink, his earbud crackled to life, startling him a little.

"You did the right thing," the Prisonmaster said.

The PM had a strange way of seeing and hearing everything down here. Victor had personally searched for hidden cameras and was never able to find a single one. Sometimes, Victor thought the Prisonmaster was the only voice of reason down here. The place had a way of making you doubt everything, even what you see with your own eyes.

"Did I?" Victor asked.

"Oh, yes. Rest assured. Now, you know I'm not supposed to divulge any details about the real-world activities of anyone sent down to site seven seven three four, but..."

"Come on. Don't be coy. Who the hell is he? Why was he sent down here?"

"You know I can't tell you that. But let's just say you were right to be suspicious of the warden's insistence on questioning Prisoner Two. He has a history with females, and the females don't always come to a happy end."

"Goddamn it."

"Don't beat yourself up, Victor. Like most sociopaths, the new warden is a gifted liar. You couldn't have seen it coming."

Victor came to visit Hardie later in his cell. He stood outside the bars, arms crossed. "Very disappointed in you, buddy."

Hardie chose to not respond. He was still bleeding from his face and his tongue felt thick in his mouth, so it was probably best if he didn't speak anyway.

"I guess I've learned my lesson. You see, we never really know what they're sending down. Could be another guard, could be another prisoner. That's part of our job. To figure it all out."

"You're making a mistake," Hardie said. "I'm supposed to be the warden."

"*Everybody's* the fuckin' warden when they come down here! That's part of the test! It's the only way to separate the heroes from the bloody villains. Eventually, your true colors emerge. Oh, yes they do. Didn't take long with you now, did it?"

"You're insane. All of you."

"In fact, you might be the most diabolical one yet. You had a lot of us fooled. Oh, yes you did. Lie after lie after lie, all delivered in that deadpan style of yours. And to think I wasted one of my beers on you!"

"That beer sucked," Hardie said.

"From now on, you'll be known as Prisoner Five. You will not answer to any other name."

"Oh, fuck you. My name's *Charlie Hardie*."

"Don't want to hear it."

"CHARLIE—"

Victor walked back to the control room across the hallway.

"—HARDIE!"

Slammed the door behind him.

Some small part of Hardie still clung to the belief that this was another test, or maybe some high-spirited hazing, a taste of the so-called torture so Hardie'd be better informed in his role as warden.

But when they all left and didn't come back...

ever...

he knew the small part of him was full of shit.

19

Prison exists to serve one purpose: locking people away from life's good things.

—Sin Soracco, *Low Bite*

Manhattan—Now

"CARE FOR ANOTHER?"

Mann realized all at once that was she awake and sitting at a bar. As promised, the Industry had deposited her into a very nice hotel. In front of her was a diamond-cut tumbler of Domaine de Canton, a ginger liqueur, that she did not remember ordering. This was not entirely strange, because she had been prepared to experience missing time. To keep the location of the prison absolutely secret, all its visitors were injected with a serum (allegedly harmless) that erased short-term memory, somewhere in the forty-to-fifty-hour range. The exact cutoff was imprecise; all at once you would snap "awake" and realize you couldn't remember what had happened over the past two days—including where you had been and what route you had taken. When Mann rolled up her sleeve and looked at the crook of her left elbow, there was a piece of cotton taped there. She peeled it back. The injection site had been healing for a few hours. She must have been given the shot earlier in the day, rested for a while, wandered down for a cocktail, then "woken up."

Until Mann slid her hand into her pocket and pulled out the folded card that housed her room key, she didn't know what city she was in. New York City, it turned out. A Hilton.

"No, thank you," Mann said, then signed the check, leaving a 20 percent tip. She then stepped outside for some air.

The sun was beginning to set, and the air was muggy and hot. Mann realized she was standing directly across from Ground Zero. Construction continued on the so-called Freedom Tower. The last time Mann had been to lower Manhattan, the site was still just a big, depressing hole in the ground.

She stepped back inside and took the elevator to the fourteenth floor, which, according to the folded card, was where she'd find her room. Mann always traveled light. Never take anything you're not fully prepared to leave behind.

At Penn Station she bought a ticket on an Acela bound for 30th Street Station, Philadelphia. Mann thought about Charlie Hardie for much of the ride down. Had he figured out the prison yet? Or had he been beaten to death upon his arrival? Of course not. Not her Charlie. The man was unkillable, right?

She hadn't thought about him in a long while. Not actively, anyway. Seeing him in the flesh, though, brought all those old bad feelings back. She tried not to show it, but he seemed to sense it anyway. The pure cold hate. Much as Mann tried to rationalize it away, the truth was . . . he had derailed her life. Utterly, completely. She thought that seeing him in that tiny little interrogation room, and knowing what fate had in store for him, would bring her some peace.

It did not.

In dreary, humid Philadelphia, Mann picked up the SUV she'd rented using her smartphone and followed 76 up to Route 611 and out to the suburbs of Montgomery County. The address had been written on the back of the folded hotel card.

The house was modest for this neighborhood, which was good. Nobody would be driving by and gawking at it. A split-level. Some tree cover, bushes, a wooden fence in need of paint. Mann parked the SUV across the street and swept the area with her eyes. The family allegedly had some guardian angels in the FBI looking over them—but as far as Mann could tell, the house was utterly exposed. Nobody on the perimeter. No sophisticated alarm systems. No one even doing drive-bys.

She removed the smartphone from her pocket and had her hand on the door handle when she heard a noise.

Behind her—

Then a form, stumbling out of the bushes.

Mann's body tensed up. Had she missed someone? Was the FBI out there? Not that it mattered, because she could flash any number of phony credentials that would ease her passage from the scene. But she would be highly disappointed in herself if she'd missed something like that.

The form darted past the SUV and into the street, casting furtive glances to the left, then the right, before jogging toward the house.

Mann squinted.

It was Charlie Hardie.

The junior version of him, anyway.

What was a young man doing out at this hour, stumbling around in the darkness outside his own house?

After a few more seconds of observation Mann had figured it out. The boy had been drinking. Look at him, how uneasy he is on his feet. He must have sneaked past Mom to go pound beers with his asshole friends somewhere in the wilds of Montgomery County. Absent father, single mother—textbook rebellion move.

So tell me, boy—what would you be drinking if I told you that your father was in some secret prison right now? Would you upgrade to vodka, maybe some coke?

She was half tempted to jump out of the SUV and tackle the boy, right there on his front lawn, put the tip of a pen under his chin and tell him it was a knife and that she was going to cut his head off. Would he act like his father and try to punch her in the eye? Would he have a wisecrack? Would she see any of the father in the son?

It was tempting.

So incredibly tempting.

But she had other work to do. The night was just beginning.

20

Imagine a thousand more such daily intrusions in your life, every hour and minute of every day, and you can grasp the source of paranoia, this anger that could consume me at any moment if I lost control.

—Jack Henry Abbott, *In the Belly of the Beast*

THE MASK.

It was much, much worse than Hardie could have imagined.

Picture your head removed from its body and imprisoned elsewhere, some cramped little metal box where the air stinks like sour breath and nothing can touch the skin of your face, not even your own fingertips.

This was a new low. Hardie's new life was smaller and more pathetic than he ever thought possible.

The first itch was a novelty. Hardie thought it wasn't so bad; okay, he could take it, it was just an itch. He could just will it away. But the itch refused to quit. You take for granted how easy it is to cure something like an itch. You do it almost unconsciously. Your nose itches, your hand flies up to your face, you take care of it. Not inside the mask. The itch was free to last as long as it wanted, because nobody could stop it. The itch continued, and grew more powerful, emboldened by the lawless space inside the stinking, hot, confining mask. Even though he knew it would do no good, Hardie's fingers scratched at the outside of the mask. He tried working his fingers under his mask, but they couldn't reach up high enough to scratch the itch.

Breathe, Hardie. Breathe.

Don't lose it just a day into this thing.

(Was it a day?)

(Two days, maybe?)

(Please let it be at least two days.)

Sleep was no escape. The moment you calmed your brain down enough to drift away, the sirens were blaring again, and the bright lights were flashing so you couldn't see anything, let alone the guards, who were forcing your back against the bars so they could take off the mask and photograph your squinty, tired, itchy face. And by the time you remembered to scratch your face they were making you put the mask back on again. Then the screaming sirens faded and the lights were cut and you'd go back to not falling asleep.

Twice a day the masks were temporarily removed for feeding. The first time, Hardie didn't even eat. He scratched at his face furiously until he saw blood on the tips of his fingers. The second time, he noted that the same old breakfast was still being served, despite the Prisonmaster's promise to do something about it. Dry, biscuitlike lumps and a thin, tasteless paste that was probably intended to be some sort of oatmeal substitute. Good to see his short tenure as warden had absolutely *zero effect* on prisoner conditions.

Then the mask went back on again, and you started counting down the time until the next head count or meal, because anything was better than wearing this heavy, choking, soul-killing mask...

And just when Hardie thought the situation couldn't be any more insufferable, the mask started to play a little slide show.

* * *

When the image of the house appeared, Hardie thought he was hallucinating. No amount of blinking would erase it, though. He realized there was a screen inside the mask, like there was in the View-Master he had when he was a kid. A tiny personal movie screen floating a few inches in front of his eyeballs.

Showing him a house—a split-level, shrouded in darkness and vaguely familiar. But he couldn't place it. Was this some home he'd guarded at some point? Why were they showing this to him?

Without warning the floating image disappeared...

...only to be replaced by an image of the same house shown from a different angle. The cement path leading up to the front door. Still night, but there was enough illumination to read the house number painted onto the black metal mailbox. It was the number that jarred Hardie's memory.

This was Kendra's house.

Specifically, the split-level he'd helped to purchase but had only seen once. The secret house, buried out there in an anonymous suburb of Philadelphia, where Kendra and Charlie, Jr., lived under her maiden name, on the off chance that the Albanian mob wouldn't be satisfied with the innocent blood already on their hands and would come looking to punish Hardie's family. The Albanians were the least of his worries now, because his new enemies—the Accident People, the Industry, a freakin' cabal, whatever—they were saying to Hardie:

Yeah, we know where they are. Look, we're standing on their front lawn in the middle of the night.

When did they take this? Was this live? Was this Mann taking these photos?

The image disappeared silently...

...and was replaced by an image from inside the house. The dim vestibule. Six stairs leading up to the living room, more stairs leading down to the den. God, please. Get them out of the house. Don't do this...

Next image:

A living room Hardie had never seen, but familiar furniture, familiar clutter. His family's possessions.

Next image, the images loading faster now...

A dark hallway, lined with framed photos. Hardie tried to see if Kendra had hung any of their old photos on the wall, but before he could make anything out—

The next image:

Farther down the hallway, headed toward the bedrooms...

Next image:

A gloved hand opening a door. Hardie burned the image of that hand into his brain. Because someday, when he found the owner of that hand, he was going to rip the appendage off the end of his arm and make him eat it...

And then:

Kendra, in bed, one bare leg draped over the covers, pillows in disarray, hair fanned out.

"NO!" Hardie shouted, but the sound was trapped inside the mask—it was like yelling inside a bank vault.

As awful as it was to watch those images—it was even more torturous when they stopped.

Because then Hardie's brain went off and running, and he continued the slide show from hell on his own, wondering if it was Mann inside the house or one of her creepy-crawling henchmen...or somebody else, someone even more fearsome, and the only reason they didn't load a new photo is because this was unfolding in real time, and now the gloved hand was pressed down over Kendra's sleeping mouth, a needle sliding into her arm...

"STOP THIS, YOU MOTHERFUCKERS! GODDAMN IT, LISTEN TO ME, LEAVE THEM ALONE! THEY HAVE NOTHING TO DO WITH ME!"

Hardie braced himself for the next image, trying to prepare himself for the worst yet *hating* himself for the images his own mind was inventing. He'd had plenty of experience seeing the things people did to each other. There was plenty of material to draw from.

But no other images appeared. Instead, a voice inside the mask, preceded by an audio crackle.

"You're going to be a good prisoner, aren't you, Five?"

The Prisonmaster.

"Oh, I have feeling you're going to be an *excellent* prisoner. This is your destiny. All your life you were preparing yourself to be here, with us."

Hardie swallowed the nuclear explosion of a scream that was forming in his throat, choking it back down into his chest, burying it.

In prison, the only place you can run is inside your own head. Eve Bell, for example, found her secret philosopher's garden and had become very skilled at whisking herself away for short periods of time. If you could escape, truly escape, into your own mental landscape, you could almost deal with the screaming sirens and horrible food and coffinlike mask.

Hardie, however, didn't like his own head.

His head was condemned space.

Unfit for human habitation.

Now and again, Charlie Hardie pictured his life as a hotel. He had spent most of his time there closing off the floors below him as he ascended higher and higher, never looking down, never wondering when he was finally going to run out of floors.

The lobby and the lower floors were his childhood—the foundation. The carpeting was shabby and almost no one was ever at the front desk, but it was a decent enough place to stay. The management did the best they could considering the neighborhood. There was a bed, four walls, food to eat. A few diversions, a few fellow travelers.

Then came the fractured, damaged floors of his adolescence, back when the idea that you could *check out of the hotel* held great appeal to him.

These were followed by the ten stories of his twenties, the military years, which he tried hard not to think about, ever, and by the time he'd reached the thirtieth floor the hotel was beginning to show its age, its limitations.

But that was okay, because that's when Hardie met Kendra.

He'd been back in Philadelphia and she'd sent him a stupid birthday card with some cartoon joke on it—a Far Side gag depicting suffering souls in hell, and a horned devil telling them, "It's not so much the heat, it's the humidity." They'd barely known each other back during his adolescence; she was a friend of a friend of his best friend, Nate Parish, and Hardie was stunned she still remembered his name, let alone cared enough to send a card.

These were the hopeful years, the time he thought he might be able to turn his hotel into something worthwhile again. At the time, he thought it would be simple: close off the bottom floors and concentrate on the floors you currently occupy. Kendra helped him with that. Her own hotel had a strange and tragic history. So they decorated the floors they were on and ignored the floors beneath them and had a boy and named him Charlie, Jr., much against Hardie's wishes. Kendra insisted. She believed boys should go on to honor their fathers, even if those fathers were working too much, and seemed to disengage a little more with every passing day...

And then one day Hardie looked inside a room he wasn't supposed to.

* * *

The last place Hardie wanted to be was inside his own head space.

He turned off the lights and continued his ascent.

This time, though, he'd run out of floors.

There was no penthouse.

There was no roof.

There was nothing up there but a cold hard empty.

And a traffic ticket, on the dining-room table.

Usually Kendra scooped up the bills, took care of them. Hardie worked with Nate day and night some weeks. He gave Kendra the checks. Kendra deposited the checks and paid for everything. So he never saw bills. Never bothered. Only reason he looked was because of the return address, Pennsylvania State Police, and he thought it was for him, some lingering piece of business. He opened it. Speeding ticket, the kind you pay by mail. He hadn't been speeding, nor had he been pulled over, nor had he traveled the turnpike anytime in the past month. Then he saw the name: Kendra Hardie. She'd been speeding on such and such a date, such and such a time, headed west on the Pennsylvania Turnpike, and Hardie couldn't figure out for the life of him what his wife was doing on the turnpike.

As much as he mocked himself for his utter lack of detective skills, Hardie had to admit that he put everything together fairly quickly. Checked their E-ZPass account, recorded the number of times Kendra had headed west on the Pennsylvania Turnpike (a lot, as it turned out, all when Charlie, Jr., was in school). Then he checked their cell phone bill for texts and calls—the standard jealous husband bullshit, stuff cops and detectives did all the time. Her text message account had gone over, way over, for three months now. About 90 percent of the texts going to the same guy.

what kind of undies

A guy Kendra knew back in high school.

how could I forget

The more Hardie dug around, the more aware he became of this whole parallel universe that Kendra seemed to be living in, and, well—

can you talk? husband around?

Hardie didn't sleep for three days straight. He lay in bed next to her, staring at the ceiling. Already condemning a large number of floors in his hotel.

But he had to be sure.

Hardie told Nate he wasn't feeling good, needed a day off. Nate praised Jesus—joked about how he could finally get some work done, and Hardie laughed along with it and then drove home and parked his car ten blocks from the house and fished out Kendra's spare set of keys for the minivan and opened up the back and tucked himself into the space where she usually put grocery bags and re-locked the car and curled up and waited. A while later Kendra unlocked the car, put on some soul music, and started driving, humming along to certain parts, singing to others. Joy in her voice. Did she ever sing in the car when it was just the two of them?

When was it ever just the two of you?

And after a long drive, much of which, Hardie knew, was turn-pike—he knew it in his mind, and he knew it by the feel of the road—she turned and lurched forward, turned again, lurched forward, then stopped. Turned off the car.

Hardie tried to imagine what the guy's house looked like. Was he rich, or did he rent some shithole town house on the outskirts of Philadelphia?

Instead it turned out to be a restaurant in a strip mall.

Hardie watched them through the window. The restaurant did a brisk trade. They sat near the back wall (smart, Kendra, away from the windows, just on the off off *off* chance someone you know wanders by). They were already deep in conversation. Kendra reached across the table, squeezed his hand. The guy smiled. She leaned forward. They—

The next few hours were a blur. Hardie took his set of the keys to his wife's car, cranked the ignition, and headed back east on the Pennsylvania Turnpike. He couldn't remember the last time he'd cried. Well, he bawled now. By the time he reached Route 1 he had calmed down. His eyes stung. He drove down Route 1 to Rhawn Street, then over to the river, where he knew a place he could dump the car and nobody would bother checking for weeks. He wiped the wheel clean, even though it was his wife's car and it wouldn't be unusual for him to drive it now and again. Then he walked home. Which was an insanely long trek from all the way down by the river. His cell phone went off about twenty minutes into his walk—Kendra, probably having worked up the nerve to call him and admit the truth. Hardie ignored it, kept walking. She tried two more times before giving up. Ten minutes later, Nate called him.

"How's it going?"

"Okay."

"You feeling better?"

"Not particularly."

Then, in that classic Nate Parish fashion, he proceeded to detail Hardie's movements for the past two hours.

"I'm guessing you're around Rhawn and Castor, right? Would take you about forty minutes to go from the restaurant down to your favorite car-dumping spot on the river, then another five, ten minutes to wipe everything down. You're too stubborn to call a cab and too pissed off to take a bus, so you're walking. How am I doing? Where y'at?"

"How did you know about the restaurant? Did she tell you?"

After a moment's hesitation, Nate said, "No. I figured that out. She said the car was stolen near Charlie's school, but there were too many holes in her story. I figure she'll give you the same story."

"So you know."

"I don't know any details, but I have an idea what's going on. I'm sorry, man. Shit gets fucked up sometimes."

"Yeah."

"Hey, you and I are going to meet up. Definitely over some beer. I'm buying."

"No, I just want to go home."

"Come on. Rhawnhurst Café. I can be there in fifteen minutes, okay?"

"What if I'm nowhere near the Rhawnhurst Café?"

"Whatever. See you then."

At that moment, Hardie had been standing at the corner of Rhawn and Castor, about six paces from the front door of the Rhawn-hurst Café. Nate had it down to the block.

Nate showed up, Hardie got drunk, came home, went to bed, again he couldn't sleep. Kendra said nothing, pretending to be furious about Hardie not calling her back all day. They started talking in the morning, after Charlie went to school, circling around each other like two street fighters with stilettos, wondering who was going to draw first blood. Hardie lashed out. Kendra maintained her innocence, claimed that she did not break her vows, that Hardie was being paranoid as usual. Hardie kept pressing, presenting the evidence he'd gathered, insisting that it would be better to have it all out in the open. Kendra swore she was innocent.

The conversation lasted for days, literally, pausing only for

Charlie's daily return home from school. Hardie thought a lot about finding this guy, beating a confession out of him. Instead he got tired of asking, tired of Kendra's obvious lies. Of course she was screwing him. Why couldn't she just admit it and put him out of his misery?

Because some stubborn part of his brain clung to her story, absurd as it was, that she did not sleep with him.

That this was all one big misunderstanding.

That he was overreacting.

That nothing had changed.

That...

Hardie couldn't solve this case so he threw himself headfirst into ones he could solve. This was around the time the situation with the Albanian gangs was heating up, and Hardie attacked them with a zeal that surprised even Nate. "They ain't fucking Kendra," Nate said at one point. "You know that, right?" Hardie told him to shut up. They hit the Albanians hard; Deke Clark told Nate he'd better watch his boy. Deke was right. Hardie got sloppy. The sloppiness got Nate and his family killed, and Hardie almost killed and sent to purgatory for his trouble.

More floors being sealed off...

But don't worry.

You can just climb higher, higher, higher.

Hardie told himself he left his family to keep them safe. He was still a moving target. People looking to hurt Hardie might choose to hurt his family instead. So his family was better off without him. Kendra didn't want him around anyway, so it was the right decision no matter how you looked at it. He packed a bag, choosing only the things that couldn't ever be re-created, reprinted, reproduced, or re-purchased. It filled a small duffel.

The day he left, his boy, Charlie, Jr., watched from the couch, video-game controller in his little eleven-year-old hands.

"Where are you going, Dad?"

Hardie couldn't lie to him. But he couldn't bring himself to tell his son the truth, either.

"I'll be back, tough guy."

Another door slammed shut in his mind, the sound of invisible workmen hammering nails into wood, starting to seal the room off, his boy crying behind it, Hardie walking away, trying to drown it out, lying to himself the whole time.

I'll be back, tough guy.

21

Hey, you bastards. I'm still here.

—Steve McQueen, *Papillon*

SOMEWHERE, IN THE darkness, was a crackle.

A tiny audible pop inside the infinite soundscape of his mask. Like the sound of a cheap metal satellite colliding with an obscure, unnamed moon.

Then, from out there, in the void, came a voice:

"Ah, hell, it's back again."

"Shit."

Static.

An Australian voice: "Who is that? Is that you, Eve?"

"Yeah. Cam?"

"Yeah, s'me. Why are these on again? After all this time?"

"I don't know. Probably want to fuck with us again. Or listen in, see what we talk about when we're all alone in our cells. *Isn't that right, you assholes?*"

"You're probably right. Spying on us again. I suppose they're bored with sucking each other's dicks."

Then came a deep, guttural voice in Italian—the prisoner known as Horsehead.

"Is that you, Silvio?"

"Uh-huh."

"Hello, Silvio. Welcome back."

"Uh-huh."

"Archie, you with us, too?"

A British accent: "We shouldn't be talking. They can listen."

"What else do we have to do? We don't have to plan our great escape over these things. Why not read poems to each other? Who has one? Eh? Anyone?"

Nobody spoke for a while. Every so often you'd hear an exhalation, loud enough to be picked up by a mask's internal microphone.

A soft, female voice:

"So...are you out there, Charlie?"

Hardie did not respond.

Eve didn't give up. Sometime later she tried again:

"Hey, Charlie, you out there?"

Faint static.

"Charlie, come on. Need to talk to you. Let me hear your voice. Even a hearty 'fuck you' would be welcome at this point."

Faint static.

"It's not your fault, Charlie. You couldn't have known. They're all sociopaths out there. Victor. Whiskey. X-Ray. Yankee. And if any of you assholes are listening, then feel free to chime in anytime! Cameron could tell you all about the guard who calls himself Victor. Couldn't you, Cam?"

"Yeah, I could."

"Why don't you tell Charlie the truth?"

"Don't want to give the *wanker* the satisfaction."

"Come on."

Cameron, the man known as Prisoner Three, sighed.

"Victor's real name is Ash. What he never tells anybody is that it's actually Ashley. I know, right? He hates to be called that. Probably why he's taken to his fake guard name. Anyway, we used to be partners. Two halves of a team back in Sydney. We solved problems for a living. He was the front man, the charmer, the talker, the snake; I was the guy in the background, on the fringes. *Ashley* would draw them out, I'd move in for the kill. We took the cases nobody else would take. We were a good team. Until we were sent here."

"Tell Charlie how you were brought here."

"Chasing a bunch of sex traffickers and we walked into a trap. Still don't know how I didn't see the signs."

"I didn't, either."

"Yeah, well, none of us did, and the moment we woke up down here everything changed. Ash lost his mind, accusing me of shit. At first I thought he was just stir-crazy, then I realized something. All this time, our entire partnership, the whole joking-around thing? The charm? It was a mask. Took coming down here for me to finally see his true face. YOU HEAR ME, YOU FUCK? I KNOW ALL ABOUT YOU. I KNOW WHAT YOU DID UP THERE."

Hardie said nothing.

Still, Eve pressed on with her case.

Namely, that the cards were stacked against Hardie from the beginning. That this prison was topsy-turvy, the good guys inside, and the bad guys out, and that was the special hell of it.

He couldn't have known.

None of them did.

Prisoner Four's real name, Eve explained, was Archie. He was a former British military man who been betrayed by his superior.

Disgusted, he'd left the U.K. and gone ping-ponging around the continental United States for the better part of a decade, helping people with their problems in return for a small fee. Nothing extravagant. Just enough to eat, buy a toothbrush, whatever. He wanted no earthly attachments.

"Tell Charlie about X-Ray," Eve urged.

"You tell him," Archie said.

"You're so modest."

"You know I'm not."

So Eve told the story.

For years, Archie had been investigating a disturbing case—one in which people were found in hotel rooms all over the U.S. (and around the world, he learned later) with their organs missing or rearranged or barely functioning or replaced by handmade parts. The victims weren't slaughtered. They were left alive...barely. As if some demented surgeon were experimenting with radical operations that tested the endurance of the flesh. This surgeon was also thought to be responsible for the death of Archie's half brother, an American military man stationed in Berlin. Archie thought he was close to catching the surgeon when he ended up here, at site 7734.

"The surgeon is the guard who calls himself X-Ray," Archie told them. "I believe he's keeping me alive to experiment on me. He has some of my brother's organs in a jar. He's just waiting until I'm healthy enough to undergo a transplant."

Hardie remained silent.

Faint static.

"Charlie, *come on*. Let me know you're there. Look, I've got something cool to share. You should be happy for me."

Static.

"Now that I've found you I've got a ninety-nine-percent success rate as a professional finder."

Static.

"Yeah, there's always one that got away, you know how it goes."

Static.

"What's that? You want to hear about that one time? Good. Anyway, this was my earliest case, when I was just starting out in the business. I was hired by a woman named Julie Lippman to find her college boyfriend. I know, sounds lame, right? This was a real case, though, and it's dogged me my whole career. Now this Lippman girl's a rich snot, and one night at a campus Christmas party she makes this joke about her boyfriend—this not-so-rich guy named Bobby—having to work for, like, an entire year before being able to afford an engagement ring. She knew she was being a snot, but meant it to be funny. She said her boy Bobby got this weird look on his face, then left not long after. She kept drinking. Didn't think much of it. Bobby was kind of a brooder that way. Besides, they were supposed to be spending the Christmas break together. She wasn't going home to her family. They were going to hang around campus and drink and fuck and give each other presents and basically avoid real life. She goes home, Bobby's in bed, already asleep. Well, the next morning she gets up and...no Bobby. She has this dim memory of him kissing her on the forehead or something, but boom, splitsville. That's when it dawns on Julie that wow, maybe he really is pissed. After a day of waiting, she knows it's true. He's super pissed. Which makes Julie super pissed. Since she assumes he went home to his parents' house, she goes home to her family and does all kinds of stupid shit. Halfway through the holiday, though, she really starts feeling bad and missing him and vows to make it all right again when they're back on campus. She gets in early and waits in his dorm room for him. Sunday, all day, waiting. Then comes the news.

Twenty-four students, dead. She gets hold of a list of victims, and sure enough, her boy Bobby's on the list. She's like, Whaaaaaaat the fuck? Bobby didn't have money to fly, Bobby was afraid to fly, where the hell would Bobby fly to, anyway, spur of the freakin' moment? It made no sense to her. She refused to accept it. The more she looked into it, the more walls she hit. Finally she hired me—her parents are loaded. Well, the more I looked into it...the stranger the whole thing was. That was my first introduction to the world beneath the real world. A world I think you're very familiar with, Charlie."

Static. A few pops and crackles on the line.

"Charlie, you there?"

Static.

"Come on, tell me your story."

Static.

"*Très* uncool, Charlie. Leave a girl hanging like that."

Static.

Nothing.

Barely a minute later Horsehead started going off in Italian. He must have heard the others' stories and decided to jump in on the act. Which wasn't all bad, because you could follow the emotion in his words. The sadness. The fury. The disgust. The loathing. The self-incrimination. Again, fury. All-consuming fury. A reckoning. A final, lingering sadness.

After that, no one spoke for a long, long time.

Still, a few shifts later, Eve tried again.

"Hey, Charlie."

Nothing.

"Come on, Charlie. Say something. Even a little 'fuck you.' Our little communication system won't last forever. They probably turn it on and off to screw with us, but so what? Doesn't mean you can't say hi or something. Let me know you're still breathing."

After a long pause.

(A long,

long

pause . . .)

"Fuck you."

Eve exclaimed, "Hallelujah! There we go! At last. He's alive, ladies and gentlemen. So go on. Tell us your story."

Tell us your story.

Right.

Eve persisted.

"Hey, you know our deal. Tell us yours."

Hardie hesitated, then figured, What harm would it do, even if the guards were listening? It would be nice to know if he could still form words.

"I was a house sitter. I tried to protect some people, but I screwed it up. They sent me here."

"They?"

"The Accident People."

"Is that what you call them? The Accident People?"

"What do you call them?"

"They're just one group in a field of many. There's a Secret America, Hardie. Beneath the one you know. Beneath everything. Run by the people who really call the shots. They're the ones who make things happen. The ones who never sleep. I've spent the past few years studying how they conceive and execute their goals. They run secret hospitals. Secret prisons. Secret airports. Secret factories. Anything you can think of in the aboveground world, there's an equivalent in the shadow world. This is the real America, the shadow structure under the structure we think is real. And here's the really weird thing, Charlie—the thing that's going to drive you right out of your mind. The more I dug, the more I learned, the more I started piecing things together, the more the truth became clear: this isn't a nefarious global plot. They espouse no particular ideology. They have no viewpoints or goals. They're so massive, so vast, they're like this big benign thug. They merely work for whoever signs the biggest check. Like Frank Zappa said—they're only in it for the money."

Static.

"Are you listening to me, Charlie?"

Yeah, Charlie Hardie was listening.

And thinking about the images they showed him inside the mask.

Hearing the prisoners' stories made Hardie realize:

This "Secret America" would never, ever leave his family alone.

Unless he forced them to stop.

22

You're stripped down to the bare essentials of what you are, and who you are as a man.

—Eddie Bunker

HARDIE STARTED WITH something small: push-ups.

One-armed, one-half push-ups, to be exact.

His old man's favorite exercise. The only exercise a man needed, he always said. And the old man's favorite punishment was a half push-up. That's when you started a traditional push-up, then stopped halfway through, with your arms nearly fully extended, back straight, knees locked, muscles working. And you stay that way for as long as you can take, or until the old man tells you to drop. Mouth off? Half push-up time. Forget to take out the trash? Half push-up time.

Get your dumb ass thrown in a secret prison, causing you to have a complete mental breakdown and a resultant moment of clarity?

Half push-up time.

His body hated it at first. Absolutely *hated* it, because it had been softened by years of watching rich people's homes and eating whatever and drinking whatever and reclining on whatever, confident that his years of strength training would still be there when he needed them. His body, of course, was full of shit. His body was weak and lazy and broken. But his head was in charge, and it ordered the body to do the half push-up. And there was nothing the body could do about it, because the head was safely ensconced in its cozy metal mask.

You can't make me do this.

Watch me.

You can't.

You will.

I won't.

You have no choice.

And the body, in fact, had no choice.

(Hardie was aware that bifurcating himself like this would probably lead to mental problems down the road, but that didn't matter, because this was the road now, and hey, you have to deal with the road as it comes.)

The guards didn't like the half push-ups, either. They would yell at him and tell him this wasn't exercise time and give him an electric jolt through the metal floor of his cell. Which was fine, because at first, Hardie couldn't do a half push-up for more than thirty, forty seconds. But he kept at it, got right back up after being thrown off by a shock. He knew there were limits. They couldn't just keep shocking the snot out of him. So they had to try something else. They had to open the cell to get to him.

Which they did, kicking him and punching him and spraying him with their wristbands full of mace and telling him to knock it off. Hardie ignored them, ignored the burning fury in his eyes, and went back to the half push-ups a few hours later anyway. After a while it became too much of a pain in the ass to open the cell. They ignored him, and only beat him every once in a while. By then, Hardie was up to three minutes. Then five.

Soon Hardie was doing full push-ups and leg squats—which killed. He did them when no one was looking. When he was caught he was shocked and beaten. Which Hardie considered to be a workout on its own, toughening his skin, his muscles. He grew to welcome the intrusions, actually.

Hardie knew that he was doing a slow-motion version of all of those insane get-back-in-shape, get-armed, build-weapons, plant-traps, don-the-body-armor, smear-war-paint-on-your-face montages from countless movies, the most egregious of which were, of course, from the *Rocky* movies, in which you could go from flabby palooka to mean lean hurting machine in as long as it took for the 1980s pop song to play itself out. What ordinarily took years could play out in a matter of verse-chorus, verse-chorus, bridge, chorus, chorus. Hardie started to imagine Rocky Balboa in the cell with him. Not to goad him on, but to be there when the monotony set in so that Hardie could turn around and call Rocky Balboa a pussy. *You're a pussy, Rock.*

Hey, whaddya mean?

A pussy, Rock.

Hey, I wouldn't be talking like that if I were—

A PUSSY, BALBOA, A BIG FAT PUSSY.

Don't get Hardie wrong; jail still sucked.

But with the same self-awareness, he understood that he'd merely adapted to his surroundings. This was nothing special. This what people did; he'd seen *Shawshank Redemption.*

And, like Tim Robbins, he had a plan.

The next shower.

Hardie knew one had to be coming at some point.

The waiting was the worst part. No watch to check, no calendar pages to rip off the wall. Just the vague notion that at some point the guards would have to release him from his cell and place him in the shower room for a few minutes.

But when?

Or had they decided to revoke his shower privileges forever?

Finally, at long last, during a long dull fuzzy moment when Hardie's brain truly tuned out of reality, Victor appeared at Hardie's cell door, with Whiskey in the backup position.

Hardie had to pull it together. Reload the plan. He'd had a plan at some point. It had been a good one, too. Both guards had their batons ready, in case Hardie decided to try anything funny. Which he totally was going to! Only he couldn't remember exactly what the hell it was...

Snap out of it. Wake up. Come on, WAKE THE FUCK UP.

"Back against the bars."

Hardie complied. Victor slid the key in hard, forcing Hardie's head to bob forward. Something beeped. The binds loosened. Hardie reached up and slipped off his mask as Victor slipped another electronic key into the cell door.

"Up."

Hardie crawled to his feet and they nudged him forward, around the block of cells and to the right, toward the shower room.

"Take your smock off," Victor said once they'd reached the door, which had a thick opaque glass panel.

"Could you turn around? I'm shy."

Whiskey poked him in the ribs with her baton.

"Lèves-toi!"

As Hardie stripped and dropped the smock to the ground, he said, "Okay, okay. Want to join me, Whiskey? Wash my back, maybe? Squeeze my testicles again?"

Whiskey's reply was to shove him inside the shower room with both hands, causing Hardie to clumsily tumble forward and slide across the tile floor.

"Guess that's a no."

And the door slammed shut and locked behind him.

Hardie climbed to his feet and waited for the water, as there were no handles on the tile wall. Just three rusted-out nozzles. And then without warning the cold water blasted him, almost knocking him down on his ass again. Once he recovered, Hardie started cleaning himself with his bare hands. No soap, but whatever. Even though the water was freezing, it felt good on his skin. More important, it cleared up his fuzzy mind. The plan came back to him. No time to psych himself up. He just had to be ready to do it NOW.

When the water died, Hardie limped back over toward the door, dripping wet, and pressed his back up against the wall. Here we go. All or nothing, do-or-die time.

The plan:

Hardie would keep his back pressed up against the disgusting tile wall, out of sight. When they opened the door, one of them would have to go in, to see what was going on. Not both of them. For both of them to go in would be stupid, and these guards were not stupid. The next move depended on speed. Hardie would grab whoever entered (probably Victor) and smash his head against the tile floor as hard as he could. It had to be done in one swift move, because one chance was all he'd have. If a fight broke out, the other guard (probably Whiskey) would jump into the shower room, and one carefully placed electric shock later the escape would be over. So the face-pummeling had to be powerful and brutal.

Next move: grabbing Victor's electric baton.

Then Hardie, if his legs would cooperate, would rush Whiskey and jam the business end of the baton into her chest and give her a jolt. Just enough to drop her to her knees, so that Hardie could snatch the keys from her belt and run over to Cameron's cell. Once *that* was open, then they all officially had a prayer. Within seconds they could be up the hallway and opening Eve's cell. Then it would be three against two, and the odds would only get better from there.

Because when you got down to it—and this occurred to Hardie in his cell days and days ago—the prisoners outnumbered the guards right now, five to four.

Okay, considering Hardie's arm and leg, maybe it was more like *four and a half* to four. Still, those were odds Hardie would take.

So he kept his bare back against the gross wall, waiting.

The door had to open any minute now.

Hardie played and replayed the move in his mind. Grabbing Victor's head by the hair and just slamming it down, using his body weight to propel it along until bone smashed against tile...

C'mon, door.

What were they waiting for?

Had to open. It just felt like forever because he was anticipating it, right?

And then, finally, the door opened.

Just not the door Hardie expected.

The opposite door opened—the one leading to Whiskey's quarters. But Victor was the one standing there.

"Over here, quick! Don't let her see you."

What the hell was this? Well, there went his brilliant plan. Had they somehow figured it out, and this was their way of defusing it? No. That made no sense. He hadn't uttered a word of the plan. It had been entirely hatched in his mind.

"Come on, mate!"

So Hardie limped over to the doorway, and saw a dirty, torn suit neatly folded on the tile floor. His old warden outfit.

"Put these on," Victor said.

"Where's Whiskey?"

"Look, you want to get out of here or not?"

Hardie dressed himself quickly. The feel of the suit on his wet skin was unpleasant, but it was better than the smock. Anything was better than the smock. All he had were the trousers and jacket, no underwear, no shirt, no belt, no socks, no shoes. But it felt like a suit of armor compared to that smock. He'd hated the smock so much he didn't even want to think the word *smock* ever again.

"This way."

They moved through Whiskey's room and then through the control booth Hardie could never see from his cage. So where were Yankee and X-Ray? And Whiskey, for that matter? Was she still waiting outside the shower door? Hardie must have slowed down because Victor was tugging on his arm, urging him forward.

"Come on."

"What is this about?"

Victor paused long enough to whisper, "You were right. It took me a while to piece everything together, but you were right, mate, and if we're going to do anything about it, we need to move now."

Victor hated this next part. It really made him feel like the world's king supreme dick. But it was a necessary part of keeping this facility running smoothly. You needed conflict, for the good of the guards, for the good of the prisoners. If you didn't let the pressure out in small, controlled doses, the whole facility was likely to explode. And shaking up the status quo helped reveal the actual traitors, the escape plots in the making.

The Prisonmaster had carefully explained this when he named

Victor the "secret warden" a little over a year ago, not long after Victor had proven himself worthy. New "wardens" may be sent to the facility, the Prisonmaster said, but Victor was still the man in charge, the one he depended upon to keep the most dangerous people on earth contained.

Victor craved the validation, the responsibility. He loved being special.

Which eased his conscience a little.

Thing was—

and Victor had *no* idea about this—

the Prisonmaster had told the other guards the exact same thing.

Victor and Hardie walked into the elevator vestibule, which was dim and quiet. Victor took Hardie's arm and led him toward a corner.

"Over here."

"I'm guessing you have some kind of escape plan that won't kill everyone down here?"

"Oh, yeah, I do."

Victor's plan was this: guide Hardie to the dark corner of the vestibule. There, Victor would pick up Hardie's electrified walking cane—confiscated when they threw him in his cell—and jam it against Hardie's heart and press the button. After Hardie did the sixty-cycle spin, Victor would sound the sirens and flash the lights, and soon everyone would realize there had been yet *another* escape attempt.

The other three guards would scramble down here and find their former "warden" holding his electrified cane and wearing his old suit jacket and trousers. Hardie would have to explain himself. Hardie would be interrogated. After all, how did he manage to escape from his cell? Where did he find his old suit? How did he recover his old weapon? Answers would have to be given. Brutal yet necessary interrogations of the prisoners would begin. Guards would be questioned, too—clearly, Hardie had a collaborator. Suspicion, naturally, would fall on Victor. Hardie himself would testify to that fact.

"But don't worry about that, Victor," the Prisonmaster explained. "This just puts you in the unique position of being able to uncover the real traitor."

Which was the whole point: find the traitor among them.

"Help me, Victor. Help keep this facility safe," the Prisonmaster had said.

"You know," Hardie said, "Prisoner Three told me something very interesting about you."

"Oh, yeah?" Victor asked. "What's that?"

Hardie gritted his teeth and jackhammered his right fist into Victor's lower back, dead bang between his kidneys, giving the punch everything he had, his entire body weight focused on that single target.

Victor yelped, twisted slightly, dropped to his knees.

"That you're a nance," Hardie said. "Whatever the hell that means."

What Cameron had actually said was that his former partner Ashley (now "Victor") had once suffered a serious lower-back injury, and that in subsequent adventures, he'd added further insult to that injury.

"That's the cunt's Achilles heel. Punch him hard enough in the small of the back and he'll fold like a fuckin' deck chair. All I want is one shot at his back. Just one, for old times' sake."

Well, Hardie was simply passing the sentiment along.

Hardie knew he didn't have much strength or time. He had to incapacitate his old buddy Victor/Ashley here quick and clean.

He was considering a chop to the throat and a few more punches to the kidneys when he saw it, over in the corner.

His cane.

That little black beauty with the curved handle and the fifty thousand volts of sheer electric hell inside.

Hardie shuffled over to it, unsheathed the end—oh, how he wished he'd realized what this puppy did when he first arrived—then came back and gave his old buddy Victor enough shocks to make him reconsider consciousness. Then after picking Victor's pockets clean of cell keys and the Smith & Wesson tactical pen, military and police edition, Hardie felt armed and crazy enough to try it.

An honest-to-God jailbreak.

He quickly made his way back down to the main floor, an excitement in his blood he hadn't felt in years.

23

*Bide your time. That's what prison teaches you, if nothing else.
Bide your time and everything becomes clear and you can act
accordingly.*

—Terence Stamp, *The Limey*

HARDIE SPRANG EVE first—her cell was the closest to the elevator
vestibule. She had been in one of her otherworldly Zen moments.
After he unlocked her mask, Eve rubbed her eyes and asked what the
hell was going on—where he got the old suit and weapons. Hardie
said he'd explain later, then offered her a choice of weapons: the pen
or the cane. Not surprisingly, she went with the pen. *Very gallant of
her,* Hardie thought. *The old man still needed his cane.*

"You know, this is probably a trap," Eve said. "They're going to
catch us and then torture the living shit out of us."

"Probably. You want me to lock you back up?"

Eve smiled. "Duh."

Cameron was next. Hardie unlocked his face mask and clapped
him on the shoulder.

"That shot to his spine?" Hardie said. "It worked. Thanks."

"You're welcome," said Cameron. "Tell me, did he cry like a little
bitch?"

Next they went around the corner and freed Archie, who was stark naked and seemingly unconcerned about it. Hardie found it a bit difficult to take seriously a man whose balls were swinging around like the pendulum on a grandfather clock, but so be it. Eve, who seemed immune to the posthypnotic sway of genitals, asked if he was up for this. Archie merely nodded. Good enough for Hardie.

Finally they came to the cell of Horsehead. The man was still curled up in a fetal position, never having fully recovered from his beating and electrocution of some time ago. The same thing that Hardie would have endured. His cell stank of urine because he repeatedly wet himself, having lost all bladder control. He twitched, and his hair stuck up in odd tufts here and there, stiff as dreads.

Hardie slid a key into the back of Horsehead's mask, but nothing happened. Horsehead cursed in Italian, then tried to take the keys from Hardie. "Hang on, let me try another one."

"Do you want to stay here?" Eve asked, pointing to the floor of his cell. "Or do you want to join us?" Pointing to the outside.

Horsehead nodded and pointed.

Yeah, he was down with the jailbreak.

Hardie tried another key, but nothing.

"We don't have time for this," Cameron said. "The mask stays on for now. We'll figure it out later."

Eve extended her hand. Horsehead, trembling, allowed himself to be pulled to a standing position. He swayed, as if intoxicated, and would have fallen back down to the floor if Cameron hadn't grabbed him and thrown one of his beefy arms over his shoulder.

"All right, let's go," Archie said.

"Wait," Eve said. "What about Prisoner Zero? We can't just leave him."

"Well, we can't bloody well carry him," Archie said. "We've already got two walking wounded." Then, with glance at Hardie, "No offense."

Hardie wanted to tell him to bloody well suck it. But Archie was right.

"We'll have to come back for him. Victor told me that X-Ray and Yankee are in there with him. If he was telling the truth."

"Where's Whiskey?" Eve asked.

"No idea."

Eve nodded. "Okay, she's gotta be in here somewhere. So let's sweep the outer ring, room by room, incapacitate the bastards, and take control of the prison. Lock them up in those cells."

"And then find a way out of this hellhole," Archie said.

"Where did you leave fuckface?" Cameron asked.

Hardie led them to the elevator room. No one was there except a still-unconscious—or faking—Ashley/Victor. Cameron knelt down beside him, touched his fingers to the guard's wrist, then to his jugular, nodded to himself. There was a sadness to his movements, as if Victor were a longtime family dog who had suddenly turned and bitten the baby. Such a creature needed to be put down, but you did not relish the task.

"Stupid *wanker*," muttered Cameron as he launched his fist into his former partner's face. The punch was a single jackhammer blow—a white-hot blast of kinetic energy, expertly focused. If Victor had been faking, he wasn't anymore. Cameron quickly stripped his former partner of his brown uniform.

"What are you doing?" Hardie asked.

"Camouflaging myself," Cameron said. "I take the lead, maybe the outfit fools 'em. Buy us a second or two of time."

The door to the break room was locked, but Hardie still had the keys from Victor's chain.

"Let me," Cameron said, holding out his hand.

Hardie hesitated, but knew it was right to hand them off. His left hand was still unreliable. Last thing he needed was to drop the damned keys.

The ragtag strike force gathered by the door: Cameron in the lead, Archie behind him, followed by Eve and Hardie, and, bringing up the rear, on his hands and knees now because he couldn't support his own body weight—Horsehead.

Hardie nudged Eve. "What about him?"

"We'll come back for him."

The odds: not great. What, three and a half tired, beaten prisoners versus three guards with weapons? Eve had a pen, and Hardie had his cane. That was it. Hardie even felt vaguely guilty about hanging on to it. The one true weapon should be put into the hands of the most able-bodied prisoner. In this case, Archie.

"You want this?" Hardie asked, showing him the cane.

But the man shook his head and showed them his balled-up fists. "These are all I need."

Cameron slid a key into the door, nothing. Tried another. Nothing. The third time, however, was the charm: a beep sounded, and the door clacked open. Cameron slipped inside the room, and—

"YEAGGGHHHHH!"

A horrible, inhuman scream as an insane amount of voltage ripped through his body.

The guards had been waiting for them.

That was because the Prisonmaster had informed Yankee and X-Ray that a jailbreak was in progress, that Victor had betrayed them, had given his former partner his keys and the uniform. He told Yankee, in English:

"This is the most dire threat we've ever faced, Yankee, and I'm counting on you to set things right."

He told X-Ray, in German:

"This is the most dire threat we've ever faced, X-Ray, and I'm counting on you to set things right."

He also told Yankee:

"You can trust X-Ray for the time being, but keep an eye on him. You're the only one I know I can trust. I'm counting on you to uncover the betrayers."

He told X-Ray, in German:

"You can trust Yankee for the time being, but keep an eye on him. You're the only one I know I can trust. I'm counting on you."

"But you need not fear," the Prisonmaster told both of them. "Because in the end, after the rebellion is quashed, there will be extra prisoners in the cells, and new wardens will surely be sent down to live among you—good men and women who will help you restore order at long last."

The Prisonmaster knew the power of hope, and, more important, how to exploit it. He'd been doing it for decades now.

Archie pushed Cameron's twitching body aside and went in, swinging his fists as though they were studded metal balls attached to leather bands. Cameron's keys went clattering to the cement floor.

Hardie thought: *Someone pick up the keys.*

Over near the door Archie traded chops and kicks with his arch-nemesis, X-Ray. Hardie dove past them, through the doorway and straight into the fray, aiming for those keys. An elbow slammed into his chest right away. Then another fist whipped across Hardie's face. Somebody kicked the keys. They shot across the floor through the open doorway and into the corner room—where food and clothes were delivered. Without those keys, they were fucked. Might as well kneel down and take their beatings just to get them over with.

Scrambling across the floor, his right leg screaming at him, threatening to cease all movement, Hardie crawled through the doorway, then reached out and wrapped his right hand around the keys. A second later a boot came down on that hand, trapping and crushing it at the same time.

Instinctively, Hardie tried to yank his hand free. It wouldn't move. The pain was unreal. Hardie thought he could feel veins bursting within the flesh sac of the thing that used to be his right hand, which was being crushed by the rubber sole of a boot from above and the sharp keys from below.

Hardie balled up his left hand into a fist and struck out, at crotch level, with all his strength. His fist struck its target. The boot released his hand. The boot turned out to belong to Whiskey.

And although she did not possess the pair of testicles that Hardie had imagined, the punch had its intended effect. Whiskey dropped to her knees, clutching at her private parts.

Yep, I've still got it, Hardie thought. *Hitting women like a pro.*

Hardie checked his hand. It still could open, but his palm was cut and punctured with key marks. There was a blur of motion to his left. Hardie looked up at the exact moment a fist smashed into the side of his head. Whiskey. She threw another punch, a sloppy but powerful left jab, muttered something profane in her own language, and followed up with a right hook that slammed Hardie back into the wall.

He also dropped the keys, and Whiskey swept them aside with a kick of her boot.

She looked like she was about to use the heel of her hand to drive a piece of his nose cartilage up into his brain when she stopped. Something crackled in her ear.

At that moment the Prisonmaster was shouting:

"Go to the break room and bar the door shut. Now! It's your only chance!"

* * *

And Hardie could hear it.

Meanwhile the two able-bodied prisoners, Archie and Eve, battled Yankee and X-Ray back into the delivery room. X-Ray tried to use his wristband mace blast, but Archie slapped his arm away and gave him a brutal head butt to his nose. Blood gushed out and clung to the wispy blond hairs hanging down from Archie's forehead. "For my brother, you cunt." X-Ray staggered backward. Through the pain, though, he heard the voice of the Prisonmaster, speaking perfect German:

"Lock them in the delivery room and get back to the control room. Now! It's your only chance!"

X-Ray grimaced and raced forward, smashing into Archie's midsection and flinging him to the side. Out of the corner of his eye, Hardie could see that Yankee was doing the same thing with Eve, smashing his way past her body, except that he was scrambling in the other direction, toward the control room.

The realization hit Hardie and Eve at the same time: the guards were splitting up . . . *to seal them in the delivery room.*

If they were trapped in a single room, it was game over.

Hardie scuttled across the floor like a crab escaping a boiling pot of water. He scooped up his cane and threw it to Eve—who caught it and wedged it between the door and the frame just as Yankee and Whiskey were pulling it shut. The guards on the other side tried, but no amount of strength was sufficient to snap that cane in half. Meanwhile Archie held it in place, so they couldn't kick it loose.

For the moment they were at a grunting, sweating impasse.

* * *

Eve, breathing heavily, lips bleeding, said, "Okay."

Hardie said, "Wait—what's okay?"

"We can't go back to the way it was. We'll never get this chance again. Got to end this thing now."

"How are we supposed to do that?"

"I'm talking about winning the fucking war, the whole thing, once and for all, change everything forever."

"Spit it out already," Archie said.

"Send one of us up and out through the elevator."

Hardie just stared at her. Do *what?*

"And trigger the death mechanism?" Archie asked.

"Hear me out," Eve continued. "One of us gets out. Escapes the facility. Finds someone on the outside. Tells the truth about this place."

"Killing everyone else," Hardie said.

"But one of us gets out," Eve added, "and the survivor has to bring the truth to the world. Hardie here knows someone who will listen. Don't you, Charlie?"

"What?" Hardie asked. "No. No way. Bad idea."

"Why?"

"Are you really prepared to kill everyone down here?" Hardie asked.

"For the greater good? Absolutely. If we don't make this strike now, we're all fucked. Things will get worse. This will go on and on and on...and nobody will know. Nobody will fucking know what went on down here! And I can't have that."

"No, she may be right," Archie said. "The question is, of course...who goes?"

"Hardie goes," Eve said.

Hardie blinked. "What? No. Unh-unh. This is insane."

"You have a wife and a son waiting for you. Besides, I have my success rate to think about. I don't complete my job if you die."

"There's another way," Hardie said. "There's always another way." He wanted to quote Batman and his thing about prisons always containing their escape, but he decided it would take too long.

"No, there's not, Charlie. You haven't been here long enough to realize that. We all have. There is no way. They designed this thing perfectly—only one exit no one would ever dare take. Well, fuck that. One of us should take it. And I think that someone should be you. Put us all out of our misery and blow the lid off this place. Don't forget everything I've told you about the people who run this pl—"

"No," Hardie said sternly. "No. There's no way I'm killing all of you."

"You don't understand—"

"No, Eve, *you* don't understand. Why do you think I'm even here? Because I let my partner and his whole family die. And you want me to do it again? To all of you?"

Archie, in all his naked glory, nodded his head. "He's right, you know."

They turned to look at him.

"I should go," he said.

"What?" Eve asked. "No. Fuck you—I don't even *know* you. Hardie goes."

Archie shook his head. "Mr. Hardie, you seem like a fine man and all, but the trick is going to be getting past these two guards and making it to the elevator while the rest of us are on defense—as you call it in American football. You were walking with a cane until very recently. What if you stumble? What if you can't make it? As I see it, we only have one shot at this. The strongest and fastest should go. There is no time for false modesty here—I am the strongest and fastest."

Archie made eye contact with each of them before continuing:

"You're all okay with this, right? Good."

And with that, he wrapped the fingers of both hands firmly around the edge of the door.

"Cover me."

With almost superhuman strength, Archie wrenched open the door and dove in.

But the guards were ready for him.

The Prisonmaster told X-Ray:

"Under the table. Pull up the tile. Use any key to unlock them. Do it now."

X-Ray quickly unlocked two weapons, keeping one for himself and passing the other to Whiskey. Now each of them had a device that resembled an electrified barbecue fork. The two prongs could be inserted deep into tissue and deliver a shock that was beyond any human being's threshold of pain. Instant bodily shutdown.

Archie charged straight at them.

Whiskey and X-Ray braced themselves, weapons behind their backs.

They did not relish this moment.

They knew the devices in their hands could potentially kill the prisoners, and they did not consider themselves to be killers.

In fact, before they were brought to this place, they were considered heroes.

Whiskey's real name was Mathilde Aslanides, and she'd made a career out of keeping people from harm. If your name appeared on a hit list, and the authorities failed or refused to protect you, Mathilde would. She knew how to hide, she knew how to fight, and until a team of vengeful assassins cornered her in a nasty Brazilian favela, she had helped save the lives of more than one hundred people. Her life was about preventing death, not becoming its agent.

In his former life, X-Ray worked on the flip side, helping people after their deaths. Under his real name—Lucas Dabrock—X-Ray was an expert at determining the *real* cause of any given death—not just what presented on the surface, not what the killers wanted you to think. If he was unable to prevent a death, then at least he could find and help punish those responsible—the ones who thought they could get away with it. Dabrock had been one of the most brilliant and sought-after pathologists in the world...until his enemies had conspired to bring him here, to this place of madness.

Now X-Ray held his weapon steady, knowing exactly where he needed to stab in order to take down the prisoner who was coming at them full bore.

At the last moment Archie dropped straight down and executed a kicking spin that knocked both guards off their feet.

In the confused tangle of bodies Archie stayed focused enough to grab one electrified barbecue fork, and, in a smooth efficient motion, plunge it into X-Ray's testicles. X-Ray's mouth made an O. Archie seized the other electrified barbecue fork just as Whiskey was about to plunge it into his heart. Whiskey was smart, determined, and excellent in battle. But she did not have Archie's upper-arm strength. It was not a matter of skill; this was down to muscle. And Archie was able to turn the fork around and jab it between Whiskey's breasts.

He triggered both electrified barbecue forks at the same moment. Both guards screamed, almost in harmony, albeit off-key.

Archie dropped the forks, scrambled up from the floor, and immediately began jogging toward the elevator vestibule.

Both X-Ray and Whiskey made a halfhearted effort to scramble after their prisoner, but they were in too much pain to move. Archie slammed the elevator-cage door shut. The guards screamed in terror. They knew what this meant.

This was death for all of them!

Archie smiled, gave him them the finger, then began to ascend.

Hardie heard the creaking, throbbing mechanism of the ancient elevator system reverberate throughout the entire facility, the screams and moans of the guards.

So this was how it was going to end.

Who was Hardie kidding? For him, everything had ended three years and God knows how many months ago—when he let Nate Parish and his family die, and when he'd survived by some quirk of medical fate. All this time he'd been a walking dead man.

A guy like Archie would go out there and punish the wicked better than any of them could.

Better than *he* could.

Archie kind of felt bad about what was about to happen.

Still, this was the absolute right thing to do. He was their best shot because Archie was a born survivor, extremely good at waiting until the right opportunity presented itself...then *seizing it*. He'd been waiting for such an opportunity ever since he'd been dropped into this infernal place. Now the chance was here, and he'd taken it. What rational being could blame him?

Still, innocent people were going to die. They had consented to the sacrifice; there was nothing he could do about it.

Archie couldn't remember exactly how long he'd been here. Not as long as the others, certainly. He kept quiet, didn't let the despair and chatter of the others affect him. That was key. Keeping your mind straight, tuning out the rest of the world's clutter.

That was why he was still sane, and why he was getting out.

After what seemed like an eternity, the elevator ground to a noisy halt. He pulled aside the door, stepped into the vestibule. Archie reached for the knob. A small voice in his head, the one he never listened to, told him: *It's going to be locked.* Archie twisted the knob. Unlocked. Archie smiled. The little voice, that annoying ghost of self-doubt, was always wrong. He was glad he hadn't let the little voice get the best of him during his long stay. That little voice would drive you mad if you weren't careful.

The doorway led to the room he dimly remembered from when he was first brought here. Table, chairs. That's right. He'd woken up handcuffed to a chair. Someone had walked in and explained the deal to him. From that very first moment, Archie started waiting for the right opportunity.

Archie walked across the room and opened the second door, which led to a small room—another vestibule, only this one was made of steel. A fancy elevator, perhaps? Holding the door, he looked behind it for any possible control panel. No buttons. Maybe this was a safe room, meant to protect the occupant. After all, the person who had explained things to him had to have left this room alive, right? Archie closed the door behind him.

The little voice inside his head screamed at him: *You're a fool!* Archie told the voice to shut up and not bother him anymore.

But there were no buttons. No secret switches. No options. No nothing. Another few minutes of searching, first calm, then frantic, led him to an unmistakable conclusion. This box led nowhere.

For the first time in his life, Archie Elder felt true despair.

Everyone in the facility waited for their deaths. Archie wouldn't waste time; he would leave as soon as possible. The only questions now were: How would they die? Gas? Electricity? Undetectable poison? A bomb? Hidden guns? And how long before it happened?

But then a very surprising thing happened.

Nothing.

Death did not come down from above. No alarms, no hidden machine guns, no sarin gas, no flooding water...nothing at all. No sound at all.

Until there was suddenly a loud mechanical *POP,* a fat spark jumping a circuit.

The elevator whirred back to life. The cage was coming back down. Hardie didn't understand until he saw Archie, head hung low, shuffling back into the delivery room.

"There's no way out," he said softly. "Just a dead end, sealed shut."

Everyone in the room, prisoners and guards alike, looked at each other, the same realization dawning on them at the same moment.

There was no death mechanism.

They were all prisoners here.

24

It's obvious what they're after — an economy of man-power — or devil-power, if you prefer. The same idea as in the cafeteria, where customers serve themselves.

—Jean-Paul Sartre, *No Exit*

THE PRISONMASTER LISTENED...and waited. He had his finger on the trigger, but he didn't want to deploy the gas until the last possible moment.

So they'd discovered the truth about the so-called death mechanism. Other groups of prisoners had figured it out, too. But not many. The death mechanism was the one lie that every inmate believed at face value. Over the years, some had tried to work their way up the elevator shaft to see if they could disable the nonexistent mechanism, but such efforts were always thwarted by the guards, sworn to uphold their duty.

Twice before, an inmate had made it up to the waiting room, intent on escape, knowing that he was damning everyone else to death.

And the result was the same: the confused inmate took the elevator back down to the main floor to report his horrifying discovery:

There is no way out!

The first time it happened, the guards reasserted their authority and slipped back into their roles. So did the prisoners, for that matter. After a while the threat of the death mechanism was a nonissue; the idea of no escape was simply their new reality. Later they were all put to death, but that was only because they had all outlived their usefulness, and the site needed to be prepared for new inmates.

The second time, however, the guards and prisoners refused to accept this, and had to be gassed, their roles reassigned.

Which would it be this time?

Yankee recovered his electric baton and stood up. "This changes nothing. We're bringing you back to your cells. Come on, X-Ray, Whiskey. Let's go."

His fellow guards, however, didn't move. They were still processing the situation.

What was wrong with these people?

All this time they had been sure of one rule: whoever left the facility basically handed everyone else a death sentence. No matter how bad it got, how much the crappy food or isolation or torture drove you out of your skull, there was that one constant: if you leave, innocent people will suffer and die.

This was still the case...

...wasn't it?

Yankee's name in the real world had been Jed Ayres, and he'd been a bartender, a soldier, a cop, and finally a mercenary and recovery specialist who loved to right wrongs. He was a man obsessed with law and order, and it was a dark day when official law broke down for him and he swore to uphold a higher law and assist those screwed by the system. For years he'd done just that, first in St. Louis, then throughout the Midwest. Jed had been great at it, too—until the rainy morning they ran his truck off the road, pried him out of the wreckage, and he woke up here as the warden of this friggin' place.

The only thing that consoled Jed was that he could still do good, still uphold the law...even in hell.

It came to Hardie all at once. He flashed back to what Mann had told him in the waiting room:

I think you're going to find working with them extremely rewarding. I mean, they're all truly good people. Heroes, really.

Yes, she had been fucking with him. Sticking it in and twisting a little. But she'd also been telling him the truth.

It was the Prisonmaster who'd been lying to them.

Feeding them bad information.

Turning them against each other.

Why?

Because this was a prison for good guys.

All of them, played off against each other endlessly. Keeping each other in check. Keeping them from meddling in the affairs of the Accident People in the outside world. One by one they were sent down here. Sorted. You ended up either as a guard or as a prisoner. The lines were drawn; the struggle never ending. Because you couldn't just have eight or nine good guys holed up in one place. Not without them teaming up and trying to mount an escape. You had to divide them. Push them. Break them. And then, when things settled into a pattern, you could shake the insect jar again and watch them all scramble for safety.

And somewhere, there was one psychotic kid holding the mayonnaise jar.

The Prisonmaster.

He was the only one who told them things, pushed them in certain directions. He'd tried it with Hardie, with his bogus crap about trying to help him escape, and bringing a "moral rectitude" to the facility.

The Prisonmaster had been playing him; he had been playing all of them.

And he was probably listening to them *right now*.

Hardie recovered his cane from the floor and used it to climb to his feet, pulling himself up the shaft one badly shaking hand at a time until he was standing. None of the guards moved to stop him. They stared at him with faraway expressions in their eyes.

"My name is Charlie Hardie. I messed with the wrong people, and they sent me down here as punishment. Probably the same for all of you, too. Think about it. Why are we were? What are we guilty of? Cameron and Victor used to be partners in the outside world. What lies has the Prisonmaster been feeding them? Feeding all of us? What proof do we have of anything? We all thought that escaping would kill the rest of us. None of us could bring ourselves to take that exit, because none of us could stand the thought of innocent blood on our hands. It's a line we refused to cross. And it's been used against us this whole time. Well, fuck that. There is a way out of here, but the only way we're going to find it is if we team up and tear this place apart brick by brick."

Hardie looked around at his fellow prisoners and realized that he was acting like a leader after all. Channeling his inner Nate Parish.

Yankee said, "Shut up. You're going back to your cell."

So that's how it will be this time, the Prisonmaster thought.

Split decision.

Well, he supposed he saw it coming. The latest addition to the facility, Charles D. Hardie, was simply too combustible. The connection between Hardie and that missing-persons investigator, Eve Bell, was enough to tip it over the edge. He would have to speak to his employers about that once again. The facility worked best when the subjects did not know each other and had no preexisting history.

That way, you could convince one man (Archie, the Brit) that another man (Lucas Dabrock, the German doctor known as X-Ray) was actually his archnemesis. And vice versa.

Or you could convince a good old law-and-order man like Jed Ayres that he'd been charged with keeping an eye on the notorious Charlie Hardie, the man who'd killed beautiful actress Lane Madden, strangling her to death in a dumpy Hollywood hotel one summer evening.

Dealing with those two Australian subjects—former partners, no less!—had been a true challenge. It had taken much effort to drive a wedge between them, but it was the only choice, really. The facility would break down without constant conflict.

Well, the Prisonmaster realized it was time to hit the reset button. Rebuild the experiment from the ground up once again.

Maybe this time he'd demand permission to dispose of one of the Australians. Pin the botched escape attempt on him.

And perhaps maybe this time he would mix among the population as a guard. Playing the role of a prisoner was always satisfying...right up until the moment it wasn't.

He whispered softly into the microphone mounted inside his metal mask:

"Good-bye."

Hardie saw it happening. One by one, a message from the Prisonmaster, delivered individually to the guards' earbuds. Heads turned quickly; hands went to ears. Yankee, then X-Ray, then finally Whiskey.

"What is it?" Hardie asked.

Yankee looked at him. "He said...good-bye?"

Whiskey nodded. *"Oui,"* she said. *"Au revoir."*

* * *

Next came the hissing from every air vent in the facility.

To Hardie, it was precisely like that moment in a nightmare when you realize that everything is *not* going to be all right.

That you are falling toward an unforgiving piece of concrete and you are not going to be rescued.

Your body *is* going to hit the ground and your blood will explode out of your useless body.

There is nothing you can do about it. There is no one to save you.

Hardie and his fellow inmates—because surely they were all inmates now—scrambled out of the room. No thoughts of fighting now; it was time for flight.

And the gas—visible as a fine, foglike mist—followed them.

Hardie nearly tripped over his cane on the way out of the room. He grabbed it, figuring if things got really bad, maybe he could shock himself unconscious to avoid the choking and vomiting and dying.

Stop it. Keep your head. There's an escape out of this prison, right, Batman? You've just got to come up with it right now. In the next two seconds.

Or you and everyone in this room will DIE.

(No pressure.)

The other inmates began to drop—that is, the ones who weren't already knocked unconscious. Hardie felt something tug at the back of his jacket. Eve. Pulling him toward her.

Hardie would have asked Eve what she was doing, but he didn't dare open his mouth. Instead he stumbled behind her, leg-cane, leg-cane, trying to keep up, feeling like an asshole because she had to practically drag him along the row of cells. There was retching and coughing all around them. Hardie stumbled. Eve slipped her hands under his arms, pulled him back to his feet. He could hear her grunting. He screamed at his legs to *work,* already. Then they were moving again, across the cement floor. The gas was spreading. Hardie's brain went woozy. Where was she leading him?

When Hardie heard the squeaky creaking of the door, he finally got it. The showers.

He felt the patter of hard water drops against his suit jacket, Eve's hands over his back, his chest. Hardie did the same, brushing her back, her shoulders, her breasts, feeling strange for touching her, even in this situation.

You couldn't consider this adultery—not in a secret prison where you were desperately trying not to die...could you?

Kendra, I can explain everything.

Hardie's head felt dizzy, as if someone were choking him and cutting off the supply of blood to his brain. He started to panic and stopped brushing Eve and started clutching at his chest, then pounding his breastbone, as if he could simply will his heart to continue to pump despite what the poison gas was telling it to do. He dropped to his knees, facing the drain, and some part of his brain that was still firing neurons—

(Find the way out yet, Batman?)

—thought it almost funny, staring into a drain as you are circling it...

And then it happened.

He thought of the way out.

Fuck you, Batman, Boy Wonder, and the rest of Gotham City, because I finally figured it out.

The drain.

THE MOTHERFUCKING DRAIN!

Hardie put his lips against her ear. "Help me." But Eve didn't understand until he guided her hands over to the drain.

The drain, which led to the steel room containing Prisoner Zero.

The grunting moron, who, Hardie now realized, was the mysterious Prisonmaster.

They wormed through the passageway in silence. They didn't dare breathe, not until they put enough distance between themselves and the poison. When they reached the steel anteroom where Hardie had been trapped (weeks? months ago?), Eve had to help up him to his feet. Hardie was proud, though. He'd managed to hang on to his cane.

"So you're thinking that Zero is the Prisonmaster," Eve said.

"There's no poison gas back here," Hardie said. "The Prisonmaster has to be someone who's nearby at all times, who can gauge situations as they evolve. Who better than the guy right next door? Who conveniently doesn't speak or move? Who has the guards take care of his every need?"

"Can't argue with your thinking. But...he's missing limbs, for Christ's sake. He does nothing but grunt."

"Ten bucks he's got a phone under that mask and can speak just fine."

They both stared at the steel door.

"Are you ready?" Hardie asked.

"Absolutely not."

"We're going to have to force this open somehow."

"Well, I didn't think this would be easy."

Eve was stunned, then, to have the door slide open at first pull. Fluorescent lights now provided erratic bursts of illumination. Both Eve and Hardie could see the interior of the chamber in little half-second microbursts. They could see that Prisoner Zero was waiting for them.

Even though he was blind, his head was twisted to the right, and he seemed to be staring right at them.

* * *

"How are ya, pal?" Hardie said.

Zero, face still hidden by the mask, merely lay there on his rusty bed. Staring at them. Immobile.

"Sure, keep playing the mute now."

Zero said nothing.

"You know the way out of here," Eve said.

"Do you really think he's going to tell us that?" Hardie asked.

"We're going to *make* him tell us."

"Guh-huh-huh-huh-huh."

"Okay, that's it, take off his mask," Hardie said to Eve, and then to the prone form of Prisoner Zero: "You try anything, I will light you up."

Eve reached around and unfastened the straps behind Prisoner Zero's head. There was no lock. When the metal mask came loose it made a wet, peeling sound, then revealed a ghastly yet boyish face. Impossibly pale skin. Eyes sealed shut under a waxlike mass of scars.

"Oh, God," Eve said.

Zero's mouth opened slightly, revealed rotted teeth, lips curled into a parody of a smile.

"Guh-huh-HUH. Guh-huh-HOOOO."

"Quit the act," Hardie said, trying not to shudder. The man was an absolute mess. "I know you can speak. Pretending is not going to help you."

"Guh-huh-huhhhhhhh . . ."

"Okay, asshole," Hardie said, but actually only managed to speak the first syllable (maybe) before something hot and vicious jumped up through the soles of his feet and made impact in the general vicinity of his testicles.

Hardie smelled burned hair and was already on the floor when he realized that someone was speaking to them. He rolled over and saw a beefy form hanging from the support beams overhead—a prisoner in a metal mask.

Horsehead.

25

Please continue. The experiment requires that you continue. It is absolutely essential that you continue. You have no other choice, you must go on.

—Instructions to participants in the July 1961 Milgram experiment

HORSEHEAD TOLD THEM, in perfect English:

"Prisoner Zero is not faking. He lost the ability to speak a few years ago. The words are all in his head, but they get lost on the way to his mouth. Not sure why. Could be the number of electric shocks he's received. Or something else altogether."

Hardie realized that the metal floor was electrified in here, just like the floors of the cells. Wired for punishment. Nonlethal, of course. Nothing in this facility could actually kill you. Just make you *wish* you were dead.

"Actually, *I* was the one who was faking this whole time."

Eve had been hit hard, too. Her body trembled as she pushed herself up to a sitting position. She squinted as she looked up at the man hanging from the ceiling.

"I don't understand. Why would you pretend to be a prisoner if you were actually the one in charge?"

"Boredom," Horsehead said. "To control a facility, it's important to see it from all sides, don't you think? And I must admit, the beatings do help keep my thinking sharp."

"Why the fuck are you doing this to us?"

"That doesn't matter," Horsehead said. "What matters is what happens in the next sixty seconds. I'm giving you the chance to decide your own fate. One of you will be my guard, one of you will be my prisoner, and we'll rewrite the rules of this facility from scratch once the others wake up from the knockout gas. Wonder who should play which role?"

Knockout gas? Hardie thought. "You sadistic fucking assssss—" he said, but once again, his comment was cut off by a hideous

WHITE

HOT

BURNING

pain that shot through Hardie's palms, spinning his body around until he landed on his chest, his nose inches from the metal floor, and all he could think was *God help me if he presses that button again.*

Horsehead jumped down to the floor. He was now wearing rubber-soled boots, Hardie noticed, so he could push that button all he wanted.

"Eve, I think it's better if you join me as a guard this time," he said, then reached around to undo the straps of his mask easily, without the need for a key. Hardie realized there had been no mask malfunction. There had never been *any* malfunction. Horsehead, as the Prisonmaster, could choose when his mask worked and when it didn't work. He could order doors open or shut at will, even as he was locked up in his cell. He could turn the communications system on or off. All he had to do was tell Prisoner Zero what to do, and Thy Will was done. That explained the wires, the isolation. The real controls to this place were somewhere in this room!

Horsehead slid the mask off and rubbed his face. "It'll be nice to not have to wear this thing for a while. It was fun at first, but..."

"Bobby?"

Hardie turned to look at Eve, who'd turned stark white.

* * *

Eve continued, her voice now an anguished wail:

"Bobby Marchione?"

Her mind tried to parse it; her mind couldn't. Like when a person from one corner of your life collides with a completely separate corner of your life.

How could Bobby Marchione be in this hole in the earth? *How could he be in charge of it?* She reached out. He instinctively flinched.

"I've finally..." she said again, almost stammering. "I've found, I've finally found..."

The shock smashed through Eve. All this time he'd been down here—one cell away from hers? *All this time.*

Why hadn't she sensed it, on some level?

"...finally found you."

What the hell was she talking about? Hardie thought. And who the hell is Bobby? Then it came back to him. The story Eve had told him about her one professional failure. The missing person she couldn't find. College student named Bobby.

All the places in the world—he was *here?*

Maybe that's why they'd sent Eve here. Just another level of torment. Send her to a secret prison thinking she'd failed, only to have her quarry a matter of yards away. Somewhere, in some plush room, a bunch of cigar-smoking assholes were probably having a good laugh over it...

"How do you know the name Bobby Marchione?" said Horsehead.

"You disappeared from Leland University in California over twenty years ago. I was hired to find you."

"This is interesting. Who hired you?"

"A woman named Julie Lippman."

"Ah, but I know you're lying. I knew you were lying the moment you told your little story in the cell a few weeks ago. What I don't know is why you would lie about something like that."

All the Zen-like control Eve seemed to possess disappeared. Her eyes were ablaze, the veins in her neck bulging.

"I'm not lying. I've been looking for you for twenty years. You don't know how hard I searched for you. How many years I spent racking my brain, following endless leads, dead ends, false trails...goddamn it, you owe me that much. Kill me if you want. I'll help you do it. But you'd better fucking tell me where you've been all this time."

"I didn't go anywhere. Bobby Marchione did."

"What do you mean?"

"Bobby Marchione just wanted to make some extra money over Christmas break."

Bobby's roommate, Pags, handed him an ad that had been posted on a corkboard in the psych-department building.

Psychological experiment, no drugs, no needles, just role-playing. For more info call...you know, one of those. Bobby Marchione wouldn't normally have even looked twice at one of those things but he saw that it wasn't some outside company. This was being run by Dr. Pritchard in the psychology department. Bobby had Pritchard freshman year, and she was an insanely dull lecturer, so he assumed this experiment would be more of the same. Boring, but not painful. And the money was too good to pass up. Twenty-five hundred dollars for a little less than two weeks. Marchione and his roommate, Chris Pagano ("Pags"), called and right away were sworn to secrecy. If they told a soul, they'd be bounced from the program. Bobby couldn't even tell his parents—Pritchard was careful to sign up only adult subjects. Sounded a little weird to Bobby, but again it was the money that attracted him. The money was so, so good. And he figured if Pags was going to do it, then why not?

The toughest part was not being able to tell Julie. Bobby knew she'd be pissed. But when he returned in the New Year with a gleaming engagement ring, he had a feeling she'd forgive him.

That was the whole point. Joking at that party about the ring. Joking, but a hard little nugget of truth within the joke, like a piece of gravel in the middle of a snowball. Bobby loved Julie, wanted to buy her everything she could ever want, starting with an engagement ring. A real ring, and right now. To let her know that he was serious.

Bobby joked with her a lot, all to make it seem like he was completely relaxed in her company. But it was a front. He was terrified she'd discover the truth.

That he was poor, came from lousy genetic stock, and had to scrape up everything he had just to be able to afford college semester by semester.

That sometimes picking up the check after their dates meant Bobby wouldn't be eating much more than boiled ramen noodles over the next three days. (He'd opted out of the meal plan.)

That really, Bobby was just spinning plates until they came crashing down...

But a ring. Oh, a ring would be a bold move. A ring would tell her, yeah, I might be nothing now, but I'm resourceful, and better things are on the horizon.

To get the ring, he had to take part in the experiment.

(Pags? He came from money. He was in it for the CD-and-beer money.)

So the night before Christmas break Bobby Marchione kissed his sweet sleeping girlfriend, Julie, on her forehead and dressed in the cold quiet dark. For a moment, he weakened and thought about writing her a note. Just a little something, so she wouldn't worry.

No.

Couldn't do that.

Pags would kill him if word got out, and Pritchard would bump both of them from the program. So instead Bobby made his way across the empty frozen campus in the middle of the night back to the small dorm room he shared with Pags. The instructions were simple: just be in your rooms by 4:00 a.m. No preparation required, other than a small bag with a few changes of clothes. Do not leave any notes or indications of where you are going. All will be explained at the test site. Bobby sat at his desk, trying to fight the urge to fall asleep. Pags sat across the room, smoking a cigarette, flicking the ashes into an empty soda can, at perfect peace with the world. Bobby was not. Bobby was beginning to wonder if this was a giant mistake. He picked up a Bic pen, pulled out a piece of typing paper, looked over his shoulder. Pags didn't seem to be paying much attention. Bobby wrote:

Dear Julie,
   This is going to be hard to explain, but

At 4:19 a.m., they came for them.

In the form of Pags. "Sorry, buddy," he said, barely able to contain his chuckling, cigarette dangling from his mouth.

"What? What the..."

Pags grabbed his roommate by the shirt, pulled him out of his chair, and forced his arms behind his back. Bobby felt cold steel on his wrists.

"The hell are you doing?" he asked.

"Shh," Pags said. "It'll all be fine. Just don't..."

Pags fell silent as he looked down at the desktop and saw the note Bobby was starting to compose. "Uh-uh-uh-uh," Pags said, then reached over, crumpled the paper up into a ball, and pitched it into the wastebasket in the middle of the room. Can't have that. At that moment Bobby's balls started to nestle up against the bottom of his lungs. What the hell had he gotten himself into?

Soon enough he found out.

The experiment: a prison scenario.

The objective: to learn more about the psychology of imprisonment.

The real objective: *classified.*

What no one knew: Dr. Pritchard supplemented her meager teaching salary with consulting work for a secret quasi-governmental agency. This agency had access to an amazing array of resources, including a secret test facility, jokingly dubbed site 7734. A number that, when seen on a digital readout and turned upside down, spelled the word *HELL*.

But Dr. Pritchard wasn't an evil person; none of them were at first. Just ambitious. Excited to push the boundaries. Eager for funding.

Student volunteers were immediately divided into two groups:

Guards.

And prisoners.

Pags, a psychology major, was a guard, naturally. Not just a guard; he was chosen to play the role of the warden. He reported directly to the Prisonmaster—Dr. Pritchard—who observed from a separate room in the facility.

Bobby was selected to be a prisoner.

Day One: Bobby and the other prisoners were treated to a version of extraordinary rendition and were "arrested" quietly all over the campus. Having told their friends and family no details, a cover story was prepared—a volunteer mission to build homes for poor families. Many of the volunteers didn't have much in the way of family, or they lived on their own. Bobby had a father who had remarried and didn't really seem to care about his firstborn son all that much anymore. As he was led away to a van parked behind the dorm complex, Bobby knew that Julie would be the only person who'd miss him. He hoped she'd understand. He wished he could have left her that note. He hoped this would all be worth it . . .

Blindfolded, Bobby asked:

"Where is this place, anyway?"

A voice assaulted him:

"PRISONERS DO NOT SPEAK! SPEAK AGAIN AND YOU WILL BE PUNISHED!"

The voice:

It sounded like Pags.

Oh, great, thought Bobby. His roommate was probably going to bust his balls this way for the rest of the school year.

Still, he wondered exactly where they were headed.

The van ride was followed by a forced march into some kind of larger vehicle—Bobby, making guesses, thought it might be a school bus. The trip was long. Excruciatingly boring. There was no landscape to gaze out upon, no conversations to strike up. Nothing to do but live inside your own head. The experience put Bobby in mind of soldiers—specifically, Vietnam-era soldiers, because he'd just written a long paper on Tim O'Brien's *The Things They Carried* before the break. Bobby remembered feeling relieved (and a little ashamed) that his generation wouldn't be drafted into a foreign war and have to deal with the senseless violence, the isolation, the loss.

Ha-ha, Bobby Marchione, joke's on you! Hope you enjoy your Christmas break in prison!

Bobby knew the trip felt like *forever* because of the sensory deprivation and all that—but *goddamn,* this trip took forever. At one point the bus even appeared to have stopped moving. He heard metal doors clanging shut. And maybe it was the lack of sleep, but Bobby felt like he was floating a little, listing back and forth gently, as if they'd parked the bus on top of the world's largest water bed.

A guard—probably Pags, that douche bag—pressed two pills into his palm.

"Swallow."

"A little water, please?"

"SWALLOW 'EM DRY, PRISONER."

Fucking Pags. Such an asshole.

So Bobby swallowed the pills. They scratched at his throat going down. After a few minutes Bobby felt his eyelids grow heavy and all conscious thought disappear into fuzzy gray.

He woke up in time for "processing."

All prisoners were stripped.

Rudely searched, by guards, including Pags, all of whom were now wearing these brown Nazi-style uniforms and mirrored shades.

Yeah, enjoy your cheap little ball grab there.

All prisoners were deloused.

(Bobby thinking: *What is* this *about? Like we've all got crab lice?*)

All prisoners were forced into cold showers with powdered soap that smelled like it had been cut with dried vomit.

Which was insanely embarrassing because he recognized some of these guards—besides that rat bastard Pags—from a few of his classes. Including the girls. Oh, yeah, this was a coed experiment, apparently. Four female guards attended to the four female prisoners, and they were *sort of* separated from the guys, but not by much. Bobby stole a few glances, which earned him screaming from one of the guards. Ridiculous.

Afterward the prisoners received their garments:

Smocks.

Rubber shoes.

And...

...that was it.

So they were all going commando for this experiment. Interesting.

Remind me again, Bobby Marchione, why you passed up the opportunity to travel back east with your hot girlfriend, Julie Lippman, in favor of being humiliated and bored out of your freakin' mind in a dank prison in the middle of nowhere.

Finally, all prisoners were given a number.

Bobby, first to be processed, was number 101.

Yay for him.

Bobby Marchione settled in for his first of fourteen nights of boredom.

Or so he thought.

The ten student volunteer guards—who quickly started giggling and referring to themselves as the "apostles of pain"—were broken up into three shifts of four guards each. Their sole objective was to control the prisoners in any manner they saw fit.

They decided to get busy right away.

Prisoner sleep should be erratic, they collectively decided. If the prisoners could be woken up at any moment with a bucket of water or a little jolt from the stun batons the guards were given (very low-wattage, of course), then maybe that would keep them off balance, easy to control.

So the first night there was much screaming and water-throwing...and some laughter, too. The prisoners knew this was all bullshit, so why get all worked up? Which left the guards feeling like idiots. Which, in turn, seriously pissed them off. Why the hell couldn't the prisoners take this seriously? They were getting paid just the same as the guards. It wasn't fair that they could just goof around while the guards did all the work.

So the guards got inventive.

* * *

Which was the real objective of the experiment: to see how far good, decent, ordinary people would go...

...when *pushed*.

By day three the experiment had devolved into bloody chaos. The more sadistic the punishments, the more the prisoners redoubled their efforts to revolt and strike back against the guards. By day four Dr. Pritchard decided to terminate the experiment. Later that same day a group of prisoners broke into her private observation room and held her hostage. By day five Dr. Pritchard was stabbed to death and a male prisoner had taken her place as Prisonmaster. The guards mounted a daring attack against the rebel prisoners, which ended in a two-day standoff. When outside observers from the quasi-governmental agency demanded that the rebel students come to their senses and surrender immediately, the students cut the communication lines. The same outside observers quickly discovered that another group of prisoners had destroyed the elevator leading down to the facility; the prisoners, apparently, had decided that no guards would be allowed to leave alive. By day six the guards had broken into the command center and retaken control of the facility. Martial law was enacted, torture. By day seven a new rebellion was formed.

Chris "Pags" Pagano became the new Prisonmaster of site 7734.

He spared his roommate's life on the condition that he agree to be a prisoner informant.

Pags was the psychology major. He came equipped with a bagful of mental tricks. The one thing he knew was that if any of them were going to make it out of there alive, he would have to assert absolute authority over the survivors.

So he became absolute ruler of the facility.

With the help of his roommate, Bobby, who remained a prisoner out in the "general population."

By the end of the first week everything had devolved into absolute savagery.

Meanwhile, in the outside world, after days of zero communication, the university held a top secret summit meeting with the quasi-governmental agency.

God knows what had happened down there in that former military installation. If word were to leak, it could destroy the university. A few people paid lip service to a rescue operation, but that was quickly ruled out in favor of containment. The quasi-governmental agency suggested a simple way to put a lid on the problem: pump cyanide down into the prison, seal it up forever, and come up with a cover story for grieving friends and family. The quasi-governmental agency, which some were referring to as the Industry even back then, said they had specialists for this sort of thing. Experts who could arrange an accident, deal with lawsuit control, deflect media inquiries. The Industry gave the university the illusion of choice; by the time it had agreed, containment plans were already in motion.

But shortly before it came time to destroy the facility and kill everyone inside, someone in the Industry thought it over. This truly was a unique opportunity, and could be useful down the road. The location was handy. Not far from the university, practically under the noses of everyone. The last place anyone would ever look. And the place could be kept running at minimal cost.

Almost self-sustaining, really.

Standing there in his secret chamber, Bobby didn't deliver this saga to Eve and Hardie. He merely said,

"Bobby and his roommate, Pags, volunteered for an experiment, and it didn't turn out the way they thought. They couldn't come home."

"You *are* Bobby Marchione," Eve said.

"I used to be," Horsehead said. "Not anymore. Just like the prisoner over there used to be Chris Pagano."

"Guh-huh-HUH. HUH. HUH!"

"Oh, God," Eve said. "Chris...?" She crawled over to the gurney and lifted herself up to look at Prisoner Zero. "I didn't even recognize him..."

Hardie didn't give two fucks about "Bobby" or "Chris" or anybody else. He needed to find a way to distract old Horsehead here and take that button away from him. *Come on, Eve, look at me. It's two against one here. If we team up we can knock old "Bobby" here on his ass.*

But she was too preoccupied with Prisoner Zero on the gurney. Did she really recognize him? Or was this some kind of angle she was playing?

"Eve, step up onto that gurney with him," Horsehead said. "The bottom is insulated. It will protect you from the shock."

"Hey," Hardie said. "No more shocks. I've had enough with the fuckin' shocks already. In fact, why don't we—"

Horsehead held up the shock trigger. "If you're going to vomit, do it now before I push this again. Because this *is* going to knock you out, and I don't want you to choke to death. Eve, get up on that gurney."

"Bobby," Eve said. "Please. There's something I have to tell you."

"No? Fine. We'll sort it out later, when you wake up."

"Listen to me, Bobby."

"Good-bye."

But before Horsehead could press the button, Eve yelled—

"It's me, Julie!"

26

I haven't the faintest idea whether this is a rack on which the lovers are tortured, or something with pegs to hold the shining cloak of romance.

— James M. Cain, in conversation with screenwriter
Vincent Lawrence

TECHNICALLY, JULIE LIPPMAN was dead.

When she couldn't find her boyfriend, Bobby Marchione, Julie asked her father, one of the biggest political donors in Pennsylvania, to call in favors from all over. Every attempt — legal or otherwise — was deflected. Nothing sinister, nothing dramatic. Just a firm invisible hand pressing back against her shoulder, and a whisper in her ear: *Oh, no you don't.* But Julie refused to give up.

She had taken advantage of two male friends, offering booze and hinting at sexual favors . . . all in return for unearthing this one little casket in a California graveyard . . .

And then *they* showed up.

Men in suits, carrying guns, blasting a warning shot into the air, threatening to blow their heads off unless they dropped to their knees and knitted their hands behind their heads. This changed everything for Julie. Now the invisible hand had a face. What kind of graveyard employed men who wore suits and swarmed out among the tombstones like professional killers?

But Julie kept such thoughts to herself even as she was charged with trespassing, a charge that caused her father great embarrassment and even more expense getting it quashed. In return she had to promise to enter a treatment facility to help deal with her grief. Julie, however, was not grieving. It was impossible to grieve over a person who was still alive. They...

THEY

...had her boyfriend somewhere, and he was being held against his will. She knew this in her heart, but she also knew it in her head. If Bobby was dead they would produce a body. And if Bobby's body was in that casket, then they wouldn't have stopped her from digging it up. No body meant that he was *alive*. And it was just a matter of time before she found him. On her own.

There were attempts at normalcy. Julie was even briefly engaged to a cop whom she'd chatted up one night at a nightclub in Old City Philadelphia to learn what she could about finding missing people. Oh, the horror and scandal in the Lippman family during those few months!

But Julie was too focused on her search for Bobby to focus on anybody, or much of anything, else. The cop went on his way; Julie continued her hunt. THEY were at the center of it all.

THEY kept resisting her.

Until finally... THEY took an interest in her.

Strange people, following her as she came and went from her downtown apartment. Bizarre pops and clicks on her phone. Pieces of mail being delivered late, bent and wrinkled. Some mail not showing up at all. THEY were watching, all right.

Which was exactly what Julie wanted.

The only way to see their faces was to make THEM come after her.

And then one night they did.

Late one icy January night Julie was attacked as she was making her way back from her car. She always parked in the same lot, traveled the same one-block route back to her apartment on Arch Street, right near a massive I-95 retaining wall. The route was desolate and rarely traveled, which made it easy to spot her spotters. In this case, however, the isolation worked against her. The man with the needle came out of the shadows.

Julie Lippman was dead.

She screamed and he punched her in the face, cutting off the sound immediately. Then his hand was around her throat and he was pressing her against the retaining wall and then rudely turning her head and stabbing her in the side of the neck with the needle. She felt the needle slide into her skin. She *snapped.* It was something in that violation-by-steel that did it; perhaps the instant realization that the same people who stole her boyfriend weren't playing games and they thought they could just show up and kill her and not lose a second of sleep over it. They shouldn't be allowed to do this. *They shouldn't be allowed to DO THIS.*

Julie Lippman was dead.

She didn't remember how she escaped, only that she found herself down by an abandoned dock on the Delaware waterfront, heart pounding, fingers raw and covered in blood. She found a dirty Dumpster full of old clothes. She left her own in a bundle by the edge of the dock, like a killer stashing them before making a getaway. She disappeared.

Julie Lippman was dead.

Twenty years ago it was easier to establish a new identity. This was the pre-9/11 world, when certain simple scams, such as applying for a Social Security number using the identity of a dead child, still worked. Much of the first year was spent re-creating herself.

Julie Lippman was dead.

"Eve Bell" was born.

The first part of her new identity came from a faded sign she glimpsed down by the dock—*STEVEDORES ONLY*, a notice from another era, when Philly had thriving ports. She would be Eve, and the name would always remind her of this moment of her birth.

The surname came from Tim O'Brien's "Sweetheart of the Song Tra Bong," the story of a young soldier who manages to have his girlfriend, Mary Anne Bell, shipped over to Vietnam.

Bobby's favorite story.

Eve Bell was everything Julie Lippman couldn't be. Eve Bell was a professional people finder who kept her own identity permanently buried—to protect her clients, protect herself. Eve Bell found dozens of people over her twenty-year career. Spouses, kids, grandparents, siblings, some of whom were happy to be found, others angry that they couldn't stay hidden. Eve Bell was smarter than Julie Lippman. Eve Bell was tougher. Eve Bell could take a punch. Eve Bell knew that to wage war against the forces of Secret America you had to become like them. Ethereal. Existing on the fringes of the normal world.

All the while she pursued her original case, hoping to find some trace of Bobby Marchione.

Bobby was her one-armed man; her cure for gamma-radiation poisoning; her one true ring.

The reason for all this.

Then one day a year ago a former FBI agent named Deacon Clark hired her to find his missing friend Charlie Hardie. The case had all the hallmarks of a Secret America grab-and-disappear. She eagerly took the case, once again thinking it would bring her closer to Bobby.

And she woke up here.

Closer to Bobby than she ever would have dreamed.

* * *

Of course, she told Bobby none of this.

She simply said,

"I faked my own death so that I could find you. But it's me. It's your Julie."

"You're not *my Julie,*" Bobby said. "You know a little about my life, and you are trying to confuse me. It's not going to work."

"Goddamn it, it's *me,* Bobby. Your sweetheart of the Song Tra Bong. You used to make fun of me for liking Prince. I still know the combination to your dorm room. Want to hear it?"

Bobby paused before replying, finger hovering on the button.

"It's twenty-four, three, fifteen, Bobby. Do you remember when you first gave me that combination, told me Pags was going away for the weekend?"

Hardie watched from the ground, where he was still twitching slightly, imagining that little tendrils of black smoke were curling off his body. The underside of Zero's gurney was full of wires and tricks. The pee tubes and all that medical stuff was a ruse; down here Bobby Whoever was at the center of this facility's communications hub. Then he saw the grooves on the metal floor, directly beneath the gurney. It took Hardie a minute to realize what he was looking at it. But when he did, hope flooded his heart for the first time since he'd been banished to this place.

"You could have found that information out from any number of sources," Bobby said. "A simple phone call to a member of the Leland University English department, for instance."

"It's me, Bobby. Touch me and you'll know I'm telling the truth."

"You're not Julie. You sound different. Smell different. I would have known. I would have known immediately."

"I haven't been Julie Lippman for close to twenty years. I had surgery to change my looks so they wouldn't know I was alive. So yeah, I am different. Just like you. We both became other people."

From the floor Hardie braced himself as he saw Eve take a step toward the Prisonmaster. The monster's button finger twitched, as if waging some internal struggle. To zap, or not to zap. Eve was not afraid. She took another step and pushed her breasts against the Prisonmaster's chest. This was no accidental touch. Hardie could tell.

So could the Prisonmaster, whose finger dropped away from the button.

"You remember, don't you?" Eve asked softly.

"No...no, you're not here. You're supposed to be in Europe now. With your husband and daughters. Two of them."

"My what? What are you talking about? I'm not married. I don't have kids. I'm standing right here in front of you. Listen to my voice, Bobby. Touch me. You used to love to touch me."

"Julie Lippman is in Prague right now, I know this, because they have eyes everywhere, and they're making sure she is safe..."

"As far as the world knows, Julie Lippman is dead and buried, just like you. A tragic little footnote. The college sweethearts who died a year apart."

"You're *lying,* Julie is alive, and she's up in the outside wor—"

"I'm standing right here in front of you!"

"NO, YOU'RE NOT, YOU'RE UP THERE AND YOU'RE SAFE AND THEY'RE LOOKING OUT FOR YOU. THEY TELL ME! THEY TELL ME ALL THE TIME!"

But now Bobby shook his head, quickly, in a trembling, pre-seizure kind of way, as if trying to shake something loose from the inside of his brain.

* * *

That was the arrangement.

Bobby would stay down here and run the secret prison, deal with whomever his employers decided to send his way. Over the years Bobby became quite skilled at manipulating the inmates—and they were *all* inmates, to be sure, prisoners and guards alike. Including Pags, who had long since lost the mental capacity to be in charge of anything, let alone this facility. Pags was good at following orders, but not much else.

In exchange, Bobby's employers promised to make sure nothing ever happened to Julie Lippman. They would be her silent guardians, using the power of their global reach to keep her safe no matter where she roamed.

They sent Bobby regular reports; he lived vicariously through them.

He would not repeat the mistake of the soldier in that story. He would not dare bring Julie to this living hell, would not let her see what he had become. That was out, forever. But he could still be part of her life, in some small way. He could spend whatever equity he'd accrued to benefit *her*.

"Is someone telling you about Julie Lippman doing all kinds of wonderful things?" Eve asked. "Bobby, I've spent the last two decades looking for missing people. I've spent the last two decades looking for you."

"They were...lying to me."

"Yeah."

"You did come after me."

"I did."

"Just like the sweetheart."

"I've got the necklace of tongues to prove it."

Bobby lifted his hand toward his head and began to make the cheesy hand signals, straight from *Purple Rain*:

I
Would
Die
4
U

And with that last letter, he pointed right at her.

Eve couldn't help herself. She giggled.

"You dick."

Hardie hated to interrupt this tender moment, but they were still trapped in a steel room with this crazy ex-boyfriend and nothing but knockout gas outside and bedrock below.

"Bobby...whatever your name is, listen."

He turned in Hardie's direction. A frown appeared, as if he were trying to figure out some complex math problem.

"Show us the way out," Hardie said. "There's gotta be one."

"It's okay, Bobby," Eve said. "You can trust him."

A strange look came over Bobby's battered face. Part hurt, part confusion. "No. You don't get it. There is no exit. No escape at all."

Prisoner Zero started to grunt. "Huh-huh. HUH-HUH-*HUHHHHHH*."

Hardie wondered what the hell he wanted.

Bobby said: "Shut up, Pags."

"HUH-HUH-*HUHHHHHHHHH*."

Zero was pointing down at the ground. The room was dark, but when Hardie went down on his knees, he could see it. The faint lines of a seam, obscured by years of grime and filth. The lines formed a square.

Bobby held up the trigger. "Go near that and I'll take you out. You won't wake up from this."

Eve moved quickly this time, throwing an arm around Bobby's throat and immobilizing his wrist.

"Julie, what are you—"

"Open it, Hardie."

"Guh-huh-huh-huhhhhh."

Hardie placed his good hand on the side of Zero's gurney and gave it a violent shove. The legs scraped against the metal floor. There it was, on the floor. In plain sight, the whole time. An escape hatch. The Prisonmaster here had positioned his old buddy over the single escape route. Hardie brushed away dirt and filth until he located the ancient handle. He had to scrape away grime with the tips of his fingers until he freed the handle.

"No!" Bobby said. "You can't open that! We'll all die!"

"What, another death mechanism? Sorry, Bob. Come up with a new trick. We're all going. You, me, and Eve..."

Hardie caught himself.

"Julie...and my new best friend up there on that gurney. We're all getting the hell out of here now."

"No no no," Bobby cried. "You don't understand. There is no escape. Not for me, not for anyone they send here. Do you think I didn't consider using that hatch myself over the past twenty years? Every day it's crossed my mind. Every fucking day! And every day I tell myself no, leaving will only punish the ones I love. I would only be punishing you. Because that's what they do, that's what they're holding over our heads. That's the real death mechanism!"

Hardie remembered the images they'd pumped into his mask. Kendra's house. The bedroom. Her sleeping form...

Eve told Bobby: "We can fight back. All of us. We can take these bastards down."

Bobby shook his head and smiled. "You have family, Mr. Hardie.

A wife and a son, isn't that right? They will be dead the moment you leave this facility. They'll see to it."

"Not if I get to *them* first. Who are they? Who are your bosses? I want names."

"That won't do you any good. You can't comprehend the complexity of the Industry—"

Eve said, "I hate to say this, Hardie, but he might be right. Once they know we've escaped, they'll be relentless. They won't hesitate to take out your family. I know how they work."

Hardie stared at the escape hatch in the floor. So that was the choice? Stay here and keep his family alive...or leave and put their lives in danger?

Hardie had spent two years in exile because he thought he'd put his family in danger. He couldn't keep hiding.

Sure, they might be in danger.

But he was the only one who could save them.

Hardie kneeled down, found the handle, brushed away the dust. "I'm going."

Eve nodded. "Go, then. I'm going to stay here and take care of Bobby."

"Not going to happen," Hardie said. "Everybody goes home. All four of us."

Eve shook her head. "You have a better chance if we all stay out of sight for a while. Ten escapees, they might notice. One, not so much. Not for a while, anyway."

A strange, giddy look came over Bobby's face. "You mean you're staying down here? With me?"

"I'm not leaving you," Eve said.

"Even after all that I've done?"

"It's not your fault."

"Okay, then," Hardie said. He refused to waste another second down here. The hatch came loose after a few violent tugs. The smell was overpowering—wet rock and mold, as though some primordial creature had just woken from an eon-long slumber and released a silent belch.

"Where will this take me?" Hardie asked.

Bobby said, "You should recognize your location once you're outside. Took me a long time to figure it out. One day they let a detail slip, and it all made sense. They'd want to pick someplace near the university, after all."

"You know, it would really be great if you just told me."

"A set of stairs should lead you to the surface. It might be a lot of stairs. We're pretty far underground."

Eve touched Bobby's face, and he leaned into her palm. His mouth opened slightly, quivering. Hardie wondered when she was going to give up the act—that she was this guy's long-lost girlfriend. It was a stunningly clever move, totally disarming their opponent. What he couldn't figure out is why she wanted to stay down here a second longer.

"Eve, I'll send help."

"Don't. Take care of your family first. We just have some unfinished business to take care of."

Some vile thoughts went through Hardie's mind. He pushed them aside, told himself to grow up. "You're sure?"

"Go to your family. Besides, I need to check on the others. I'm presuming everyone's going to be waking up sooner rather than later."

"I can help."

"*Go*," Eve insisted. "Leave this to me. This is no hardship. I've been at war with Secret America for two decades now. Thanks to this place, I now have an army. And we're going to kick their asses."

Hardie was two steps down before Bobby spoke to him one last time.

"Doyle, Gedney, Abrams."

"What?" Hardie asked.

"They're the ones who put you down here. The ones who fund this place."

Hardie repeated the names in his head. *Doyle, Gedney, Abrams.*

He started down the staircase then stopped, turned around, and picked up his old-man cane from the floor. He almost gave Eve and Bobby one last good-bye, but they were otherwise engaged.

Hardie left them alone.

She caressed his scarred, pale face with her fingertips. She hadn't touched Bobby Marchione in twenty-one years. The last time had been that last night before Christmas break, when he'd brushed her forehead with his lips and whispered good-bye to her. But she touched his forehead, and leaned forward to kiss him there, and she knew it wasn't really him. The real Bobby had died down here two decades ago. Which is why she calmly wrapped the mike wire around his neck and pulled both ends in opposite directions as hard as she could.

In the movies there was some killer move where you could quickly and compassionately snap someone's neck by pushing on his chin while cradling the back of his head. Or some such shit.

But Eve Bell didn't know such a move, so she had to resort to strangling her former boyfriend, sweet goofy Bobby Marchione, with his own electrocution trigger wire, and she was able to see the anger, followed by the hurt and confusion, followed by (she hoped) a little bit of understanding before the light finally went out of his eyes.

It took longer than she could have imagined, almost longer than she could bear.

* * *

There it was—her 100-percent success rate.

Eve Bell, professional finder, had cleared her docket. She could take it easy now, couldn't she? Retire. Kick back, enjoy life. She knew, though, that this wouldn't happen. She hadn't cleared her docket. Her success rate was not 100 percent. She had to find the most elusive person of all: a college student named Julie Lippman. Fucked-up spoiled chick who lost her boyfriend and spent the rest of her life throwing a tantrum about it.

Where was Julie Lippman?

Eve thought about it and realized that she wasn't worth looking for. Julie wasn't missing. Julie had died a long, long time ago, just like her boyfriend, Bobby.

27

If you go down into the darkness, you must expect it to leave traces on you coming up. If you do come up.
— Derek Raymond, *The Hidden Files*

A SHORT FLIGHT of steps led down to a skinny hallway, which in turn led to a narrow spiral staircase. Hardie made his way through the hallway in the dark, using the cane for balance. The stale air reeked of something wet and dead and ancient. He was loath to touch anything. Even walking through the passageway in bare feet was disgusting enough.

Then he slammed into the staircase, and he began climbing.

The metal stairs were caked with years of dust and grime and rust. Hardie tried not to think of what he was crunching underfoot. He kept climbing. After a while his heart began to pump wildly, warning him to slow down, take it easy. Hardie would not slow down or take it easy, because he didn't want to stop and realize that he couldn't move any farther. And then he'd die here, inside the stairway between Hell and whatever was Up There. So no. No stopping. Keep going. He even thought it seemed like *they* knew Hardie was ascending, so they had a construction crew working like crazy up top, adding four new flights of stairs for every single flight Hardie cleared. He didn't care. He kept going...

* * *

And then, the final flight, and a steel door, which Hardie expected to be locked with a dead bolt, possibly even professionally welded shut. It wasn't. The knob was one of those that turns from the inside, no matter what, even if it's locked from the outside. The steel door opened up into...

Oh, God.

Another prison?

More cages and bars and walkways and staircases. The only difference was that this prison allowed sunlight to pour through dirty windows. Hardie hadn't seen light in so long it hurt his eyes.

This prison was also completely deserted, as if the Rapture had taken place while he was underground. Down a hallway of flaking paint, empty cells, dirty floors—nothing. Nobody. Hardie pushed his way through a set of doors. And another empty room. A mess hall, from the looks of the galley kitchen and scuffed-up tile floors, where tables and chairs used to be. Where was he? Why was no one up here?

Another set of doors, another hallway, and finally, within a steel cage, a room with a long table. Lined up on the table were rows of shoes, men's, all sizes—all of them straight out of the last century. Hardie walked over to the cage door and pulled on the handle. It opened.

Down the hall—murmuring. Hardie panicked. Maybe it was a good thing he'd been alone. Perhaps he'd wandered into the closed wing of a working prison. And once these new guards saw him, he'd be back in the same position. Or worse. There was a push-bar door on the left, leading outside. Should he?

The murmuring grew louder; someone laughed.

Hardie slammed through the door.

The sounds, the sun, the noise—all of it disorienting.

There were people everywhere. Not in uniforms of any kind, but in everyday street clothes. It was sunny out. No, not quite sunny. Just bright, somehow, even beneath a vast, gloomy sky. A cold wind sliced right through him. People were everywhere. That was the confusing thing. Holding bottles of water, laughing, smiling, taking pictures, despite the fact that this looked very much like the grounds of a prison. Barbed wire. Hardie made his way down a steep wide concrete path trying to understand where the hell he was. There was a sign mounted on a concrete wall. The wall had blue-and-tan streaks on it from faded paint jobs over the years. On the wall above the sign were thin red letters proclaiming:

INDIANS

WELCOME

And the sign itself:

UNITED STATES

PENITENTIARY

ALCATRAZ ISLAND AREA 12 ACRES

1½ MILES TO TRANSPORT DOCK

ONLY GOVERNMENT BOATS PERMITTED

OTHERS MUST KEEP OFF 200 YARDS

NO ONE ALLOWED ASHORE

WITHOUT A PASS

Fuck me, Hardie thought. *Oh, fuck me fucking stupid.*

The most secure secret prison in the world, site number 7734, was located far beneath the world's most notorious inescapable prison...which was now a tourist attraction.

They—whoever *they* were—had a sick, sick sense of humor.

He couldn't wander around like this, wearing nothing but a jacket and trousers. He ducked back into the building, went to the shoe room, and selected a pair of black brogans in his size. No socks, but Hardie didn't care. Felt good to have something on his feet again.

The murmuring, it turned out, came from one of the gift shops. Hardie buttoned up his coat, hoping no one would notice his bare chest, then eased into the shop. Everybody was busy looking at souvenir rocks, calendars, CDs, comic books. Hardie saw a stack of black T-shirts, sizes S to XXXL. He took an XL, rolled it up tight, moved behind a bookcase, and slid it into his trouser pocket. Stealing from a prison gift shop; this was a new low, even for him. He made it out of the shop without any alarms going off, then found a quiet corner. Only after he put on the T-shirt did he realize what he'd selected: ALCATRAZ SWIM TEAM.

He buttoned up, looked for a men's room.

Found one. Straight out of the 1920s, fixtures and everything, but kept tidy for visitors. New soap, new paper-towel dispenser, new signage.

And a large clean mirror, hanging over a row of sinks.

Hardie put his palms on the cold ceramic tile under the mirror and looked at himself.

You.

You look familiar.

But you're not me.

You kind of remind me of... my dad.

No; not exactly my father. My father wouldn't have let himself go like that.

But old like my father.

Weary like him.

Look at you.

Unruly hair, grown out from a buzz cut. Reddened eyes, dry lips, the skin looking like it had been shrink-wrapped to his skull.

Hardie reached out and touched the glass, on the off chance that it wasn't a real mirror. Maybe it was a carnival's trick mirror, installed here to amuse the tourists. Cold, hard glass beneath his fingers. Cold, hard skull beneath his skin.

Hardie had no idea how long he'd been out, how much time the memory shot had taken away, or even how long he'd spent down in that prison. But surely it couldn't have been long enough to do *this* to him.

"How are you doing, handsome?" he said softly.

Hardie had three names, thanks to Bobby Marchione:

Doyle.

Gedney.

Abrams.

Hardie would have to pay them a visit to discuss his recent employment. Not alone; he needed Deke at his side. That's what he should do first. Call Deke, tell him that he was alive, that the crazy beautiful missing-persons expert he'd hired had completed the job after all. And, more important, Deke needed to send a small army of feds to raid that damned place, rescue the sorry bastards trapped down there before—the first shot in the larger war.

Hardie looked down at his ripped, dirty, bloodied suit. He walked over and caught his reflection in the glass of a tourist information booth. He looked like a crazy homeless man who'd somehow managed to camp out on the island. He had no ID. He probably stank, too, although it was hard to tell, thanks to the relentless odor of mildew and cold rock in his nasal cavity. So it would probably be a little tricky, introducing himself to some poor tourist and asking to borrow his cell.

Instead, Hardie wandered into a crowd until he found one to steal.

Not a proud moment, but too bad. He saw a black-onyx slab sticking out of the top of a blue leather Coach purse. Hardie figured the woman could afford to replace it easily enough. He'd make it up to her later. Send her flowers.

The snatch was easy; just a bump then a lift. He slid the phone into his trouser pocket and went off to the holding area, where people sat on dark gray metal benches waiting for the next ferry back to San Francisco. Tourists cleared a spot for him as he approached.

Hardie pulled the phone out of his pocket and tried to look for the On button.

He couldn't find it.

What kind of phone was this, anyway?

He didn't recognize the brand name, nor did he see any buttons that made rational sense. Come on. Had Hardie been locked up for so long that they went and changed all the cell phones already?

At long last his trembling fingers tripped something and the screen lit up. A green bar appeared on the screen, with a tiny lock icon at the end of it. Hardie touched the lock. The phone gave off a small annoyed shudder; the screen bounced. But nothing unlocked. *Come on, already.* Why did he have to steal the phone of a paranoid who locks it? There was no way to enter a PIN or anything. Hardie jabbed a thumb at the screen. A tiny shudder; a screen bounce; nothing else. The irony was not lost on him. He'd just managed to escape a super-secret inescapable prison facility; now he was having trouble getting past the pixelated image of a lock on a goddamned cell phone.

There was a teenage girl sitting on the bench. Hardie looked at her, cleared his throat.

"Uh, my phone is locked. You know how to unlock it, by chance?"

The girl's eyes crawled over in Hardie's vague direction, assessed him in a second, then returned to their original position. Thin white wires hung down from her ears.

"Don't worry about it," Hardie said. "I'll figure it out."

After a few more stabs and shudders, Hardie started sliding his fingers around the screen, as though he were trying to massage it to life. The green bar moved! But then the lock appeared again. He slid the bar and held it open, wondering if that would do the trick. No. The lock reappeared. Someday he was going to laugh about this. Not now, but someday. Maybe. Sitting in Deke's backyard, watching him grill. *So there was this one time I escaped from a secret prison but I couldn't call for help because . . . get this . . . the green bar wouldn't stay open! Isn't that a scream!*

At long last he figured it out: you had to slide the bar over, then linger for a second until the phone unlocked. There. Done. But now came a new problem: where were the numbers on the phone? After some more faffing about, Hardie's thumb found a handset icon, and when he touched it a nine-digit keypad popped up on the screen.

The main number came back to him almost instantly. Hardie listened to the automated welcome message, then thumbed the zero and asked the operator to transfer him to Agent Deacon Clark's office.

"I'm sorry, he's no longer with the agency. Can I direct your call to someone else in the agency?"

"What? No . . . Where did he go?"

"Let me direct your call to another agent."

"Hang on . . ."

Hardie's mind went cold and panicked. If Deke was no longer

with the FBI, did that mean that Kendra and Charlie, Jr., no longer had FBI protection? He tried to think of the names of Deke's colleagues and came up with one.

"Can you transfer me to Agent Jim Glackin?"

"I'm sorry, he's no longer with the agency. Let me direct you to—"

Hardie interrupted. "Who's in charge of the joint FBI–Philly PD task force?"

"Transferring you now."

An agent whose name he didn't recognize—some Agent Wilkowski—told him that he wasn't available, but if he would leave his name and number, he'd get right back to him, or he could e-mail him at...

No, no e-mail.

God, Kendra and Charlie...

Beep.

"I'm calling for Agent Deke Clark, and it's extremely important I reach him right away. My name is Charlie Hardie. I used to work with your task force a couple of years ago. If you can have Deke call me back immediately, I'd..."

The phone was stolen; he didn't know what number to leave. But this was the FBI. He probably wouldn't have to. The number would pop up on caller ID instantly.

"Just have Deke call me immediately."

Hardie ended the call, slid the phone back into his pocket, and looked out onto the gloomy bay. The ferryboat was approaching. His journey back across the River Styx. He felt his heart racing. Too much sensory detail to absorb. Too many people holding too many things. Phones and cameralike gadgets he didn't recognize. Designer names that sounded like parodies, the kind they'd run in *Mad* magazine. That's what you get when you put yourself in exile for a few years, he supposed, then ended up cooling your heels in a secret prison.

He wandered over to the entrance to the ferry walkway, wondering how he was going to pull off this little scam. He hadn't come here as a tourist; he had no ticket. Somehow he'd have to slip back onto that boat.

He glanced at the information on the board, announcing new events and tours at Alcatraz for the coming season. Glimpsed the dates idly, wondering what month it was.

According to the coming-events flyer, it was almost August. Typical cold San Francisco summer weather.

But then he happened upon the year.

Hardie blinked.

It...

...it couldn't be.

28

What we'll be calling on is good old-fashioned blunt-force trauma. Horsepower. Heavy-duty, cast-iron, pile-drivin' punches that will have to hurt so much they'll rattle his ancestors.

—Tony Burton, *Rocky Balboa*

Philadelphia—Now

DEKE WAS MAKING deviled eggs when the FBI called.

Ellie was crazy about deviled eggs at picnics. But she couldn't make them. Correction: of course she knew *how* to make them. Wasn't nothing to them. Boil the eggs until hard, halve 'em lengthwise, scoop out the yolks, mix 'em with a little dry mustard, mayonnaise, and seasonings, then scoop the filling back into the white rubbery shells.

But if Ellie made them, for some reason, she couldn't properly enjoy them. Weird, sure. But Deke didn't care. Because if something this easy was enough to make his woman happy, especially the way he'd been behaving, then he'd boil eggs all day long. He took two teaspoons and started scooping the yellow deviled part into the hollow inside the white halves. He was halfway through when his younger daughter yelled, "Dad!" and told him his cell was going off.

He recognized the name right away.

"Wilkowski? What's up, man?"

Deke may have left the department, but he kept his hand in. He was teaching criminal justice, and it helped to be able to draw on a pool of guest speakers. Wilkowski was one of them.

"Got an interesting call a little while ago," Wilkowski said.

"Yeah? Interesting how?"

"You holding on to something steady?"

They'd traced the call to a cell phone in San Francisco. Deke packed a bag—his habit of having a go bag ready was long forgotten. He hadn't stayed anywhere *without* his family in what...five years? Ellie always packed, so there was no need to think about it these days.

But he didn't think about the right kind of clothes for San Francisco in August as much as whether he'd need a gun or not.

Deke's own, purchased the day after he left the bureau, was locked in a box at the bottom of his closest. Just in case somebody showed up one day to make trouble for him, or to follow through on a threat. Deke fished the key out of his side-table drawer, kneeled down in the bottom of the closet.

Charlie Hardie, do you see what you have me doing?

His former colleague had asked: "You think it's him?"

"Play me the message," Deke had said.

Wilkowski did.

Deke listened to it, felt his blood literally chill in his veins and the tips of his fingers tingle.

After a while and a dry swallow he said, "No. That doesn't sound like him."

"Well, we're going to have someone out there follow up."

"Probably a smart idea," Deke said. "Let me know what you hear." Already rehearsing in his mind what he was going to tell Ellie.

Goddamn—where have you been, Charlie?

And how did you get out?

29

FIVE YEARS.

He'd been gone five years.

No; scratch that—

They had stolen five years from him.

The Industry.

Secret America.

The Accident People.

Who-the-fuck-ever.

FIVE YEARS

in white-hot neon, burning the gray pulp of his brain.

Hardie himself had thrown away two years during his time in self-imposed exile as a house sitter. Now...add five more to that? Seven years total? He thought about Charlie, Jr. How old would he be now? Once, he'd read that over the course of seven years every cell in your body dies and is replaced. Every seven years you are a different person, physically.

Five years stolen, seven years total.

Five fucking years.

Mann had tried to tell him, hadn't she? In her own way, she'd tried. Water under a very old bridge.

Five fucking...

The men responsible?

The men who had stolen a chunk of his life?

Three names:

Gedney.

Doyle.

And Abrams.

Or to put it another way:

Gedney, Doyle & Abrams.

Not just three names, but a law firm. Somehow Hardie was able to use the Web browser on "his" phone to look it up. Downtown, right off Market Street. In the Flood Building, not far from the corner of Market and Powell.

Hardie was standing there now. Watching from a Muni bench across the street, pretending to be homeless.

(Pretending? Dude, you are *homeless.)*

He'd done his homework. Five minutes on a public-library computer revealed jack shit; but Nate Parish had taught him how to dig deeper. Hardie found their faces in a local legal newsletter, in a photo taken at a glitzy bash. All three of them. He memorized their features, staring at them long enough to burn the newsprint into his mind's eye. The men were not quite what Hardie expected.

That didn't matter, though. He posted himself outside. Waited. This part of Market Street was busy with shoppers, tourists, buskers. The cable-car turntable was down here. Everybody paid attention to that, not so much to him. Which was good.

Years ago, while on a case with Nate Parish, Hardie had hung out in the Kensington section of Philly, dressed as a homeless man, trying to catch a serial strangler-rapist. Kensington was where they'd filmed much of *Rocky*. The neighborhood was struggling back in the 1970s; more than thirty years later, it was in a virtual death grip. After streetwalkers started turning up dead, the neighborhood accused the cops of doing nothing. Nate wondered about that. So Hardie told Kendra he'd be gone for two weeks and went undercover. He learned how to blend in, where to scrounge clothes, where to get soup handouts, fresh needles, the whole nine. In the end Hardie cornered the strangler and had to restrain himself from breaking the scumbag's head. The strangler turned out to be a deputy district attorney—one who'd been on local television news that very afternoon calling for the strangler's immediate capture and prosecution. Which Nate had suspected all along. Don't ask Hardie how. All he knew was that after he'd spent two weeks on the street, Kendra refused to go near him until at least a dozen showers later.

Hardie used those same street skills now—in San Francisco.

Nate, you'd be proud of me. I can still act like a bum.

I can still stalk powerful men who prey on the weak.

Hardie saw Doyle pop out of the Flood Building first. The impulse was strong to walk across the street and just tear the man apart, rip entire chunks of flesh from his skeleton. But Hardie took a deep breath, willed his blood to cool, waited. He had to do this right.

Gedney was next, the short prick. Two on his checklist. All he needed was the third—Abrams.

Hardie quickly learned Gedney's and Doyle's comings and goings. Gedney stayed close to the Market Street office except for occasional jaunts to the St. Francis Hotel a few blocks up the street, where he would visit his usual suite. Doyle was more predictable. Almost every day he spent five to six hours at a garage down by the Embarcadero.

Abrams, though—a constant no-show.

The clock was ticking. If they knew what happened down in site 7734, they weren't letting on. Presumably Eve got out, along with the rest of them. Eve, preparing to go to war with her army of heroes. The quiet couldn't last forever, though; soon, Eve would strike her first blow. Any day now Gedney, Doyle, and Abrams could disappear.

Hardie decided to start with Gedney and Doyle.

He'd kill one, make the other lead him to Abrams.

Hardie strolled into the ornate marble lobby, hung a quick right at the oversize grandfather clock, and made his way toward the elevators. To the casual observer he looked presentable enough. Jacket, thrift-store shirt, no tie. He was also reasonably sure that security would be preoccupied, what with the fire and everything behind the hotel.

The fire he'd set just a few minutes ago, using three road flares he'd picked up from an unguarded construction vehicle on Market Street and a whole lot of trash stored in an alley beside the hotel.

Hardie saw a wood-paneled restaurant in the lobby. It was the dead zone between lunch and dinner; nothing save a red velvet rope guarded the place. Hardie slipped past it and snatched up a steak knife from a serving tray, then left just as quickly to catch an elevator.

The hallways up here were wide enough to park cars along one side while still leaving a lane free for traffic. He passed wide, vertigo-inducing windows that looked out upon the newer wing of the hotel across the way. Gedney's suite, of course, would be facing Union Square. Only the best for the captains of the Industry.

Hardie braced himself for maybe a stray security guard or two disguised as a member of the hotel staff, but there wasn't a soul in sight.

He didn't go through the pretense of knocking; there was no time for his wire-hanger trick, either. He used his good arm to balance himself as his good foot slammed into the space to the immediate left of the key-card reader.

Gedney was perched on one of the two beds inside, watching a movie on a flat-screen TV. He was fully dressed in a gray suit, with a tie and everything, only he had kicked off his shoes and socks. Which struck Hardie as a strange way to relax. Why didn't the man loosen his tie? Hardie kick-slammed the door shut behind him, then closed the distance between him and Gedney. He put the tip of the steak knife under Gedney's chin. Gedney wore a blank expression. Not even mildly curious, as if he'd been expecting such a thing to happen.

"Where have I been for five years?"

Gedney inched up cautiously on the bed but said nothing. His eyes narrowed.

"Did you hear me? Where the fuck have I been?"

"Please don't take what I'm about to say as a sign of disrespect, because that's not what I'm intending. But who are you?"

"Charlie Hardie."

Gedney seemed to search his memory bank for a few moments. His eyes drifted away from Hardie, as if the answer were on the next bed.

"Did you FUCKING hear me?"

Then Gedney exhaled slightly. "Of course I remember, Mr. Hardie. Unkillable Chuck, isn't that what they used to call you? I liked that. I enjoyed the stories about you."

"Five years."

"It has been a long time."

"I have no problem chopping your head off."

"I believe you, Mr. Hardie. I really do. And a man in your

position—well, I can't say I blame you. But you have it all wrong. They could have flushed you down the toilet right then, like a gold-fish. But I had a feeling about you. I knew you were talented, and could be useful to us. You still can. Let's talk."

"I don't want to talk unless you care to explain where I've been for five years."

Gedney frowned. "I'm guessing that site seven seven three four has been compromised. That's a real bummer."

"Why did you send me there? Why didn't you just kill me?"

"Kill you?" Gedney asked. "Why? When you could serve as lever-age?"

"What do you mean, leverage?"

"Every once in a while someone comes along trying to make trou-ble," Gedney explained. "Guy like you, for instance. Raises a big fuss, laboring under the delusion that he's doing something heroic. But all you're doing is getting in the way. So we send heroes like you to site seven seven three four. A special prison. A prison for heroes. See, we couldn't send heroes like you to an ordinary prison. You'd just join forces and eventually escape. I mean, that's the kind of thing heroes do, right? So we came up with something special—a way to keep heroes pitted against their fellow heroes, in a state of perpetual conflict. The machinery was already in place; we just had to take ad-vantage of it."

"Bobby Marchione," Hardie said. "The prison experiment."

"Exactly. And this is what I'm talking about. Sure, we could have killed him along with everybody else. But that would have been shortsighted. That would have meant ignoring a unique situation that we could use to our advantage. A place for all you heroic types. But it seems you've found a way out, which either makes you a hero, or something else al—"

Gedney moved quickly, slapping away Hardie's knife hand,

bouncing off the bed and tackling Hardie right in his center of gravity. Hardie dropped the knife. Hardie dropped his cane. Hardie went down hard. Pain exploded in his lower spine. What he wouldn't give for his old body back. Gedney, meanwhile, kept on trucking. On the other side of the room were three doors, side by side—one leading to the hallway and the others, presumably, to a bathroom and a closet. Three guesses which one Gedney would be choosing.

Hardie cursed himself for his stupidity as he rolled over. To lose it all so quickly in a matter of moments...

But Gedney surprised him by launching himself into the bathroom and slamming the door shut behind him.

Thank you, God.

Hope you'll forgive me for what I am about to do.

Hardie pulled himself up from the floor, stumbling a bit as he recovered his cane and the knife. But the stumble was fortunate, because as Hardie raced for the door a bullet blasted through the wood, whizzing by his face before burying itself in the plaster across the room. Another second and it would have buried itself inside Hardie's head.

Ah.

No wonder he chose the bathroom.

Gedney had a gun in there.

Gedney was very glad to have a motherfuckin' gun in here.

Never thought he'd ever, ever have to use it, though—this was the St. Francis Hotel. Survivor of the 1906 earthquake. Site of countless Industry meetings over the decades, not a single incident. A safe zone. A dead zone. Like a womb, surveillance-wise.

A womb with a revolver hidden away.

Not so much to use on outsiders breaking in, but in case a meeting went...south.

Whatever its intended purpose, Gedney was glad to have the revolver. He kept it trained on the door. He didn't think Hardie would just give up and go away. And he didn't think he was lucky enough to have hit the bastard with that first shot. So the next move would be Hardie's; the finishing move would be Gedney's. That, or somebody had heard the shot and already called downstairs, but that was unlikely. Big old pile like the St. Francis muffled sound pretty well. Gedney would know.

So the play was simple. Hardie would either come through that door, or launch something through that door, or try to lure him out of the bathroom with some ruse. No matter what, all Gedney had to do was keep his back to the wall, keep the gun pointed at the door, and shoot when he saw Hardie.

Gedney had infinite patience; Hardie clearly did not. Or he wouldn't have marched here straight from the prison to exact his revenge. Gedney fixed his grip on the gun and took a deep, cleansing breath. He was about to consider how infinite patience usually prevailed in these kinds of situations when the tile behind him exploded.

Not all of it—just a half-dollar-size hole. But through it, Hardie jammed the business end of the cane into the back of Gedney's little skull and pulled the trigger. The man cried out and the gun dropped out of his hands and made a sharp clank as it landed on the tile floor.

Hardie had gone in through the wall of the walk-in closet, which he accessed through the second door. He listened, tried to remember Gedney's height. Then he used all his might to force the cane through the wall. He might have missed completely. The cane might have snapped. But there was no way he was going through that bathroom door—it was a suicide move. Better this than nothing.

After he pulled the cane out of the hole in the wall, Hardie shook it free of plaster dust as he walked back around to the bathroom. He kicked in the door, crouched down, recovered the gun, slid it into the back of his trousers. Then he picked up Gedney, who was dazed and bleeding, and slowly dragged him across the carpet.

Gedney woke up to find his face pressed up against the cool glass of the window in his room. His eyes rolled down, saw bustling Union Square below.

"Where's Abrams?"

"You won't do this," Gedney said. "You won't put me through this window."

"Oh, I won't?" Hardie asked, keeping his grip firm against Gedney's back, supporting both of them with his one good leg. The gun he kept pressed against Gedney's head.

"That's Powell Street directly below us. Too many people down there. Throw me out the window and I'll be taking innocent lives with me."

"You're assuming I'm going to push you. Maybe I'll just blow your head off."

"You would have already done it. You want something from me, don't you? Information. Or maybe a deal. Isn't that right, Mr. Hardie? You're a bruiser but you're not a stupid man."

Hardie thought about this.

"Good point. Let's go for a walk, then. You're not going to give me any trouble, will you? I don't think you're stupid, either."

"But why go anywhere? We can talk right here. No eavesdropping. The walls are soundproofed."

"Unh-unh. I've got a special place in mind."

With the gun pressed against the base of his spine, Gedney was forced into the hallway. Again Hardie marveled at how huge the spaces were in this old hotel. You could fit entire rooms in the hallways. Then again, maybe they just seemed wide because he'd been cooped up inside a mildewy cell under Alcatraz for Christ knows how long.

"We really should have stayed in the room," Gedney said, and right away Hardie pushed him forward, making him walk faster and faster until he was in a light jog and nervously turning his head backward, trying to find Hardie's eyes and muttering, "What you are doing?" but Hardie just kept pushing him faster and faster until they were actually running, Hardie's left knee screaming like you wouldn't believe. But it didn't matter, because this was a short run, ending when they reached the bank of picture windows and Hardie threw Gedney's body through the glass.

And just before that moment, Hardie whispered: "Bobby Marchione says hello."

Gedney's screaming, twisting body fell at least ten stories down to the roof of the structure that connected the old St. Francis Hotel to its new wing.

No innocent people down there.

On the roof.

Hardie didn't need any information from Gedney after all. Hardie had picked up the man's smartphone, checked the address book. Abrams had five addresses. All L.A.

Maybe Doyle would help him pinpoint the correct one.

30

*It's an odd thing, but anyone who disappears is said to be seen
in San Francisco.*

—Oscar Wilde

HARDIE RAPPED THREE times on the metal door of the garage. Some
stooge in a jumpsuit answered. Before the door was even half opened
Hardie jammed the tip of his cane into the man's ample belly and
gave the button a squeeze. The stooge's eyes rolled back in his head;
the stooge went down. Pressing his cane to the ground, Hardie slid
himself in through the open doorway, kicked the door shut behind
him.

Two other guys in jumpsuits were already up and yelling and racing toward Hardie. One of them had a tire iron. The other, a gun.
Hardie spun himself around, leaned against the nearest car.

Reached into his jacket pocket, where he kept the gun.

But the guy with the tire iron reached Hardie first, which is probably why his partner with the gun hesitated. No need to waste a
bullet on an intruder when you could just cave in his head with a
piece of metal. They hadn't seen what had happened to their buddy;
they assumed this was just some crazy old geezer with a cane.

Hardie lifted his cane. The jumpsuit smacked it to the side with his tire iron. Hardie felt the shock of the blow all the way up his arm, across his shoulder, and down into his chest. The tire iron went up, and then began its swift descent toward Hardie's face. Hardie let himself drop down to his ass and grunt as he swung the cane back around. The tire iron struck the car so hard it created tiny white sparks. Hardie thrust the cane up under the guy's ribs, hoping there had been enough time for the damned thing to recharge. He thumbed the button and—

CLICK

Nothing.

The guy lifted the iron again. Hardie used his free hand to reach into his jacket pocket.

BLAM

The guy was flying backward into the side of another vehicle.

The third guy, the one with the gun, screamed, took aim, fired.

Almost at the same time, Hardie twisted the gun around in his jacket and fired again.

The first bullet went SPACK into the car.

The second bullet ripped through Hardie's jacket and sliced through the third guy's stomach.

He moaned, dropped to the floor.

Hardie removed the warm gun from his jacket, aimed, and gave the third another one in the head, then turned his attention to the second guy in the jumpsuit and shot him in the head, too.

As soon as Hardie struggled up from the floor, a man in a pair of greasy overalls came bursting into the room, cursing about all the noise. Hardie nearly shot him in the head until he recognized him as Doyle, the second lawyer.

Doyle looked down and saw the bodies, then Hardie. Recognition washed over his face.

"You."

Hardie raised the gun an inch. "Don't move."

Doyle moved like he was on fire.

Shit.

What was it with these lawyers bolting like jackrabbits? Did they all run track in their spare time?

But he couldn't risk shooting and accidentally killing the son of a bitch.

Not before he talked about Abrams.

Hardie hurled himself toward Doyle, limping as fast he could. He ended up catching him and bodychecking him into a table. Doyle's hands reached out wildly for the closest sharp tool or blunt object. There was no time to fuck around. Hardie put the cane under Doyle's neck and pulled back hard, as if doing a barbell pull-up. Doyle's cry was choked out immediately. But then he shifted his body weight back onto Hardie. No cane, no support. Hardie's right leg tried to support the weight, but it was too much. It shook wildly before giving out. Both men tumbled to the floor, Hardie hanging on to his cane as if it were the only thing preventing him from a sixty-story drop to a hard sidewalk.

"Where's Abrams?"

"Eat me."

"Which address in L.A.? Tell me and you'll live."

"Eat your mother."

The contact file on Gedney's phone had five L.A. addresses. House in Holmby Hills. House along the Venice Canals. Office in Century City. Some building in Arcadia, California. Some other building in Thousand Oaks, California. So which one would it be? The revenge clock was ticking.

And only Doyle knew the magic answer.

Hardie briefly considered running through the addresses one by one, but he expected Doyle to say pretty much the same thing. Shame he couldn't have hung out with Bobby a little while longer in that hellhole. Hardie was sure the man would have had some fantastic interrogation tips to share. So instead he settled for choking Doyle with the cane until he passed out. There was a certain finesse to doing such a thing. You want them out, but not out forever.

After he was sure Doyle was unconscious, Hardie relaxed his grip and rolled away. He was exhausted down to the marrow in his bones. He couldn't remember feeling so tired. Old Man Hardie.

He reached out and put his hand against the nearest vehicle—the big black car he'd seen when he first entered the garage. Using the cane and the car, Hardie somehow made it back up to his feet. Only then did he realize what he was touching.

Jesus Christ.

He hadn't seen this thing in more than five years.

The Coma Car.

Well, technically, it was a Lincoln Town Car. But the last time Hardie had seen this—or its older cousin, because this thing looked brand-new—he'd only been able to enjoy it from the inside. While unconscious.

And it was the last thing he remembered before waking up in prison.

A trunk-release trigger was mounted under the dash. Hardie popped it, then walked around to the back to fully admire Doyle's ingenuity. As he remembered, the trunk contained a fully functional life-support system. Complex and expertly engineered, to be sure, but even a first-year nursing student could figure out how the needles and hoses and wires would be inserted in a living human being.

"Doyle, buddy, we're going to Hollywood," muttered Hardie.

Which is when he heard movement behind him.

* * *

"Charlie?"

Deke Clark.

More or less the last person Hardie expected to see in this garage. Deke—who'd really gotten *old*. Still, he held a gun, classic two-hand grip.

"Hi, Deke."

"Where the fuck have you been, man." A statement, not a question.

"They sent me away."

"I know. Believe me, I know. They sent me pictures. I've been looking for you for five years. I hired people to go looking for you. But you vanished without a trace."

"Well, I'm back. So what are we going to do?"

Deke looked around the garage, saw the bodies lying in pools of their own blood. "You do that?"

"You would have, too."

"Who's the guy on the floor?"

"His name's Doyle. He's one of the ones who sent me away."

"Law firm of Gedney, Doyle, and Abrams," Deke said, then sighed. "The police found Gedney. On the roof of the St. Francis."

"Yeah. He's another one who sent me away. There's this one. Doyle. Fuckin' Abrams will be next."

Deke tensed up. "You don't understand, man. Stop for a minute and consider your situation. The world thinks you're a killer. That's right. Far as everyone's concerned, you killed an innocent woman five years ago and went on the run. Now you show up and start killing more people? Don't you realize the road you're headed down?"

"You don't know what these sons of bitches did to me."

"I know, Charlie. Believe me...I. *Know*. They've been threatening to do the same thing to me, Ellie, everyone close to me. They deserve to die screaming for what they've done. But this isn't how we fight them. We drag their asses out into the light and we *burn* them."

Hardie said nothing. Deke Clark was one of the smartest and toughest guys he'd ever worked with—besides Nate Parish, of course—but now his eyes were full of fear. Maybe Hardie would have been the same way had the roles been reversed.

"Come on, Charlie. Let's go. Let's get out of here."

"No. I'm not finished."

"Finished *what?* You have nothing to finish. You come back with me and you start explaining. Other people will finish this. You? You're done. You don't have to do this anymore. We can get help. You've got to stop now and come home."

Home.

That's when it occurred to Hardie.

"Do you still have people on Kendra and Charlie?" he asked.

Deke swallowed. "They're fine. Perfectly safe."

"You're not answering my question. Does the bureau still have a detail on my wife and son?"

Deke couldn't lie; he was practically incapable of it. Hardie knew that.

"Listen, Charlie..."

"Goddamn it, how long you been retired?" Hardie asked. "The person who answered the phone said you were gone."

"It's been a while, man. Look, back when you went missing..."

"How long have Kendra and Charlie been without protection, goddamn it!?"

After a quiet beat, Deke said: "I look after them."

"What, do you sleep in your fucking car outside their house and keep constant vigil? Does Ellie join you? You living your life making sure nobody kills my family? Who's watching your family? You got a detail for that?"

"Hardie..."

Hardie leaned on the cane and turned away from Deke. All this time he could relax with one assumption: that his wife and son were being looked after. Deacon Clark was the fuckin' Boy Scout of the Philly branch of the FBI; his word was bond, you needed nothing else. He'd never imagine Deke leaving the FBI. Never. No way. The man was one drunken night away from having J. Edgar Hoover tattooed on his dick. Hardie had always comforted himself with knowing that Deke would never fall down on the job. Even if Hardie were to die, Deke would honor his promise.

But his family was wide open, exposed.

And right now in the worst danger of their lives.

All because of him.

Deke couldn't tell if the man was crying or ready to collapse or laughing from nervous exhaustion or what. All he knew was that it was finally time for Charlie Hardie to come home. He slipped the gun inside his jacket pocket and walked over to Hardie, put his hands on his shoulders, told him everything was going to be okay, even though it probably wasn't. Right here, in this room, were three men Charlie had killed. Another on a roof just a dozen blocks away. No matter what had happened, you can't make murder go away. He could feel Hardie trembling a little under his touch.

Look at him. With a cane and everything. If the moment weren't so horrible Deke would have maybe found a little amusement in the notion of Charlie Hardie, baddest man in Philadelphia, having to get around with a cane.

Didn't explain where he'd been the past five years.

"Come on, Hardie," Deke said softly. "It's going to be all right."

Deke briefly looked past Hardie to see the interior of the trunk. At first it looked like somebody had shoved a bunch of medical gear back here—oxygen tanks, IV bags, tubing. But then he saw how neatly it was all arranged. "What the hell is that?"

Deke was so mesmerized by the contents of the trunk that he didn't feel the tip of the cane against his chest until it was too late.

He barely felt the shock.

31

The question is not when he's gonna stop, but who is gonna stop him.

—Cleavon Little, *Vanishing Point*

HARDIE DROVE THE big bad black Lincoln Coma Car down the Pacific Coast Highway.

If you're going to check out the gorgeous California coast, might as well do it in style—with someone special on life support in the secret trunk.

They stopped in Big Sur. Hardie had a burger and a beer in a small place called Ripplewood. The beer hit him hard. He used to have a high tolerance, but five-plus years on the secret-hospital-and-prison wagon must have killed it. His head swam. Not good. He couldn't afford to be drunk for the next twelve hours. Hardie ordered three glasses of ice water. The waitress didn't even flinch—she brought all three and one straw, as though she knew the deal.

Back outside, and once he was sure nobody was around, Hardie popped the trunk and slapped Doyle until his eyes opened. He hadn't gotten everything perfect back here in the trunk of the Coma Car—and Hardie was no doctor. But the fucker was securely bound, at the very least. And guaranteed to be super uncomfortable.

"So, which address?"

Doyle tried to spit on Hardie, who jumped back, but caught some of the saliva on his hand anyway. Hardie leaned over and press-wiped it on Doyle's overalls, which only made Hardie's hand greasy *and* wet. Disgusting. Doyle leered at him.

"Okay, then," Hardie said. He punched Doyle in the head twice, then closed the trunk.

The scenery along the Pacific was breathtaking and beautiful, that much was true. But what they didn't tell you about the Pacific Coast Highway was that it pretty much went on forever. Repeated itself, too, to the point where you could have sworn you'd passed this exact same eye-popping view of a canyon overlooking the perfect blue ocean just a few minutes ago. It was an orgy of supermodels at sixty-five miles per hour, all beauty, no imperfections, and after a while it just made your dick want to shrivel up from all the splendor.

God, that beer had really hit Hardie.

Near the Hearst Castle, Hardie found a place to pull over and stretch his throbbing right leg. He tried to use cruise control, but one near collision convinced him he was better off regulating his own speed. It was tough, though, using his left leg on the brake and accelerator. His right leg just wasn't trustworthy. Who knows if it ever would be.

Hey, asshole—you're the one who got shot in the head. I served you well until then. Remember that.

You're right, leg. You're right.

There was a lonely stretch of beach not far from where a group of enormous sea lions basked in the sun, rolling around in the wet sand. Hardie once read that sea lions, though cuddly, could be quite ferocious. Maybe having a thousand-pound creature snapping a bite out of his leg would convince Doyle to cough up the address...

Instead Hardie drove farther, to a more secluded spot, pulled over, and decided to try again. He woke Doyle by twisting a crimp in his breathing tube. The man's eyes popped open, and his face turned a sickly cyanotic color, but he still refused to pinpoint Abrams's address.

A one-in-five shot; those odds sucked. If he was going to win this, he needed to trap Abrams immediately. A break-in at one of the other addresses would only serve as a tip-off.

Hardie continued down the California coast as the sun dropped down onto the flat gray slate of the Pacific.

Morro Bay at night.

Even in the gloom you could see the BIG FUCKING ROCK right in the middle of the water, as if a killer meteorite had crash-landed on earth. But instead of wiping out the human race, it just decided to kick back off the California coast for a while. With the sun down, it was chilly as hell out here, wet salty air lashing your skin.

Might be mildly romantic, if it were just him and Kendra out here, lounging around the seaport restaurants, maybe even holding hands and looking at the big fucking rock.

Instead, Hardie found himself with Doyle—his new main squeeze. Hardie found a quiet, desolate space behind an abandoned store and opened the trunk again. Hardie wasn't going to ask this time. He popped the hood and started in with his fists, beating Doyle for a solid minute, not really worried about killing him because, you know—the bastard was already on life support.

"Not asking you again," Hardie said.

Doyle spat blood. Like, everywhere. But he didn't say a word.

Well, that went well.

Hardie slammed the trunk lid shut.

An hour later, as he passed Santa Barbara and the early rays of the sun seemed to warm up the entire universe, he got an idea.

Finally—

Hello, L.A. Can't say I've missed you.

Feels like I just left you.

Only that was five-plus fucking years ago.

But you haven't changed.

Not really.

Your streets still confuse me with all your sprawl. Your hills still scare the shit out of me—no offense, but I think it'll be a long time before I go anywhere near the Hollywood sign, thank you very much. You're still vain and wrapped up in yourself, which, frankly, is good, because I don't want you even noticing I'm here. Just want to talk to one of your citizens for a while.

Hardie drove the car into the long-term parking lot at Los Angeles International Airport, took a ticket, instantly crumpled it his fist, and let it drop to the ground. The entire parking lot was a multilevel garage. He chose the top level. Right in the baking sun. Few cars were up here at this early hour of the morning.

Hardie opened the trunk. Doyle was already awake, as though he were waiting for him. Hardie put his hand on the breathing tube, but before he yanked it out of the man's mouth, he told him the deal.

"This is the last time I'm going to ask you for that address. If you say nothing, I'm going to pull the battery and leave you to die in this car. It'll probably take a while. I don't imagine it will be a very pleasant death. Understand?"

Doyle nodded.

Hardie pulled the tube.

As soon as Doyle coughed up some phlegm and blood, he said in a raspy voice: "The Arcadia address."

Hardie blinked.

"If you're..."

"I'm not. Abrams is always there. Fuck—fucking let me out of this thing!"

"No. You should take another nap. If you're telling the truth, I'll come back and let you go."

"You won't. You're going to leave me to die here, aren't you, you prick?"

Hardie slammed the lid shut, walked around to the front of the car. Then he popped the hood, unplugged both of the batteries he found, closed the hood again, and walked away.

Yeah, he was.

32

Just walkin' in the rain, gettin' soakin' wet...
   —The Prisonaires, "Just Walkin' in the Rain"

YEAH, THIS WAS IT.

Hardie had a suspicion this might be the place, but it wasn't until he saw the loading area—through which he entered now—that he completely and for sure *recognized* the place.

This was where they'd stuffed him into that life-support trunk...what was it, more than five years ago?

And see, it felt like just yesterday they'd sentenced him to a life of unconsciousness and forced detention.

With each step Hardie steeled himself to be ready to open fire. Left hand on the cane, right hand on the gun. Left arm was still the weakest but he still felt the cane was the wisest choice for that hand. He could fall, he could be knocked down—but at least he'd still be able to shoot no matter what. And there would be nothing worse than to raise his left arm to blow somebody away only to discover that *oops, sorry, body, the left hand is unable to take your call right now, please try again later.*

Hardie fully expected to be blowing people away any second now.

If his memory served—and this place was the last thing Hardie remembered before waking up, handcuffed, in that room with that bitch Mann—then this secret little hospital facility should be absolutely crawling with armed guards. He needed to move as quickly as a man with a cane could move. The first gunshot would alert the rest; then it would be a simple matter of Hardie having enough bullets to take out every person between himself and Abrams.

Curiously, the loading area was deserted. No resistance as Hardie made his way up a cement ramp. No locked doors. No one guarding the hallway leading back to offices and operating rooms.

Abrams was sitting at a desk in a small office when Hardie walked in. Just sitting there, newspaper in front of her, remnants of a grapefruit and a glass of orange juice next to it. Hardie had caught her having a morning snack.

Hardie showed her the gun, cane-stepping toward the desk, saying, "Don't move."

"Okay, I won't move," she said. "What can I do for you?"

Hardie shoved the gun into her mouth. He even heard the metal chip her tooth enamel. Smudged her lipstick, too.

"Nugh," Abrams said, wincing.

"You stole five years of my life. I've killed your partners. Gedney first, then Doyle. I'm going to kill you next unless we reach some kind of arrangement. I don't want your word. I want an honest-to-fucking-god arrangement, or however you pieces of shit do things. Airtight, locked down, the whole thing. You've done it before, you're going to do it now."

Abrams, mouth wrapped around Hardie's ballistic "cock," waited to see if Hardie was finished speaking. Eyes wide open and patient.

"Do you understand me?" Hardie asked.

Abrams nodded gently, the gun moving up and down in Hardie's hand slightly.

Hardie slid the gun out of her mouth. A trail of saliva followed with it. Abrams wiped her lips with the back of her hand, smearing more lipstick. She felt her front teeth, felt the chip. Shook her head, disappointed.

"Why don't you have a seat?" she said. "I promise I won't move, if that's what you're worried about."

"No."

"Your leg must be killing you by now. Seems you've got—"

"Shut the fuck up. There's only one thing I want to hear from you. And that's how you're going to convince me that nothing else will happen to me or my family."

"I suppose giving you my word wouldn't do the trick, huh?"

Hardie flashed back to Eve, down in the prison, giving him a look: *Duh.*

"Okay," Abrams said. "Let's get down to it, then. You claim we stole five years of your life, and for that, you killed Gedney."

"And Doyle."

"We'll get to that in a minute. From where I sit, however, we did *not* steal five years of your life. You were in a coma for almost four of those years, and then in physical rehabilitation at a facility in Grand Island, Nebraska, for about a year. And sure, you could make the claim that we put you in that coma. But you were not responding to traditional amounts of anesthesia, as I recall, and you were in danger of hurting yourself. We had to take action to save your life."

"I was in . . . a *what?*"

"A coma. And not our fault, Mr. Hardie. We were endeavoring to save your life. You were scouted. And we thought you'd be ideal for future projects. While you caused the Industry more than a little grief, we all saw it as a trade-off. Yes, Lee Harvey Oswald killed the president of the United States. But that kid sure can shoot, so let's get him on board. Do you understand?"

"What are you talking about? I don't remember..."

"Of course you don't. Throughout the therapy sessions you were stubborn. Incorrigible, actually. A tremendous pain in the ass. Oh, you played along enough to actually bring your body back online, to some degree. But our staff knew you were up to something. And as soon as you deemed yourself physically fit, you tried to escape."

"Guess I didn't pull it off."

"You came close. Killed quite a few people, too."

This was a lot like hearing about all the great fun you had while stinking drunk just before you passed out on the lawn. All the pain, none of the satisfaction.

"So," Abrams continued, "we decided that you weren't the right man for the project we had in mind at the time. Still, you were a potential asset, and we never just throw away our assets. You were sent to site seven seven three four with a group of other potential assets. Your memory loss is normal. We wipe out about a year's worth before sending anyone down there. Keeps the place secret."

"Right."

"Of course, site seven seven three four is useless to us now. Not long after you did away with Mr. Gedney, we sent a team down there and found it abandoned. Not a single living being. Not a single corpse."

"Whoopsie."

"No matter. That's another issue entirely. I'm just trying to impress upon you that this claim that we stole five years of your life is really kind of silly. Not sure what we're guilty of, other than trying to save your life and protecting our interests."

"Gee, if only your pals had explained it to me that way," Hardie said.

Abrams smiled. "The fact that you escaped...that's truly remarkable. Makes me see your potential in a whole new light."

"Not interested. Let's talk terms, or you can join your pals Gedney and Doyle right now."

"Just Gedney."

"Huh?"

"If you shoot me, I'll only be seeing Gedney. That is, if you believe in life after death. Which I do not. But whatever."

"Doyle's dead."

"Mr. Doyle is alive and on his way to the hospital. We were talking to him from the back of the vehicle—there's a wireless communications system back there. It cut out a little on the Pacific Coast Highway, but we were able to tell him how long to hold out, what to say to bring you here."

"Why? Why not just kill me on the open road? You could probably have blown up the car by remote."

Abrams sighed. "You're not listening to me, Mr. Hardie. You're still an asset. Blowing you up would get us what, exactly? A warm, tingly feeling inside? Grow up."

Oh, how Hardie's trigger finger twitched. One little squeeze, a spray of skin and bone and blood . . .

"I see you're impatient. So here's our offer. We still want you for this project. Gedney wasn't sure, but Gedney's dead. And unlike your stint in site seven seven three four, this project is aboveboard. We'll tell you everything. Exactly what's expected of you. In short, one year of service, doing what you do best."

"What's that?"

"Guarding something."

Hardie thought about it, then shot Abrams in the face.

Okay, he didn't.

He badly wanted to, and the fantasy sequence that ran through his mind was so, so tempting. But instead Hardie asked,

"What do you want me to guard?"

"Agree and we'll tell you everything."

"What do I get in return?"

"A clean slate. Do this job for us and in one year you can walk away. Go back to your life, if you want."

"And if I refuse?"

Abrams shrugged and showed him her palms. "Look, I don't have to sell you on our capabilities. Your wife and son have been left unmolested. If you decide to kill me and continue on with this rampage of yours, it won't end well. For any of us."

Hardie thought about it, then shot Abrams in the face.

Wanted to.

Wanted to oh so fucking badly.

But for years now Hardie had been doing just what he wanted, and where had that gotten him?

Sometimes your guts know it before you do. You're about to take a step off a curb and your guts are screaming *NO NO NO YOU FUCKING MORON* but you feel your foot leave the cement anyway, hanging in the air, thinking that when you set it down again in 1.4 seconds you're going to find solid ground beneath you, just like the billion other times you lifted your foot with the intention of putting it down again. You think your gut is wrong, your gut is being paranoid, just take a step, just like you've always done…

Hardie placed the gun on the desktop, nodded, took a step back, balancing himself on his cane.

Abrams allowed herself a polite smile, then settled back into her chair.

Almost immediately armed gunmen poured into the room, automatic weapons in their hands. They were trained; they'd clearly practiced this move a hundred times before. They surrounded Hardie in such a way that if he went for his gun on the desk his arm would be separated from the rest of his body by a flurry of bullets.

That didn't mean he didn't think about it, though.

One second to fall forward...

Another second to grab the gun...

One last second to pull the trigger and destroy her face.

Surely he could endure the agony of a hundred bullets blasting through his body, severing veins and shattering bone and spraying gray matter for three seconds?

Yeah. Right.

"That was a wise choice," Abrams said. "You probably could have killed me, but you wouldn't have made it out of this room alive. Your family would have died within the hour, too. We have Mann and her team assembled in Philadelphia right now. And while it may have felt good to take my life, that would not have done a thing to change our operations. I am not the be-all and end-all of the Industry. I'm just an employee. Just like you."

Hardie looked around the room, all those guns pointed at him, the utter hopelessness of it all.

He laughed. "I should have just run."

"We would have found you."

"I should have pulled the trigger," Hardie said. "You're going to kill me anyway."

Abrams smiled and leaned back in her chair, put her feet up on the desk. She wore boots with heels tall and sharp enough to lobotomize a man through his eye sockets.

"Oh, Mr. Hardie," she said. "It's much worse than that."

33

You always makin' big plans for tomorrow, you know why?
Because you always fuckin' up today.
— Roberto Benigni, *Down by Law*

PEOPLE ALL OVER Southern California heard the explosion—a kind of end-of-the-world roar that brought certain Santa Barbara residents to their windows, fearing the worst. When you looked up into the pale blue sky you saw the missile and the trail of fire almost as long as the missile itself and your heart seized—but for just a moment. Because this missile—a rocket, actually, 235 feet tall—was zooming away from Southern California at 17,500 miles per hour, not screaming toward it.

Older residents, though, were used to such launches. Vandenberg Air Force Base was nearby, and ever since the 1960s the government had been launching all kinds of space shit up from Slick Six—the nickname for Space Launch Complex-6.

The newcomers, on the other hand, were mesmerized by the sight, at least once the initial fear drained away. They summoned their kids and went outside to their perfectly maintained lawns and pointed up at the sky, idly wondering if they should invest in a telescope. Might be cool to show the kids these kinds of things. Or maybe start looking up at the stars on a regular basis.

Within the hour, however, the explosion and the rocket and the fire trail and the telescope and everything else were forgotten, and people got back to their lives. Miracles are cool and all. But there are things to do.

Hardie woke up cold.

Freezing cold.

He opened his eyes.

No memory problems this time. There had been no need for a shot. The training had been important; he needed to remember every piece of it. There was a checklist of duties to perform.

But this morning he indulged himself and looked in on his family first.

Kendra was making chicken soup. Both she and Charlie, Jr., were fighting colds. Kendra had already taken apart the chicken and was now chopping thick carrot slices. Made him nervous to watch her fingers move so quickly, chop chop chop chop chop chop chop, even though her fingers were curled under, just as they were supposed to be. Still, fingers could slip. And if something should happen...

Charlie, Jr., was in the living room, holding up an imaginary gun and blasting away digital opponents on a flat screen. Nothing real, except the anger on his face. You could tell when he got off a particularly gory shot, because his eyes lit up in a certain way. Partly appalled, partly amused.

Hardie's family.

They were right there in front of him.

Actually, they weren't. Their *digital images* were right there in front of Hardie, on the screen. His actual wife and son—their flesh-and-blood bodies—were far, far below.

He should be passing over them soon, actually.

THANKS & PRAISE

If I could round up everyone who supported me during the writing of *Hell and Gone* and put them in a secret prison somewhere, those walls would contain the coolest people on earth.

First, I would use fabric hoods and plastic wrist-tie cuffs on a group of people I like to call...*the Wardens.*

My keeper and minder for thirteen-plus years now has been the lovable yet hardboiled **David Hale Smith.** This book is dedicated to him, not just for his faith in me, and his unflagging support and advice since the turn of the last century, but because he's the kind of agent who inspires you in the present while keeping an eye on the bigger picture. I love DHS like a brother and without him I couldn't have found my way through the novel you're holding in your hands (or on your favorite e-reading device) (or direct mental implant if this is the year 2019).

By his side, smacking their batons against their gloved palms, are the amazing Richard Pine, Lauren Smythe, Danny and Heather Baror, Angela Cheng Caplan, Shauyi Tai, Jessica Tscha, and Kim Yau, as well as the whole (chain) gang at Inkwell Management.

In the brand-new Mulholland Wing of my secret prison you'll find John Schoenfelder, Miriam Parker, Wes Miller, Michael Pietsch,

Luisa Frontino, Theresa Giacopasi, Betsy Uhrig, Barbara Clark, Christine Valentine, and the rest of the stellar Little, Brown team. Some may question the wisdom of incarcerating my publishers, but you have to understand: they trapped me in a karaoke prison during BookExpo America 2011 and refused to let me out until I did my drunken Jim Morrison impression. It wasn't pretty; they deserve the sentence they've received.

In an adjoining office in the control tower is Ruth Tross and the amazing Mulholland UK team. Their office has the wet bar, and they know *exactly* why. Next door you'll find Kristof Kurz, Frank Dabrock, and the rest of the team at Heyne in Germany.

My official prison doc, and the man who keeps me from making serious medical blunders in all of my books, is the legendary Lou Boxer. He's the most *noir* guy in all of Greater Philadelphia, yet an absolute sweetheart. Explain *that* one...

I would also forcibly (yet lovingly) detain certain people I like to call *the Prisoners*—those unfortunate souls doomed to a life sentence of breaking rocks in the tough-yet-fertile fields of publishing. This list includes the lifers and the new fish (and I'll let you sort out who's who):

Megan Abbott, Cameron Ashley, Janelle Asselin, Brian Azzarello, Jed Ayres, Josh Bazell, Eric Beetner, Stephen Blackmoore, Juliet Blackwell, Linda Brown, Ed Brubaker, Aldo Calcagno, Jon Cavalier, Sarah Cavalier, Stephanie "Mos Stef" Crawford, Scott and Sandi Cupp, Warren Ellis, Peter Farris, Erin Faye, Ed Fee, Joshua Hale Fialkov, James Frey, Joe Gangemi, Sara Gran, Allan "Sunshine" Guthrie, Charlaine Harris, Charlie Huston, Tania Hutchison, John Jordan, McKenna Jordan, Ruth Jordan (mystery nerd trivia: only *two* of the previous three Jordans are related!), Vince Keenan, Anne Kimbol, Katie Kubert, Ellen Clair Lamb, Terrill Lankford, Joe Lansdale, Simon Le Bon, Paul Leyden, Laura Lippman, Sophie Littlefield, Elizabeth-Amber Love, Mike MacLean, Mike Marts, David Macho, Patrick Millikin, Scott Montgomery, Lauren O'Brien, Jon Page, Barbara Peters, Ed and Kate Pettit, Keith Rawson, David Ready, Marc Resnick, Janet Rudolph, Jonathan Santlofer, David Schow, Joe Schreiber, Brett Simon, Jason Starr, Evelyn Taylor, Mark Ward, Dave "Vigoda" White, Elizabeth A. White.

I'm sure I've forgotten a ton of potential inmates here; my apologies in advance, and please go easy on me during my sentencing hearing.

Living nearby, in a private residence near the secret prison—all Alcatraz-style, natch—is my family: Meredith, Parker, and Sarah, who are incredibly understanding when I disappear into the prison of my own making (in the basement office of our northeast Philadelphia home) for long stretches of time.

And finally, a word of thanks to my former high school English teacher James Roach, who showed us *Cool Hand Luke* during a series of classes one week. Wish you'd stop bein' so good to me, cap'n...

About the Author

Duane Swierczynski is the author of several crime thrillers, including *Fun and Games*, Book One of the Hardie Trilogy. He's written for Marvel Comics's Punisher MAX, Cable, Deadpool, Immortal Iron Fist, Werewolf by Night, and Black Widow series, and has collaborated with *CSI* creator Anthony E. Zuiker on the bestselling Level 26 series of "digi-novels." He lives in the City of Brotherly Love with his wife, son, and daughter. Visit him at www.duaneswierczynski.com or twitter.com/swierczy.

...and what about Charlie Hardie?

In March 2012, Charlie Hardie's story continues in *Point and Shoot*, the conclusion of the Hardie Trilogy. Following is an excerpt from the novel's opening pages.

This isn't going to have a happy ending.

—Morgan Freeman, *Se7en*

Philadelphia—Now

Of all the shocks Kendra Hardie had endured over the past few hours—the dropped call from her son, the chilling messages on the alarm keypad, the thudding footfalls on the roof, the wrenching sounds in the very guts of her house, the missing gun, and the awful realization of how quickly her situation had become hopeless—none of that compared to the shock of hearing that voice on the other end of the phone line:

"It's me."

Kendra's mind froze. There was a moment of temporal dislocation, distant memory colliding with the present.

Me.

Could that really be...you?

It *sounds* like you, but...

No.

Can't be you.

But then how do I know, deep in my soul, that it is you?

"Are you there? Listen to me, Kendra, I know this is going to sound crazy, but you have to listen to me. You and the boy are in serious danger. You need to get out of the house now and just start driving. Drive *anywhere*. Don't tell me where, because they're definitely listening, but just go, go as fast as you fucking can. I'll find you guys when it's safe."

Kendra swallowed hard, looked at the face of the satellite receiver. 3:13 a.m. A little more than four hours since she had stepped into her own home and into a living nightmare. Eighteen hours since she had last seen her son. And almost eight years since she'd last heard her ex-husband's voice. Yet there it was on the line, at the very nexus of the nightmare.

"Kendra? Are you there? Can you hear me?"

"I'm here, Charlie. But I can't leave."

"You have to leave, Kendra, please just trust me on this..."

"I can't leave because they've already called and told me I *can't* leave."

Earlier in the evening Kendra had been out with a friend downtown, at a Cuban restaurant on Second Street in Old City, but found that she wasn't really into the food, didn't want to finish her mojito, and was tired of hearing about her friend's first-world problems, such as problems with interior decorators and the headache of maintaining three vacation homes on the Delaware shore. Kendra excused herself and just... *left*. Paid for half of the tab and split, handed the valet her stub, and drove back to the northern suburbs, leaving poor Derek to complain to somebody else about having too much money. Maybe one of the Cuban-exile waiters would give a shit.

It had been that kind of listless, annoyance-filled week, and Kendra now felt foolish for thinking that a night of moderate drinking and inane conversation could turn that around.

During the drive home her son, CJ, had called. He told her he was just calling to check in—which was just about as unusual as the president of the United States dropping you an e-mail just to see how everything was going. CJ didn't check in, *ever*. As CJ grew to manhood, he became increasingly like his father, with the delightful ability to cut off all emotional circuitry with the flick of an invisible switch. All the abuse her son had been dishing out over the years had hardened her into exactly the kind of mother she'd vowed never to become. The kind of mother who said things like,

"Cut the shit, CJ. What happened?"

"Nothing, Mom. I just . . ."

Mom. Oooh, that was another red flag. CJ hadn't called her Mom in . . . months? CJ barely spoke to her, and when he did, it was little more than a grunt.

A tiny ball of worry had begun to form in Kendra's stomach. Was he hurt? Was he calling from a hospital or a police station? Her body tensed, and she prepared to change direction and gun the accelerator.

"Where are you?"

"I'm at home, everything's fine. Look, Mom, I know this is going to sound weird, but . . . what did you do with Dad's old stuff?"

"What? Why are you asking me about that?"

First "Mom," now . . . *Dad?* For the past seven years CJ hadn't referred to his father as anything but "asshole" or "cocksucker" or "psycho." Before Kendra had a chance to hear CJ's answer, the phone beeped and went dead. NO SERVICE.

Kendra continued in the same direction but gunned the accelerator just the same, all the way up the Schuylkill Expressway, then through the endless traffic lights up Broad Street, and finally along the hills and curves of Old York Road out to the fringes of Abington

Township. Home. She didn't bother pulling the car into the garage, leaving it parked out on the street. Something in CJ's voice...no, *everything* about CJ's voice was completely wrong. Dad's old stuff? What was that about? Why did he suddenly want to see the few possessions his father had left behind? The thought that CJ might be drinking again crossed Kendra's mind, but his voice wasn't slurred. If anything, it was completely clear and focused, in stark contrast to the moody grunts she usually received.

And whenever CJ did go on a binge, his heart filled with raw hate for his father, not fuzzy nostalgia.

"CJ?"

The alarm unit on the wall to the left of the door beeped insistently until Kendra keyed in the code. She closed the door behind her, locked it, then reengaged the system. It beeped again. All set.

"CJ, answer me!"

And then began the nightmare.

No CJ, not anywhere. No trace of him in his room, no telltale glasses or dishes in the sink. The house was *exactly* as Kendra had left it when she left for Old City earlier in the evening. Had CJ even called from home? The call had come from his cell, so he could be anywhere right now.

Not knowing what else to do, Kendra tried him again on her phone, but still—NO SERVICE. What was that about? She could understand a dropped call when speeding down the Schuylkill, as if a guardian angel had tweaked the signal to prevent you from sparking a twelve-car pileup on the most dangerous road in Philadelphia. But in her own home?

Maybe she could get a better signal outside. Kendra went back to the front door and keyed in the code. Two digits in, however, her finger stopped and hung in midair before the 6 key.

The digital readout, which usually delivered straightforward messages such as SYSTEM ENGAGED or PLEASE ENTER ACCESS CODE, now told her something else:

STAY RIGHT WHERE YOU ARE.

"The fuck?" Kendra muttered, then lowered her finger for a second before blinking hard and stabbing the 6 button anyway, followed by the 2. Which should have disengaged the system. This time, however, there was no reassuring beep. There was nothing at all, except:

KENDRA, THAT WON'T HELP.

Then:

DON'T MAKE A SOUND.
DON'T MOVE.
NOT UNTIL WE CALL YOU.

And Kendra, much to her own disgust, did exactly as she was told, staying perfectly still and silent...

...for about two seconds before realizing *Fuck this* and grabbing the handle of her front door. She twisted the knob, pulled. The door didn't move, as if it had been cemented in place. What? She hadn't engaged the deadbolts when she'd come in just a minute ago...

The phone in her hand buzzed to life. There was SERVICE, suddenly. The name on the display: INCOMING CALL / CJ.

Oh, thank God. She thumbed the accept button, expecting to hear her son's voice, maybe even hoping he'd call her *Mom* again.

But instead, it had been someone else.

* * *

Now, four agonizing hours later, during which Kendra had heard the sounds of her own house being turned against her...she was listening to the voice of her ex-husband—an accused murderer long thought to be dead. And he had the audacity to be grilling her!

"Who told you that? Who told you you were dead?"

"They called me and said if I left the house I was dead."

"*Fuck.* Did you call the police? Anyone at all?"

"They told me not to call anyone or do anything else except wait."

"Wait for what?"

There was a burst of static on the line, and then another voice came on. The one who'd called four hours earlier, from CJ's phone.

The evil icy-voiced bitch queen who had her son, and who claimed to have the house surrounded.

"Hey, Charlie! It's your old pal Mann here. So good to hear your voice after all this time. Well, that magical day has finally arrived. In about thirty seconds we're going to kill the phones, and the power, and everything else in your wife's house. We've got her surrounded; I know every square inch of every house in a five-block radius. You of all people know how thorough we are."

Charlie ignored the other voice.

"Kendra, where's the boy?"

"Shhhh now, Charlie. It's rude to interrupt. You're wasting precious seconds. I know what you're going to say. You're going to tell me that if I touch one hair on your family's head, you'll rip me apart one limb at a time...or maybe some other colorful metaphor? Well, you know, that's just not gonna happen. Because you lost this one, Chuck. There's not going to be any cavalry rushing in, no last-minute saves, no magic escapes. And you know what's going to happen next?"

* * *

What *should* have been going through Kendra's mind at this moment was something along the lines of:

Charlie, where the hell have you been and why have you surfaced now? The last time we spoke it was a stupid and petty conversation about a late credit card bill, and I think the last word I spoke to you before disconnecting was *whatever.*

Or maybe:

Charlie, why didn't you call me before tonight? Do you how many late nights I stared at the ceiling, trying to actually physically will you to call me? Not to change anything or explain anything, but to just to tell me what happened? Do you know how hard the *not knowing* was? How much it consumed me over the years, digging in deep, way past the regret and guilt and into the very core of me?

But instead Kendra thought:

Goddamn you, Charlie.

Goddamn you for doing this to us.

"What's going to happen next is," the ice bitch queen continued, "your family's going to die. And there's not a fucking thing you can do to stop me."

If Kendra had any doubts about the voice on the other end of the line belonging to her husband, they vanished when he spoke again. Because his words were infused with a rock-hard defiance that had once been familiar to her, over a decade ago.

Charlie Hardie told the ice bitch queen,

"I can stop you."